We All Have A Story To Tell

Memories of Another time

Stories From the First Half of the Twentieth Century
By Family and Friends

Book I: 1900-1941

by
Robert H. Wells
Editor and Contributor

Bloomington, IN Milton Keynes, UK

AuthorHouse™
1663 Liberty Drive, Suite 200
Bloomington, IN 47403
www.authorhouse.com
Phone: 1-800-839-8640

AuthorHouse™ UK Ltd.
500 Avebury Boulevard
Central Milton Keynes, MK9 2BE
www.authorhouse.co.uk
Phone: 08001974150

© 2006 Robert H. Wells. All rights reserved.

This book may not be duplicated in any way without the expressed written consent
of the publisher, except in the form of brief excerpts or quotations for purposes of
review. The information contained may not be duplicated in other books, databases or
any other medium without the written consent of the publisher or author. Publication
December 2003

2nd Publication May 2004

First published by AuthorHouse 9/18/2006

First Published by Katerina Press—A Vanity Publication
23635 Community St.
West Hills, California
91304

ISBN: 1-4259-3518-4 (sc)
ISBN: 1-4259-3520-6 (dj)

Printed in the United States of America
Bloomington, Indiana

This book is printed on acid-free paper.

Dedication

*To my sister Barbara, brothers Dean and Gene
Sister Marydith*

*And in memory of
Brother Wayland Lee Wells*

*As well to
The many friends
Who
Contributed
Their memories
To this book*

Table of Contents

Chapter 1	Introduction Robert H. Wells	1
Chapter 2	Growing up in the early Twentieth Century Frederick George Greaves	9
Chapter 3	Making a Life without a Father Ernest Giffen	21
Chapter 4	Growing up in Early Los Angeles Nort Sanders	25
Chapter 5	An Alaskan Adventure Howard Rustad	29
Chapter 6	A Coal Miner's Daughter Hazel Schmeil	37
Chapter 7	Disease and Family Survival Robert H. Wells	51
Chapter 8	A Rural Upbringing Harriet Gladys Wilkerson	57
Chapter 9	A Will to Live John Van Beekum	71
Chapter 10	A Child's Memories of the 1920's MaryBelle Preston Wells	87
Chapter 11	Reaching for A College Education Patricia Murphy Burns	103
Chapter 12	Westward Migration Alexander J. Sharp	117
Chapter 13	Relief Checks Kept our Family Going Harold E. "Sam" Haight	129

Chapter 14	My Father Worked Theodore 'Ted' Lumpkin	133
Chapter 15	Growing up Poor Robert H. Wells	137
Chapter 16	Malnutrition and Other Things Robert Martens	147
Chapter 17	1933: A Summer's Adventure Charles B. Downer	155
Chapter 18	Family, Cars and Other Things Frank S. Preston	167
Chapter 19	The Appeal of Physics Henry Fairbank	183
Chapter 20	Summer Adventures in Iowa Frank Steele Preston	193
Chapter 22	Preparing for War Robert H. Wells	201
Chapter 23	Shipbuilding in WW I & WW II Frederick G. Greaves	211
Index of Contributors		217

CHAPTER 1

*I*NTRODUCTION

By
Robert H. Wells

GROWING UP in the aftermath of the "War to end all Wars"; formed
and influenced by the years of the Great Depression and finding my
college years interrupted by three and one half years of military service
in WW II, my own life experience bridges a significant portion of the
first half of this countries existence in the Twentieth Century.

I mention that because this book serves up the memories of family
and friends taking part in the life and actions of that period of time.
The thesis of this book is that the changes in structure and purpose
occurring in the first half of the twentieth Century makes it one of the
most important periods of time in this country 's history.

While the founding of the country was probably of greater historical
significance than the first half of the 20th century, it was accomplished
in a much shorter time span and at the time affected a much smaller
portion of the population.

The second half of the 19th century with its Civil War or war of
Rebellion was critical to assuring that the United States remained as one
country. The fact that it took a Civil War to make this one country was
not without cost. For the peoples of this country it left a lasting sense
of division and bitterness still not entirely reconciled. The war itself was
all consuming. A vast portion of the people of this country was involved
in the struggle. And the death toll exceeded that of all wars we have
engaged in before or since. In its final outcome it can be and often is
seen as possibly the most significant event in this country's history.

Nevertheless, it is my belief that the first half of the twentieth century might be seen as this countries most significant period of challenge and change. The challenge, a continuing one, was marked with its two world wars and a Great Depression that at times threatened the survival of a people as well as the nature of our government. It was also a time of industrialization and the electrification of the country. Within that framework were broad significant scientific advances that included the invention of the automobile, the airplane and of both penicillin and the atomic bomb.

Not least and perhaps as important if not more important were social advances that not only equalized to a great extent the rights and status of women but led to a greater acceptance of our responsibility for the welfare of others, including a beginning acceptance of other races. Taken altogether those changes and advances must be seen as laying the foundation of one of the most if not the most significant growth and testing periods in this country's history.

History has been defined as "a chronological record of events, as of the life or development of a people or an institution, often including an explanation of or commentary on those events". History may also be seen as "the events forming the subject matter of a historical account. b. Something that belongs to the past".

Much of our written history adheres to that general definition. However, there is another kind of history, that which reflects the personal memories of the individual living in a given period of time. History can also be seen as a "narrative of events; a story".

In that last sense then, it is my belief that history, to be meaningful, is also very much that of each individual's participation and contribution to the making of that history. The actions of individuals in their own time determines the direction of those times as well as of the major events that will be known to future generations as history.

Having had the good fortune to share in the experiences of that first half of the twentieth century and, more importantly, to have known people and heard the stories of those same people who lived during much of the early twentieth century, I consider it my duty as well as my pleasure to share some of their memories with you.

MEMORIES OF ANOTHER TIME

*   *   *

Of the mosaic of memories collected for this book many deal with small incidents that stood out in the daily struggle of living. Some few also offer stories of great adventure, of daring, of survival, moments for the most part related to incidents and accidents of war.

It should be noted that these are the stories of my family and of friends I have been able to persuade to share their stories with me. Many who contributed their memories to this story are no longer among the living and the other stories were all told to me or in some instances shared with me in writing while they were somewhere in their "Golden Years". They all lived what we refer to and they considered to be "normal" lives. For the most part they did not see themselves as makers of history. Rather, their stories and occasional adventures were a taken for granted aspect of the lives they lived.

They had no reason to think their lives and their adventures would be of any interest to others. In fact, and for the most part, no one had expressed an interest even as they tried to share the story of some of their more adventurous activities with family and friends.

As a people we tend to live in the here and now. For the most part we aren't interested in what went before us, the "stuff" that we refer to as "history". And above all, we don't want to learn from the history of past actions, past changes and most critically, past mistakes. As individuals and as a people, we are much too omnipotent to believe the past has anything to do with our present.

In a sense then, the stories I am presenting are of the taken for granted adventures of living that others did not appear to be interested in. Yet, as you will see, they are stories of survival, of adventure, of occasional heroism and above all, of character that reflects on us as the people we were and the people we became. One common thread shared by all these stories is that they are told matter of factly, with no elaboration and seldom any sense of how the narrator felt or believed and almost always, without any sense of the narrator's emotional involvement in the action.

In presenting these stories I have begun with the oldest of these storytellers and the small adventures they had to share. The stories from both farm and city continue through the trials and struggles of the Great Depression years and on through WW II as told in Book II.

Much of the population was rural during the early part of the Twentieth Century. The tools of industrialization were just beginning to be a part of our culture. As a personal example, until the mid 1930's my father depended on a team of horses to haul logs from the woods to the sawmill and firewood to our home, to haul gravel from the creek bed to local construction projects, to plow, to haul hay and in every instance, to see his team of horses as a supplement to and enhancement of his labor.

In bringing to you these otherwise untold and unheard stories, my own awareness of the fact the stories of most of us remain untold was brought to my attention when I realized that the story of my own parents was an otherwise story untold. The fact I lived with them for seventeen years only brought to my attention how little I knew about them. And yet, the fact they lived full lives through three depressions, two world wars, faced death from illnesses now readily controlled by medications then unknown and managed to raise to adulthood 6 children is a miracle for which I am grateful. I can even speculate how they managed the multiple demands that made such an achievement possible. But of the stories that they might have told me of the specifics of that accomplishment I have almost no knowledge.

My parents were born in the 1890's. As a result they had their own role in the major and significant activities of that first half of the twentieth century. My mother's family came west starting in Scotland, then Illinois and on to the state of Washington while it was still a territory. There her father mined coal near the town of Roslyn, Washington where she was born. Her teen years were marked by the near death experience from an illness identified as rheumatic fever and complicated by a Tetanus infection that left her with a damaged heart and a locked jaw. During WW I she worked in Seattle, Washington as a telephone switchboard operator.

My father's family left their Missouri farm in 1908 to claim newly opening homestead lands in Idaho. There, major diseases took two of his brothers and his father. As a soldier in WW I he became a victim of the worldwide flu pan-epidemic. The fact he survived when millions

MEMORIES OF ANOTHER TIME

died was mostly due to a hardy constitution aided by the nursing care of his mother.

Both parents having survived the depressions of the 1890's, 1907, 1920-21 were, as a result, as prepared to handle the Great Depression of 1929-1940 as any low-income, day labor dependent couple could be. With an eventual six children to house, feed and clothe during the years of the Great Depression they faced what might be considered their greatest personal test.

Unfortunately, their memories of that experience were not recorded. If they had been it would not have been a story of adventure and derring-do. Rather, it would have been the story of the daily struggle of making ends meet, of hard work, self denial and the small successes of making it through another day with all members of their family fed and housed.

In arranging the stories in this book, the very first stories are told by friends and acquaintances of their lives in the first part of the century. The very first story tells us of a now unknown form of education, the role of apprenticeship in our education system. Farm life, city life and an Alaskan adventure offer glimpses of the demands and opportunities of the early part of the century. These stories are followed by several glimpses into life experiences in the 1920's.

Then there are the stories of surviving the Great Depression of 1929 through 1939. Within those stories we often get no more than a glimpse of the social and psychic toll involved in that long struggle. That period occurred during my own formative years. I identify much of my character with the struggles and lessons learned in a time with no seeming future and therefore no expectation that life could be so different as I now find it.

We often look back longingly to what we refer to as the "Good Old Days". Many of you as readers and possibly even as participants in those days will need to determine for yourself the good to be found in those days! For those of us living through those times we have to believe there must have been some good there because we survived but the specifics of that good, when the memory focuses so much on the trauma of those hard times, are often hard to identify. For some the closeness of family and shared struggle is often seen as the remembered positive.

On the other hand, an all too common memory is that of the hardships and the hopelessness of that period, often seen as an all encompassing force destructive to and greatly limiting any hope of a future. One sad and seemingly universal effect seen if not then understood was often the picture of seemingly emasculated fathers. With no job, no hope and the desperation that comes with responsibility of a family to support and no means to do so, their burden of unending failure could be overwhelming.

For the children of the family, closeness in the physical sense of sharing limited living space and resources was certainly an important factor in their lives. That may have mitigated in part their father's sense of defeat and worthlessness, a defeat they believed themselves to be a part of and at some level, responsible for.

In spite of apparent difficulties and hopelessness, the human spirit demands and even lives by hope. With hope, life is given a focus. An example of this may be seen in the effort to achieve an education at a time when higher education had importance only if you were planning to enter the professions of teacher, lawyer, doctor, engineering, the ministry. Obtaining a college education had little relevance to the usual jobs available to most workers of that time. Even so, as a goal it made life worth the effort embodied in achieving that goal.

John Van Beekum's matter of fact story of surviving with a badly damaged body and constant pain to the kind of achievement that can be seen as heroic can be seen as a lesson in hope and struggle we can all empathize with.

Mostly though, these stories deal with the ever day struggles of the people of a time now hard to visualize in this modern age. Living as we do in an age of TV and man journeying to the moon, it is hard to visualize an age of the horse drawn vehicle, the first airplanes and automobiles, electricity lighting the home, the occasional phone, home gardens and home cooking, horse and steam powered farm equipment and the importance of physical, hard labor in doing the work of the world. Even the struggle to obtain an advanced education when the high school diploma was the norm of general achievement and the college degree was gained by perhaps five percent of the population. My parents, for example had grade school and two years of high school for my mother to represent their educational achievement.

As you read these stories I hope you will allow yourself to visualize the people telling these stories as real people like yourself but living in the kind of situations you have not shared in our modern world. With that under standing you can think of them as like your parents, other relatives or older friends and always as people just like yourself, only living in a different time and without the advantages you live with and take for granted.

CHAPTER 2
GROWING UP IN THE EARLY TWENTIETH CENTURY

By
Frederick George Greaves

I WAS BORN on November 6, 1892. I don't know whether my father, Charles H. Hicks had an opportunity to make my acquaintance before he left for the Yukon or not. It never occurred to me to ask my mother during her lifetime. Some time in 1892 Charles joined the throng of impoverished and hopeful young men who took part in the Alaska Yukon gold rush. No word was ever heard from him from that time forward, and it has been assumed that he died on the Yukon trail, becoming one of many such casualties.

It seems logical that when my father did not return from Alaska and our family was in dire circumstances my maternal great-grandparents welcomed my maternal grandmother, my mother and me into their home. We moved into two or three rooms on the second floor.

The Great Depression of 1893 was in the offing. As my great-grandfather had a large house, he not only took in our little family; they also had living with them a cousin with their son and daughter.

I have some vivid recollections of the house. There was a fence alongside the house, on the side where both front porches were located. A cabinet shop was in the rear. Apparently, as a toddler I had a habit of running away. Grandfather fixed up a rope running along the fence, to which he attached a short rope with a ring, which slid along the fence rope. When I was tied to this rope it gave me the run of the yard.

9

Grandmother was a seamstress and made for me a Lord Fauntleroy suit, which little boys were dressed in for special occasions. It featured short pants worn with long stockings. The suit was elaborately cut, with ruffles at the sleeves. I had long curls. One day Uncle Art came to see us. Without a word to my mother he took me to the barber and had my haircut. My mother cried when she saw me, but I'm sure I was cooler and happier.

When I was between six and seven mother married George E. Greaves. Both of them took great pains to tell me that now we were a family I should stop calling him Uncle George because he was my step-father. Dad Greaves explained that he was adopting me and therefore he hoped I would always use the name of Greaves.

While living not far from Edgar Emmerson's print shop I attended kindergarten in the home of his wife Nellie. One day she gave a party for us kids and Mother dressed me up in my Lord Fauntleroy suit. On my way to the party I slipped and fell into a mud puddle and my pretty suit was ruined.

My first half brother was born September 24, 1899. Later Mother gave birth to twins, a boy and a girl. The boy died at about three months and the girl at about six months. Both had weak hearts. It was a very sad time for our family.

My folks were not very well off, so money for playthings was not available. It occurred to me that I could build a wagon out of a soapbox if I could get a set of wheels. Uncle Bert found a set and fastened them to the bottom of a wooden box and put a long handle from one end of the box's bottom. I probably had some help from Dad or Uncle Bert because the wheels and handle were quite secure. When Saturday came around Mother sent me to the grocery store a few blocks away. Nothing would do but I should take my cart to bring back the groceries.

Among other supplies there were two dozen eggs. As I had pulled the cart all the way to the grocery and part of the way back I decided my cousin should take a turn at it. She said, "I should say not. You're the man, you should do all the pulling." I said, "If you don't pull it some of the way, we'll just leave it right here." She said, "Well, I won't," where-upon I let go of the handle and as the cart was not too well balanced it tipped over backwards and away went the eggs.

MEMORIES OF ANOTHER TIME

Needless to say, when we got back Aunt Jenny was so angry she gave me a spanking. When I got home I got another.

At about that time automobiles were beginning to be produced by quite a few companies. Dad was an expert engine assembler. He was a journeyman machinist, having served an apprenticeship at the Erie Railroad shops. He moved around to various auto-building shops in Cleveland, wherever he could earn the highest wages. Urban transportation not being good he generally moved our home to be near the shop where he worked, so I never went to the same school for more than about a year.

Dad was also a very experienced railroad locomotive specialist. The railroads were expanding rapidly in those days so he had no difficulty getting jobs and was quite well known in certain railroad circles. However, his health was very poor. He was constantly seeking a better climate and easier work. He also was highly sensitive, and frequently quit a job if someone crossed him in any way. He was never discharged, and in fact was sought after and seemingly could always step from one job to another in short order.

At Topeka he was working for the Santa Fe Railroad. During the summer I caught the "Kansas Chiggers" from lolling around on the grass. These little insects bury themselves into the skin and cause tremendous itching. The method of getting them to come out was to wash yourself with kerosene, which I finally did. Getting rid of the kerosene odor and grease from one's body was almost as bad as the chiggers.

While at Topeka Dad was asked to go down to Chickasaw, Indian Territory {now Oklahoma}, to take charge of the locomotive repair shop. It was winter. I remember sitting in the railroad station at Topeka waiting for a late train far into the early hours of the morning. I was shivering while lying on the hard wooden seats trying to sleep.

When we got to Chickasaw it was raining and the town was in terrible condition. The main street was knee deep in red gumbo mud, and all that could be seen was Indians, all muddy and mean looking. Dad got the family settled in a dingy room in a hotel {a small two-story frame building} and when he got to the shops he found there was a strike on. While he was not a union man, neither was he going to be a strikebreaker, and what was most pertinent was that he had not been told there was a strike.

As we were traveling on passes, Dad went to the division superintendent and requested passes back to Topeka. The superintendent refused, saying it was not his fault and besides he did not have the authority. Dad knew Mr. Lovett, the President of the railroad, so he sent a telegram to Lovett in Chicago. Within twenty-four hours a wire came back instructing the superintendent to give Dad passes for the family to return to Topeka. Believe me, Mother was happy that we would be able to leave Chickasaw, and the sooner the better.

Naturally, someone in Topeka was responsible. Dad was unhappy enough to decide to leave Topeka as soon as possible. He learned that a similar position was open at the Gulf, Colorado and Santa Fe shops at Cleburne, Texas, which at that time was a subsidiary railroad to the main line Santa Fe.

The first thing we knew, we were in Cleburne. It is situated on the Brazos River, about 40 miles southwest of Fort Worth, and the same distance from Dallas.

Living in Cleburne was a totally new experience. We stayed at a boarding house at first, operated by a southern family who had moved to Texas from Tennessee immediately after the Civil War. When we arrived in Cleburne in early February 1903, they were suffering from a silver thaw, which really was a blizzard where it had rained and frozen. Everything was shut down. There were no cabs or any type of conveyance at the railroad station. The only person on the platform as we got off the train was a very elderly southerner with a short beard, who was chewing tobacco.

Dad said to him, "Pardon me, but can you tell me how to get to the nearest hotel or boarding house?" The old fellow looked the five of us over critically, then said, "Where you all from?" Dad answered, "We're from Ohio." The man answered, "Humph. Some more of those damn northern invaders." He turned on his heel and walked away. The stationmaster directed us to a boarding house.

There were at least fifteen boarders at this large house. We had two rooms. It was temporary until our furniture arrived. The food was typically southern—grits, chicken, potatoes, corn bread and biscuits from white flour. Several of the men were from the north. They got very tired of the biscuits, which generally were quite hard. Some of the men worked with Dad at the shop, and he said they played handball with

MEMORIES OF ANOTHER TIME

the biscuits at lunchtime. These men finally persuaded the landlady to let my mother bake some good homemade bread. After that she baked every week while we were there.

I got a job taking orders for enlargements of photographs, especially portraits, which were hand-colored by artists and mounted in fancy frames. I worked there for two weeks, took two orders, earning about $4.00, and then caught the mumps. Mother kept me in the room and brought my meals up from the dining room. One of the boarders worked at the post office. When he found out I had the mumps he told the landlady it was him or the kid who would have to get out for the duration. The landlady said, "Well, he stays in his room and there are five of them and only one of you; so I guess it will be you." He moved out and ironically was then the only one in the house to get the mumps besides me.

As soon as I went to school I found that if you were a northerner you were not only ostracized, but also your contemporaries would endeavor to pick a fight with you. When the boys asked me if my parents were from Ohio I learned to say that my ancestors were from England, after which they would tell me how the north had treated the south so badly. Their parents, and particularly their grandparents, had lost their homes in the Civil War, which apparently was still being fought in the schoolyard. There were stone battles between north and the south across the creek, with a few of the boys getting hurt. The authorities then put a stop to it.

After we moved from the boarding house we lived across the street from a school, but since I was in sixth grade I had to go down town to the central school. It was a large frame building and each room had its own heating system—a large cast iron pot-bellied stove in the center of the room.

We had a young female teacher from the north. She was quite small, probably weighing not over 115 lbs., and she was very nice. In our class were several young cowpunchers that at age 18 or 20 had come back to get some schooling.

It was customary in cold weather for the janitor to place a bucket of coal alongside the stove. About the middle of the morning and afternoon the teacher would instruct one of the boys to feed some coal into the stove. It was also customary for the teacher to call on the janitor for a bundle of switches if any of the boys got obstreperous.

One morning she told one of the cowpunchers to feed the stove. When he did, there were several loud explosions. Apparently, someone had placed some cartridges in the coal bucket. The teacher jumped to the conclusion that the cowpuncher was guilty, and sent a younger boy to the janitor to obtain switches. Then she called the cowpuncher to the cloakroom, apparently expecting him to stand still while she administered the usual switching. In less time than it takes to tell it, he came back into the room with the teacher in his arms, sat her down in her chair, and said, "Wal', I guess I'm too old for school. I'm going home."

In 1904-05 Cleburne was a typical small town of about 3,000 people. There was a public square and courthouse in its center. The main business district was on the four streets facing the square. A few of the stores were not permanent, and about once a year an outfit selling shoes would rent a store and put on a big sale. I got a job with them selling baby shoes, which were a loss leader for five cents a pair. Some of the women buying them expected as much as if they were a dollar a pair. One morning the proprietor sent me to the bank to get a dollar's worth of nickels. I was all excited at being trusted by him and rushed up to the teller saying, "Please give me a nickel's worth of dollars." He said something like, "Next Sunday when we are closed."

Walking from home to town I passed the Episcopal Church. In the evening on my way home the rector would be standing at his front gate smoking. He always spoke to me in a friendly way and we became acquainted. One day he said, "Where do you go to Sunday school, Fred?" I said that occasionally we went to the Methodist church. On Saturdays he had a Boys Brigade in the churchyard, and I often stood outside the fence watching. One day he said, "Fred, I saw you watching our boys on Saturday. You could join us if you would like to, although we usually limit membership to our church." I asked Dad and Mother if I could join and they said, "sure, go ahead if you like."

Reverend Johnson, the Episcopal minister, was from England and was not married. He seemed to take a liking to me and I to him. After I had belonged to the Brigade for a while he asked if I would like to

MEMORIES OF ANOTHER TIME   15

come to his Sunday school, and again my folks said, "OK, if you wish." Later, the Reverend asked me to join the choir, which I did.

One day he said, "You know, Fred, I'm not supposed to have a person singing in the choir unless they belong to the church. I don't want to pressure you, but if you would like, the Bishop is coming in a few weeks and that would be the time to join." My folks thought that would be all right, so I started to learn the catechism. Three weeks later Dad decided to move back to Hammond, Indiana. He had been offered superintendency at a locomotive rebuilding shop in Hegewisch, Illinois. That was in almost walking distance of Hammond. So I did not become an Episcopalian.

We moved onto a ten-acre farm at the East End of Hammond, near South Chicago, Illinois. Dad thought he would go into the chicken raising business on the side, with a man named Jack Thompson and me as assistants.

Our farm was across from the Hammond city-park, and I enjoyed playing in the park whenever I had the opportunity. The farm was mostly in corn, except for some vegetables, including a large plot of asparagus, and a small plot of horseradish.

I went to school part of the time. I was in the eighth grade at Hammond Central School. Then I went to work as a machinist apprentice at the locomotive shop where Dad was superintendent. Later I spent some months as a pattern-maker apprentice, and then as a boilermaker apprentice. I didn't spend much time in any one trade to get really proficient, but it did give me a good idea of each. This stood me in good stead later when I studied engineering.

I was about fourteen years old but very small for my age. By that time there was a child labor law, and the inspectors would not believe I was much over eleven. My age had to be proved to them to allow me to work in the shops.

While going to school it was my job to feed the chickens, cut the asparagus, etc. I had an agreement with Dad and was getting small wages for this work. However, one Saturday there was a Sunday school picnic in the park. I knew quite a few of the children. They invited me to join in their games. I became so engrossed that I forgot all about the time until Jack Thompson came over and told me I better go home and take care of the chickens. I wasn't on the best of terms with Jack because he teased me so much, so I didn't obey him. I did go home later, but it was after the time the chickens should have been fed.

Dad wasn't feeling very good physically, so when I got home he really jumped on me hard. He gave me a tongue-lashing like never before, and it seemed to me it was not called for at all. He said that if I couldn't live up to my obligations at home I could just find another home. I told him I would just do that, whereupon I went into my bedroom and packed a few clothes.

It was late in the evening, but still not dark. Mother was greatly disturbed and said, "You must not go without having something to eat, and you had better ask your father for some money—he owes you a little." I said no; I would get along somehow. Mother packed a lunch and with my knapsack I started out. The C & E.I. Railroad ran just in back of the farm, so I started down the tracks. I had gone about three hundred feet when my brother Art came running after me with tears running down his cheeks. He said, "Dad wants you to come back. He says he didn't mean all he said." It didn't take any more for me to turn around, because by that time I was beginning to wonder just what I would do.

When I got back Dad had cooled off and talked to me as a real father. We made up. During all our years together Dad never gave me a whipping, and there were times I reckon I deserved one.

*   *   *

Several times in my life I have had close calls with death, and one was when I was working in the locomotive shop with Dad. By taking the train to Hegewisch and going into Hammond, we could then take an interurban car out to the farm. Passenger trains were just beginning to use the vestibule type car, which is all that is used now. When the train starts up, the doors to the outside on the vestibule are closed.

One of the trains stopped at Hegewisch, not far from the shop, at just a few minutes after quitting time. I was a bit late getting away from the shop and the train was pulling out just as I reached the station. Before I knew it most of the cars had passed me. Rather than miss the train I dropped my lunch bucket and stepped onto the step below the closed door. My hands were on the grab irons on the outside of the car,

MEMORIES OF ANOTHER TIME

and my feet were on the step, with my body projecting about one and a half or two feet outward. I could not let go to open the door without falling off. By that time the train was up to speed and nobody knew I was there. I tried kicking at the bottom of the door with one foot, because men were walking through the vestibule, but owing to the noise of the train nobody heard me.

By this time I was really scared. I knew it would not be long before I would fall off, and that would be the end. Just about then, who should come through the vestibule but Dad! He told me later that he didn't know what caused him to look out the window but he did, and he immediately opened the door and pulled me inside. That really taught me a good lesson, and it sure made me appreciate Dad more than ever.

The locomotive shop ran out of work so Dad procured a job with the Rambler auto building plant in Kenosha, Wisconsin as an engine inspector. He had considerable experience on auto engines; having assembled the first engine put into a Peerless auto {one of the very early high-class cars}. Dad helped me apprentice as a tool grinder, at which trade I worked about six months.

Then I saw an ad for a boy to become an apprentice to be a pharmacist. At the time I felt I would very much like to be a druggist so I applied and landed the job. The job was with the Kradwell Drug Company. At that time in Wisconsin if one worked about five years in a drug store and passed the examination, you could get a license.

After I worked a few months at the drugstore Dad was offered a better job with the Kiselkar Company at Hartford, Wisconsin so we moved to Hartford. With Dad's help I secured a job with the company for which he worked, as a clerk and roustabout, picking up time slips, helping with the shipping of parts, etc.

The Kissel plant was much smaller than the Rambler plant and had many more parts of their car made for them by others. They were the first company in the United States to put out a car with a four-cylinder engine. Apparently they purchased the design drawings, because when we got there they did not have a mechanical engineer on their staff. They did have a body designer and assistant.

Being of German descent, Dad spoke excellent German, and Hartford was almost completely settled with people of German extraction. One day the foundry foreman told Dad there was a mechanical engineer {expert engine designer} from Germany working as a laborer in the foundry. Largely because he could not speak English he had not let many folks know about his ability. Dad talked to the man, Herman Palmer. He was the son of the designer of the Palmer-Singer car of Germany. Dad then spoke to George Kissell. As a result Mr. Palmer was brought into the office and given a drawing board next to my desk.

Palmer immediately set to work redesigning the engine to make it easier to build. It was my first contact with an engineer. Mr. Palmer used me as much as he could to learn to speak English fluently, so we became well acquainted. He let me look at his engineering books, but as they were written in German I didn't get much out of them except to whet my desire to learn engineering.

The work was quite heavy for Dad, and his health was very poor. Since he was also an experienced railroad clerk he applied for a position at the Milwaukee Railroad's main office in Milwaukee. He also felt the schools and living conditions would be much better in Milwaukee for us boys.

At the time the Milwaukee Road was extending its road to the Pacific Coast, so John W. Taylor, the Chief Storekeeper in charge of all store departments, immediately hired Dad. Dad started working in Milwaukee and for a month or two came home to Hartford on weekends. This was about 1908. To help move the family to Milwaukee Dad learned of an opportunity for me in the Milwaukee store department of the railroad. I obtained a job as shipping clerk in the brass goods section, which handled all brass fittings and valves required for locomotives, passenger and freight cars.

Milwaukee turned out to be the nicest place we had lived up to that time, although Dad often spoke about wishing he could go back to Tacoma, Washington in the Puget Sound area. He had been out there about 1893, when times were very bad and he couldn't get a job, so had returned to Cleveland.

About the time the Milwaukee Road completed it extension, someone at the Falk Company, which was next door to the Milwaukee shops, told Mr. Taylor they needed a man to organize and run a store department for them. Mr. Taylor recommended Dad because work was slacking off on the railroad and he had to cut his force. Dad took on the Falk job, and shortly thereafter he asked me if I would like to be

MEMORIES OF ANOTHER TIME   19

his receiving clerk. I took the job at $75.00 per month, which in those days was good money for a lad about 18 years old.

In the meantime I had learned that I could study engineering at the University of Wisconsin night school. They had just opened an extension school as an experiment and I became one of their first students. I made good grades in drafting, and decided it would be wise to try to get started in an engineering office. Dad encouraged me in this idea.

I spoke to Mr. Andrew, head of the kerosene engine department at Falk's, and he said all he could offer at the time was a job as blueprint boy in beginner detail draftsman at $50.00 per month. That was a big drop in pay for me; however Dad said there was no opportunity for advancement in the store department where I had been working, and Mr. Andrews felt that an increase in salary would be available in a few months, so I became a blueprint boy.

Shortly after I went to work for Andrews, the Falk Company decided to discontinue making the engines. Fortunately there was an opening for a junior draftsman in the new herringbone gear department engineering office, under Mr. Percy Day, Chief Engineer. Mr. Day was a fine engineer and I obtained some good experience under him.

A few months later Dad Greaves died from a severe heart attack. He practically died in my arms immediately after eating a heavy meal. Dad had no insurance, as no company would insure him because of his heart.

My salary was still only $50.00 per month. It was imperative that I earn more money, as I was now sole support of the family. I spoke to Mr. Falk myself. He said he couldn't give me a raise and suggested we move into poorer quarters because at $33.00 per month we were paying too much in rent. As there were five of us we needed a house with two bedrooms.

Mr. Falk raised my dander, and I asked folks about where I might find a better job. Someone told me the T.L. Smith Company, manufacturers of concrete mixers, might have an opening. I called on Mr. Brackenbury, chief engineer of that department, and he promptly offered me $75.00 a month so I left Falk's.

By that time I had met a young woman and we had fallen in love. Ottilie Mueller and I were practically engaged to be married, but Dad's passing made us agree that the marriage was quite a long way off.

Because John Bayne had been Dad's best friend, I naturally wrote to him about Dad's death. He was a locomotive engineer working on the new line being extended to Seattle-Tacoma. He responded to my letter asking if I would like to apply for a position in Seattle as a draftsman. He boosted the idea by telling me what a wonderful part of the country Puget Sound was, and how he wished he had come out there earlier in life.

I wrote back telling him that if a job with sufficient increase in pay justified it, I would certainly give the matter serious consideration. He obtained the name of J.V. Paterson, president of Seattle Construction and Dry Dock Company, which had several good Navy contracts for vessels.

I wrote an application to Mr. Paterson, giving him an outline of my experience. To my great surprise I received an offer of a job as a detail mechanical draftsman by return mail and offering $100.00 per month. This was $25.00 a month more than I was making so after serious consideration, I accepted the job, and on April 13, 1914, arrived in Seattle.

John Bayne met me and took me down to introduce me to Mr. Paterson. The next day I was turned over to Mr. Allen, the chief draftsman.

Knowing nothing about ships everything was new to me. Except for the weather, the first three weeks in Seattle were very depressing. I did not immediately make friends, because I needed to learn about ships as fast as possible.

By July I was pretty well settled in my job and sent for Mother and my three half brothers. I found a new five-room house on the outskirts of the city. The rent was $12.00 per month. There were no sidewalks or even grading. There were tree stumps in front of the house. Soon after we moved in, the street was graded and it proved to be a good home for about four years.

CHAPTER 3
MAKING A LIFE WITHOUT A FATHER

By
Ernest Giffen

In 1903, before my second birthday, we moved to Fowler, a small farming community in Fresno County. That year the first automobile to be owned by a resident of Fowler was brought to town.

My father was a minister who had spent much of his life organizing or serving as a minister to newly organized churches.

Following the death of his first wife, my father married my mother. From that union they had three children. My two sisters are younger than I am. We moved to Fowler, California in 1903, then to the Yakima Valley in Washington for a few years. We then returned to the old home at Fowler, where my father, whose health had not been good for many years, died shortly after my tenth birthday.

I had been doing farm chores that were expected of boys growing up on a farm, but after father went, I took on an increasing number of chores. Mother secured some work as a substitute teacher. Within a few years, I was delivering milk to town on my bicycle. I remember that the first work I had away from home was for a neighbor at 75 cents a day.

My schooling at Fowler was uneventful. The grammar school was an eight-grade school, and for the most part, one grade to a room. The high school was the county four-year high school. It lacked many of the enriching courses, which could be provided by a larger school. Many of the boys found it necessary to be absent from school a good deal to help with the farm work.

Part of my high school time was during the First World War. We had two years with rather good crops and were able to sell them at higher than usual prices. With our newfound "riches", we were able to install inside plumbing in the house. Up till then, we had pumped our water from a well with a hand pump and carried it into the house in a bucket. Our bathing facilities consisted of a galvanized washtub in the middle of the kitchen floor. The old fashioned outhouse provided other sanitary facilities. We had no electricity in the house, nor did we have electricity when we sold the farm in 1922. The old kerosene lamps provided our light at night. When I was a junior in high school, we purchased our first automobile.

I went to Occidental College in 1920. For most of the first two years I lived in the men's dormitory, then for two years with my family who had moved to Eagle Rock in 1922. I secured a job as a janitor, which I maintained for four years, and I also worked in the college cafeteria for four years. I was able to find other work, particularly on weekends. During my senior year, I was teaching assistant in the Philosophy Department.

During college I participated in track and cross-country, was on the debating team for awhile, worked on the college newspaper, spent some time on the annual literary journal, and spent a good deal of time with my college sweetheart. In between these various activities, I was able to complete my class work adequately, and graduated with honors.

Shortly after graduation I was married, and we left for the University of California at Berkeley where I had been awarded a teaching fellowship in the Philosophy Department. As I recall, my stipend was $62.50 a month. I had saved money from my employment during college. In Berkeley we rented a very meagerly furnished apartment.

We soon did what many other students were doing--we supplemented our furniture with storage cabinets, closets and cupboards made from apple or orange boxes, which in those days were made from wood rather than cardboard. We also soon learned the stores and markets that had the most reasonable prices on food.

MEMORIES OF ANOTHER TIME

Much of our recreation centered around cultural and other events on the campus that either had no admission charge or very low priced admission.

Not too long after my wife became pregnant, she became ill and the doctor tried various treatments. However, a proper diagnosis was not made until after the birth of our son in September. At that time we learned that she had tuberculosis. I gave up my teaching fellowship and we returned to Los Angeles. There I was able to secure work as a gardener, which, while not paying much, did provide quite a little flexibility, so that I could be away from work as needed. My wife passed away in February 1926, and my son, then five months old, and I moved in with my mother and my two sisters. I secured a job delivering Sparkletts drinking water in the Hollywood area.

While working on this delivery job, I had been in contact with grammar and high school friends in Fresno County, and had been offered the job of Child Welfare Supervisor in the Fresno County Schools, if I could secure the necessary credential. This was a new certificate created by the State Department of Education in "Child Welfare and Attendance," which was an upgrading of the previous "truant officer" credential.

I arranged a meeting with the state superintendent of public instruction, and he authorized the issuance of the certificate to me if I successfully completed certain designated courses in summer school and would continue attending summer school for several years thereafter. I did complete the required courses.

I bought a car, a four-cylinder Dodge sedan, which for me was a new experience. I moved with mother, my two sisters and my son to Fresno where as I recall, my salary was a magnificent $200 a month. I remained in Fresno for five years, attending summer school and taking courses in education and social work.

In 1931, I returned to the University at Berkeley and secured another teaching assistant job. In June 1934, for health reasons, I returned to Southern California. This was in the depths of the Depression.

I looked continuously for work, until finally in December of 1934, with the assistance of a college classmate, I was able to get employment with the State Emergency Relief Administration and was assigned to the Pasadena office. As I recall, my salary was $90 a month for working six days a week. I worked for a while as a complaint clerk, then had a caseload both in investigation and supervision, and my final assignment was helping with a study and survey of self-help cooperatives. During employment with the State Emergency Relief Administration, I became engaged to a fellow worker.

In the meantime, I had taken the Los Angeles County civil service examination for Deputy Probation Officer. I remained with SRA until I received notice of my appointment as a DPO, and in February 1937, began work in the Los Angeles County Probation Department.

February 1937 was still in the Great Depression. The base pay for the Deputy Probation Officer was $150 a month, and everybody was taking a 10% cut. However, $135 was so much more than I had been getting at SRA that Betty and I figured we could make it and were married several months after I went to work. We had my son from a previous marriage and eventually added two boys and one girl to our family. All of my children are still living, and I have 14 grandchildren and four great-grandchildren.

*   *   *

Addendum: From the foregoing no hint is given that he was widowed, lonely and plagued by arthritis to the point of immobilizing him in a wheel chair for the latter years of his life. True to his upbringing, he played the hand he was dealt without complaining.

CHAPTER 4

GROWING UP IN EARLY LOS ANGELES

By
Nort Sanders

IN THOSE pre - radio and pre – TV days social visitation was customary with Sunday activity including "motoring" in the country or picking up friends and sight - seeing around town and the suburbs. Oddly, my folks always had me going to Sunday school but I never recall either ever attending church. Papa was regarded as an authority on the bible and I recall his discussing and explaining it to friends on several occasions.

Papa owned one of the first automobiles that scared the horses in Los Angeles. Some of my first memories involve the excitement of getting up at 3:00 AM, dressing, packing clothing and food, loading the car and taking off for the Castro ranch. I recall my folks outfitted in dust - protective clothing. Mother carried a parasol for protection from the sun. Roads were unpaved, single lanes with "turnouts" for passing, and in the mountains, navigating blind curves and sounding the horn to warn approaching vehicles did little for my mother's serenity.

It was always a relief to reach Santa Maria and turn inward toward the ranch country. The ranch was situated in the beautiful foothills and consisted of hundreds of acres of level and mountain land covered with live oaks and frequent streams.

My father bought - or had made for me - a small saddle. I rode my horse right along with the others as we went into the hills to locate or move cattle. My mother and I spent at least a month each summer with the Castro's until I was 11 or 12.

We did a lot of camping, often with Uncle Jim's family. I had a BB gun at first, then a .22 automatic rifle and did some hunting with a small shotgun. I found killing birds and animals not to my liking and never resumed it.

On a number of occasions we took the steamer to Catalina Island and stayed in the "Tent City".

The number of playmates in the neighborhood, mostly boys, offset the disadvantage of being "an only child". Down at the corner of 8th street was a large double vacant lot that became our year - around sports and recreation area. Across the street was a tennis court that was also available for our use.

I grew up in the Wilshire district of Los Angeles when the city was at its finest: bursting with an adolescence that was the envy of the country, where the future held only promises and opportunities and a good part of Iowa was moving to Long Beach.

The climate was the envy of the world with air so clean it sparkled. For a nickel you could ride for miles on the Yellow cars through a seemingly endless metropolis. The Red Cars in the country's finest inter - urban transportation system could take you, sometimes at 70 MPH, anywhere in Southern California far faster than you could drive. It always seemed most of the time you were traveling through orange groves. Neighbors did a lot of visiting.

You belonged to a Boy Scout troop; mine was #8 and met at the Presbyterian Church at 3rd and Western where I also attended Sunday school.

Frequently, while in elementary school, I'd take a small, packed bag with me to school on Fridays, then take the street car down town, go to the Pacific Electric Station, purchase a round trip ticket then board one of the "Big Red Cars" headed for Newport - Balboa. Upon arrival I took the ferry across to the island. From there I would hike up to Garnet Street to find Grandma and Grandpa eagerly waiting my arrival. It was at their home on Balboa Island I spent most of my week - ends as well as Easter and summer vacations.

Grandma and Grandpa were a case of "opposites attracting each other." She was the epitome of poise, refinement and an old - fashioned delicacy of manner and presence. Grandpa had been a bit of a 'rounder' and had lost an eye in a bar fight. Finding peppermints in his left coat pocket, it never occurred to me that they constituted an excellent cover for an otherwise alcoholic breath.

Grandpa had a couple of rowboats and an outboard motor. We often fished in the Bay and usually with success.

Until I started Junior High School, ours was a consistently happy home. It was a popular locale for visiting relatives.

Nevertheless, it was there the saddest event of my life occurred. I had selected Lad while still a newborn pup. I trained him and his devotion and intelligence was the talk of the neighborhood. Each afternoon upon returning from Virgil Jr. High School I would find Lad waiting out on the front lawn to greet me. When skating he was always my "tow" and was my "tag along" when I went anywhere in the neighborhood. When run over and killed by a car, I was distraught for days. This was the only tragedy I have experienced.

A few blocks west of us was a large farmhouse with a water tower with enclosed nests for birds and pigeons. I used to take a gunnysack, climb the tower after dark, reach into the cubbyholes and usually find a pigeon or two.

About a mile west we found two swimming holes, "Sandys" and "Four Dead Cats." These were our outdoor Jonathan Clubs where we skinny - dipped, then enjoyed the sophistication of smoking corn silk, sawdust, or coffee cigarettes while drying off.

It was during the world - wide Flu plague, circa 1917, that I came down with a severe case of Diphtheria that nearly cost me my life. I survived but recovery was slow. I was crippled with damaged vision and kept out of school for almost a year.

My physical and visual restrictions took some getting used to; I'd been adept and active in all sports and always was an avid reader. Eventually, I could resume reading but even after I returned to school I had to forego all athletics and gym activity for a year.

My employment record began with a small, weekly route delivering the Literary Digest at 10 cents per copy; shortly thereafter I had a Shopping Guide route. Every Friday a truck would dump two large bundles of these in front of the house and my evening would be occupied in tri - folding these papers in preparation for depositing some 100 of them on residential doors Saturday morning. A bicycle riding teen "paymaster" would locate us and pay us the couple of dollars due.

Saturday afternoons I also did house - to - house distribution of the weekly list of movies to be shown at the neighborhood movie house. As the shows were changed almost daily and I had earned free entry; my alleged nightly trips to study at the library experienced a constant array of detours offering additional explanation why I never attained Rhodes scholar status.

CHAPTER 5

AN ALASKAN ADVENTURE

By
Howard Rustad

MY FATHER was born in early day Wisconsin at Fort Rossacree. Grandmother's most exciting memory was of the time he was in his crib and the Indians came one day and asked her for food. She said "No". One of the Indians grabbed my father from the crib and started off. He got his food all right.

My father had to go to work and support the family when he was 12 years old. He spent one summer driving cattle from the Black Hills down into the Mississippi River area where they were shipped by boat south.

Moving west in 1888, he landed in Seattle and thought he was in heaven. Instead of snow it was rain and it was warmer. He always talked about the dry rain of Seattle. He said you could be out in the rain and it would dry as fast as it hit you.

He apparently had been in Seattle but a short time when the Seattle fire started in a paint shop. The fire was uncontrollable and didn't stop until it had burned out all of the main buildings in downtown Seattle.

With all the buildings destroyed he figured it was a good time to go into business for himself. By this time in his life he had worked at a number of trades with moderate success. With downtown Seattle needing to be rebuilt he figured there was an immediate need for plumbing and heating supplies so he started a shop above Fourth Avenue.

I was encouraged to help around the store. My father would always ask me if I would like to go with him when he went to meet customers. I remember one day he said, "I just got a call from Billy the Muggs. How would you like to go with me and see what they want?"

Billy the Muggs was quite a good-sized store. It catered largely to loggers. It was only a block and a half from father's business. We walked up there. It was the first saloon I had ever been in. I noticed there was a bar on each side the whole length of the building. There was only one entrance in the middle. There was nobody at the bar with the exception of one man drinking beer and a barkeeper at each bar. My father was told to go down stairs. The whole downstairs was about the same size as the room above but it was just full of men.

The loggers would come in the winter because they couldn't work. They would buy a beer or two then go downstairs to spend their day reading papers, playing cards, snoozing or what have you. It provided a comfortable place for them to while away the winter months when there was no work.

While still in the basement area he said "I've got to go to Chinatown, how would you like to go?" He opened a door inside the room leading into a tunnel.

When Seattle burned down, they raised the main street up and run all the electrical and piping at the old level. All the businesses in downtown Seattle were heated by steam from a central steam plant.

We zigzagged for a ways until my father opened a door to the worst smell of my life. These Chinese stores carry everything. We went upstairs to the store. That was the kind of thing that opened my eyes to things most kids don't get a chance to see.

My father always kept his older employees. One was named Lawrence. He had been in the Civil War. He became head of the local veterans group, the GAR. [Grand Army of the Republic] He always had a lot of his GAR fellows come in to visit for a while. Years later I took him with me on a trip to Bremerton. There he was treated like a "Big Shot".

When the Depression hit my father's business just went to pot. He had enough coming in to drag along but he needed my help to keep everything going. Of course Kathryn and I were married in 1930. The plumbers and Steamfitters were only averaging one hour a day of work and my father would say, "I only wish I was making as much as they did".

MEMORIES OF ANOTHER TIME   31

*   *   *

My mother was born in Scotland and immigrated to the United States
by way of Canada. One story she told me of life in Scotland has stuck
in my memory.

The day before the family was to sail for America her father asked
her to go over and pay the fishmonger. He wanted to get that paid up
before they left. When she got there the fishmonger was just pulling
out a couple fish for a small boy. He was there to buy a fish for the family. One was a fairly good-sized fish with the head cut off. The other
was quite a bit smaller but with the head still on. The fishmonger said,
"Which one do you want?" The kid pointed to the one with the head
on it. The fishmonger said "but there is a lot more meat on the other".
The little boy said "But the head is my share."

Her family left Scotland when my mother was seventeen. My grandfather died not long after and left a lot of young children. My mother
was next oldest. That left my mother to support that family and bring
them up. She was in high school when she was orphaned.

*   *   *

My sophomore year in high school the YMCA agreed to supply high
school kids to the canneries up in Alaska during the summer. Adult
labor was scarce due to the military call up for WW I. A private railroad
car was held for us at the railroad station to take us up to Bellingham.
There we got on a cannery boat taking us to the cannery.

They had Blacks in the hold, the steerage. We were first class. We
were thirteen days going up on the Bering Sea to Port Moller.

On the trip up we traveled the Inside Passage to Ketchican and
then went out the Dixon entrance over to Kodiak Island. The passage
into Kodiak itself is quite narrow. A lot of boats couldn't get in there.
We came out again and went down the Alaska Peninsula. We had some
pretty rough weather approaching Kodiak. The boat would be riding
on top of the waves but they had to cut the speed down because of the
danger of ripping the sides out on the bare spots.

I didn't get sick, in fact, I don't get sick. I might get sick the first meal that's all. I won't stay inside if it is rough. If you walk you can level everything off. It's the changing all the time that makes you sick.

There were fifty blacks in steerage. They went on strike immediately they got off the boat. They didn't work all summer. They fished for food. They got what they called cucumber fish. They smelled like cucumbers.

We didn't have much to do. There was an Indian village within a quarter of a mile. We did have a sea lion came up to the cannery and they [the Indians] rushed over to get it up on the beach.

On the way up there was a wealthy kid with us who went to our school. At the time we left his family had given him a rifle. All he did all day long was take that rifle apart and put it back together. He wouldn't go out and look at any scenery. He came up for meals and that's about all he did.

One night it sounded like the boat blew up. He had accidentally fired his rifle. The bullet went through the wall into the next cabin, parted the hair of a man in that cabin, went through the door, splitting it and then went through a lifeboat. The Captain was as mad as could be and confiscated the rifle.

Pretty near all the kids had rifles but I couldn't see having a rifle up there. The only wild life in the area was the Kodiak bear. And who was going to tackle a Kodiak bear? I never was interested in hunting and fishing.

Once we got there, there wasn't much salmon. I was through work by ten o'clock in the morning. My job was to take the trays with the canned fish and slide them off onto a dolly and then carry them into storage to cool. Instead of being busy all the time, we were getting very little fish. We were paid by the day. I came back after paying board, room and transportation with $145.00 which was more than I could have made in Seattle. The wages were clear and in between jobs you could longshore or stevedore and make extra money. I didn't work at that.

When we got up there they assigned the kid who had had his rifle confiscated to my cabin. There were two of us to a room in a string of rooms in one building. Each room had a stove inside and a stairway out.

MEMORIES OF ANOTHER TIME

Without a rifle he took to collecting. He got a ground squirrel and put it in a barrel and kept it by our entrance. He bought Wolverine furs from the Indians.

One day I came in and found a Kodiak bear skin taking up most of the wall. It smelled to high heaven. I said "You take that thing out of here". He said, "I got no place to put it". I said, "Put it outside". Finally what he did was pack away the Wolverine skins so he could hang the bearskin on the wall. Eventually, you got so used to the smell you hardly knew it was there.

When he ran out of things like that to do I took him out to collect and press flowers. I had taken Botany that year and there were a great number of very beautiful flowers in the area.

In later years in Seattle, during rough weather, he was crushed to death between the pontoons of his seaplane and the dock.

We pitched horseshoes when not working. I picked up a lot of black stones on the beach that I had a hunch were silver oxide. Where we were it was very sandy with some small rocks.

In the cemetery the persons buried would be covered by the sandy soil, then the water would wash the sand out and leave the person uncovered. Then they would rebury them.

One night a volcano maybe fifteen miles away blew. I didn't wake up for it. There was just one big blast, that was all.

On the Fourth of July at midnight we decided to go down and jump in the ocean. We took all our clothes off. We did get in the ocean and it was cold. The Indian village was no more than a quarter mile away. They and their squaws all came down. We decided we better get dressed again.

Coming home we were two and a half days in the icy straits with nothing but the log and our compass to keep us posted. We hit within a mile of the entrance to icy straits.

*   *   *

I had another sea adventure some years later in 1923. The Dorothy Alexander was the smallest of the Alexander boats. Even so it must have had three or four hundred passengers. The boat was to leave Seattle at midnight and pick up somebody at four o'clock in the morning off

Victoria. It started to snow just as the boat left. By morning there was three inches of snow on the decks. They had to go half speed so instead of four o'clock it was eight o'clock in the morning when we reached Victoria. We spent quite a bit of the day getting out through the straits of Juan d' Fuca.

When we got outside we hit the roughest sea they had had in years. Many, many smaller boats went down during that storm. We traveled down the Washington coast. It was so rough only five of us came down to eat. One was a girl about my age, about 22 I guess. We just walked the decks all the time because we didn't want to get down where everybody was sick. That night we didn't seem to get sick. No one came on deck or for meals until we got to San Francisco. I walked alone in the morning and together with the girl in the afternoon when the sun was warmer.

One morning I was walking the promenade deck alone when I just happened to look up and here was the biggest wave coming I ever saw in my life. It was probably several hundred feet away. I ran as fast as I could to a passage within a hundred feet of where I was. As I cleared the passage three or four feet of water came right behind me. It would have taken me down the other deck and that would have been the last of me if I hadn't seen it. That wave might have been eighty feet high. They call them rogue waves.

When we got down to southern California I was on deck about seven o'clock in the morning as I remember. There were about eight or ten people on the foredeck. We were talking while taking in the balmy, fragrant air and clear skies. I thought, "Gee, this is wonderful place". I happened to look back over my left shoulder to a place near the top of the hill. I said "I'm going to live up there someday" and I pointed to it. I never thought of that again until thirty years later when we bought a lot and built a house up there. I remember this so vividly because it was so different from what we had just been through. I just thought that it was a wonderful place to live. I didn't know I would ever live up there but I was just feeling that way that day.

My two roommates on the boat were Canadians. They took me in tow. That was nice because they had been traveling off and on. They were both carpenters. The older one knew how to pick out a boarding place. Two of us would go in the building to see if we liked the setup.

MEMORIES OF ANOTHER TIME

Then we would say, "Well, we will have to talk it over with our friend". That gave us a way to get out. Finally we saw this place at sixth and Alvarado across from Westlake Park. The older fellow said, "There will be something doing in this place". They had a beautiful big living room with a fireplace and piano. It was a mansion that had been dropped down to being a boarding house. We got one big front bedroom. We were there most of the year.

*   *   *

Back in Seattle, the Depression came along. I had seven or eight draftsmen working for me then. I had to let one after another go. Eventually they came to me and said I was to be next but if I would run a warehouse while the country was in a depression, they would give me my old job back when times got better.

I didn't have any college degree. I had had to give up the University because of illnesses. My education really started when I went to work.

One of the kids was going to the University of Washington days and working nights. He was graduating and his job was open. So I requested the watchman's job so I could go back to school. Working full time it took me twelve years to finally get my engineering degree.

CHAPTER 6

A COAL MINER'S DAUGHTER

By
Hazel Schmeil

I WAS BORN at home in Roslyn, Kittitas Co., Washington on July 15, 1904 to Arthur Thompson born October 26, 1878 and wife Agnes, formerly Hewitson, born March 28 1878.

One of the first things that I remember of my early life was the Christmas that my brother Carol was born. I was sitting by the oven door, crying because Mama was sick, and Î was sure that Santa Claus would forget to come to our house.

We always had a tree in the parlor. On Christmas morning, we would have our stocking and then breakfast before gifts. The presents would be unwrapped under the tree. Mom always had a good dinner of us.

Papa was bringing the wash from the outside clothes line, and they were frozen stiff. The north wind was blowing, and the ground was covered with snow. Those winters in Montana were really rugged.

The next morning everything turned out right, as Santa had come, and later there was a baby brother for us. Later in the week I visited the neighbors and told them that I had a baby brother, and he would be a boy till he was a man and his name was "the sun moon and starzy boy."

We were living in Red Lodge, Montana at the time that Carol was born but later moved to Bear Creek, a smaller town but closer to the mines where our father worked. In those days the men walked to their work, so tried to be as near as possible to the job.

37

Bear Creek was a small town and very muddy. We were forever cleaning mud from our shoes. We lived in a very small house there, and I remember after my sister Dorothy was born, mother was very ill with blood poisoning and Dad brought a bull pup home. We kept it in a small box in the house and Dad thought he would look better with his ears clipped short, also his tail, so he cut them off. Every time the pup bumped either end, he would howl in pain! Poor mother, she fussed at Dad for it, as she couldn't stand the noise of the dog and all us children.

I think about that time, one of mother's friends took me home to help out. I was unhappy there away from my parents. When she took me to visit I would not go back with her. She tried to bribe me with a new doll, but I preferred to stay with the family.

When Aunt Betty was visiting us in Bear Creek I burned my hand really bad. Mom had hired a horse and buggy to take us to a picnic. Aunt Betty was making fun of my burns and putting my arm in a sling. However, my hand had blood poisoning and she didn't laugh anymore.

We moved back to Red Lodge again as I remember living in a very large apartment over the blacksmith shop. The place must have been partly furnished as when Mama was looking through some of the dresser drawers she found signs of mice. I was very proud of myself when I found the nest with tiny pink mice in it! She was horrified and made me drop them.

I thought the blacksmith was a nice man. Quite often on our way in, he would offer me a nickel if I would sing for him. The temptation was great, but I was too bashful. Edna offered to sing, so I guess she collected the money.

Red Lodge is a small city but it seemed big when I was there. Papa would take us on long walks on Sunday while Mama fixed the Sunday dinner. It seemed such a long way home, and his legs were long and he took very long steps and walked too fast. Mama took us to Sunday school in the morning, which was on the other side of town. It was a long walk there, too!

The only thing that I remember about my first day at school was the little girl in the red silk dress. I was sure she came from a rich family, to wear such a beautiful dress. She ran away the first day.

MEMORIES OF ANOTHER TIME

I was helping my Dad clean up the yard after a severe winter. The glass in one of the windows had blown out, and buried in the snow. After it had melted away, Dad usually cleaned the yard. I thought if I broke it into little pieces, it would be easier to remove. I had a rock and was pounding it up when a small piece flew up and hit me in the eye. I ran in crying to Mama. She said the color from my eyes was running down my face. The Doctor said it just missed the sight in my eye. It was painful for me to lie in bed, so many nights Mama sat up with a pillow on her lap, and my head on it.

One Christmas when we were in Red Lodge, Montana, times were bad and we were so hard up that Mama made all the toys. Best remembered were calico dolls and animals from the scrap bag that we always seemed to have. That Christmas was a joyful time, even if we did not have much. We were together as a family.

My responsibilities on holidays included making beds, emptying the pot and helping with the dishes. I liked to help Mom with the cooking.

We always had good homemade bread, also vegetable soup. Sunday was special with pot roast, mashed potatoes and gravy and always a yummy lemon pie. My Dad would call me pie face, as I would clean up my plate first and get ready for more pie.

There was a river in back of our house. Dad used to go fishing after work. While we were living there a little boy drowned one spring evening. When they took him from the river someone came to the house for a blanket to wrap him in. Later the family returned a new blanket.

Work there for Dad was poor so he went back to Roslyn, Washington to work. He took Sister Edna with him, so Mama would have one less to care for. She stayed with our grandparents and he stayed part of the time there and some of the time with his sister Sarah, who also lived there. After he had enough money saved, he sent for us to join him.

We then moved to Ronald, two miles west of Roslyn, and lived in our Grandpa's little house. He had two houses on the same lot. The one we used was very small. There were three rooms, but I think that the kitchen was unfinished as we only used two rooms at first. Later we used the kitchen, too.

After we moved to Grandpa's big house, there was an epidemic of scarlet fever, and we lost my little sister Dorothy. We were in quarantine for several weeks. I think I was the only one in the family that did not get it. My parents had to take my sister to the cemetery on the back road, with no service or people there. By now there were only five of their nine children left.

When we were living at that house Mama was sick and spent some time in the hospital. My sister Myrtle took over much of the care of the children. It was quite a job for her as she was only in her early teens. Aunt Sarah would come some times and help her with the work.

My parents bought a large two-story five-bedroom house down the street where we lived the rest of the time until I was married. It was never painted. It had a shed in back where Mom did the family laundry and the boarders had their bath after working in the mine. The toilet was up the hill at the back of the lot.

As there was lots of room there Mom thought she could help out by taking in boarders. Her first paying guest was a schoolteacher. They put a bed in the parlor with the piano for her. She stayed several years with us. Her home was in Cle Elum and she went home every weekend.

Dad used to play the piano. I think he played by ear, having played the big horn in the band. When he was in the band marching in the parade, I liked to stop and ask for a nickel to spend; knowing if he didn't have one, one of the other players would come up with it.

The Fourth of July was always a big time for us, with the parade and big celebration in Roslyn. We saved our money for then. My grandfather Hewitson always had a booth where we could win something. We went on the train to Roslyn and sometimes walked, as it was only a couple of miles.

I went every Saturday to Roslyn to take piano lessons from my cousin. I thought she played beautifully and loved to have her play for me. One time when I was going for my lesson I washed my hair and rinsed with olive oil in the water. I was so proud when she asked me what I had done to my hair. Mom had a fit when she saw it and had me wash it out.

Ronald was a small town. There was no church there. Much of our religious services were held in the school. Mom usually went and took us with her. One year the Presbyterian minister would come once a week

MEMORIES OF ANOTHER TIME
41

for service and the next year, the Episcopal minister would come. In the summer we had vacation Bible school. We looked forward to that time. They always had a big picnic and program the last day.

My Mother's parents lived in Roslyn across the street from the Episcopal Church. When we went to visit them they would take us to church.

My grandmother was very strict with us. I remember when she gave us lunch outside. I didn't like the sandwich and threw it on the ground in the ashes. When she said I had to eat it, I put the sandwich down the outdoor toilet.

My first revelation of the Lord was one morning while lying in bed. I had a large picture of Christ hanging by my bed. While looking at it very intensively, I started to cry for no reason. I have thought since that He was calling me to come serve Him.

The school in Ronald burned one night. We were sure that it was the end of school for us but they fixed up the hall in Jonesville and put us there while the school was rebuilt.

I used to take my crocheting to school. One day when I was in the outside restroom, as I bent over, my crochet hook went through my pocket and stuck in my leg. I tried to get it out but just couldn't. One of the girls had to get the teacher to do it. I was really embarrassed, as it was a man teacher. I did not put my work in my pocket after that!

I was looking forward to graduation from the eighth grade, as it was quite a big thing. When it came time to graduate I did not have that pleasure because there was not enough students to put one on.

I went to high school in Roslyn the next year. We had to walk the two miles to school most of the time. Sometimes we went on the train for a nickel. The train took the miners to work in the morning and returned for them in the afternoon. That was the right time for the high school students to go to school.

I was in the tenth grade when the flu epidemic of 1918 was with us. Both my parents were down with it so I stayed out of school a few days to help take care of them. When I returned with my excuse, the principal said it was an unexcused absence and I had to make up the time by staying every night for a period of time. That meant I would miss my ride and have to walk alone the two miles home. Since it was winter it would be getting dark before I could reach home so I skipped out the first two days.

We usually walked on the railroad track. If a train came we had to get off the track and onto the deep snow while it was passing. The first couple days, I took off as usual but then the principal cornered me and put me in her office between classes so she could watch me. I had only been in there a few days when the Superintendent came in one day. He asked me what I was doing there and I gave him the whole story. He did not say much to me but later the principal came in and dismissed me. That was the end of staying in.

At noon, a few of us would take our lunch and go down town to the ice cream and lunch place, where we would buy a cup of coffee and eat lunch. Usually one of the gang would buy lunch. The owner was very kind to let us eat there. I think he looked for us every day and was disappointed when we did not show up.

The highlight of my junior year was the Junior Prom. We shopped for material for my dress. A friend of Myrtle's offered to make it. It was cerise meline and was made with a large collar and sleeveless. I felt like a princess that night.

To make a little money I washed dishes for a neighbor who had boarders. She promised to pay me 25 cents a night. When I got there a stack of dishes were piled high in the sink. I think she saved them the whole day for me. During the month, my cat Annabelle visited them and ate the canary she had on her front porch. There went my hard-earned money! Mother made me quit the job when she made me pay for the bird.

I also did some babysitting for 50 cents for all night, doing the supper dishes while they got dressed to go out.

Myrtle came home to have Mother take care of her when Jack was born. Edna and I waited on the front porch for the baby, feeling sure it would be a girl. Imagine our disappointment when they announced it was a boy. We insisted on calling him Mary. He was a husky baby and looked more like a boy, so we finally had to give up and accept him.

One time Edna and I were up in the hills close to home one spring evening when we met the neighbor's cow. She seemed tame so we got the bright idea of getting some free milk. One of us ran home and found a tin cup. We started following bossy around the hills. She was very tame

MEMORIES OF ANOTHER TIME 43

but reluctant to be milked again. Edna was doing the work and I was encouraging her! Since bossy had already been milked that evening, there wasn't much milk to be had. It was beginning to get dark by then so we took our milk home to present to Mother.

She wasn't as happy as we were and said it was the same as stealing. She made us take the milk to the owner of the cow and tell them what we had done. We got to the door with it. I pushed Edna ahead and when they opened the door, she said, "We milked your cow", and then she started crying! Mother came in behind us and they all had a good laugh but it didn't make us feel any better. I think that it was a good lesson in honesty for us.

As a teenager I would describe myself as shy, not pretty. I liked to read. I had my nose in a Bible.

I was in my early teens when World War I was over and I remember the celebrations everyone had.

I think it was about that time I began dating Jimmy. James C. "Jimmy" Norris, born in Roslyn, was just returned from service in the Navy in WW I. There he had last served on a sub-chaser patrolling Atlantic Coast waters. It was later believed that it was during that time he contacted the nephritis that took his life in 1927.

My mother and his mother got together and arranged for our first date. I was sixteen years old. They both went with us in the car to the movie in Roslyn. When we went for a ride, both our mothers went along. Later we were allowed to go alone. Cars in those days were un-common, so they never went anyplace partly empty.

After dating Jimmy for a number of months, we thought we were in love enough to get married. It was customary for the boy to ask the father for his daughter's hand. I was very nervous that night but Mother assured me that Dad would give his consent. I think Dad thought a lot of Jim, and maybe was a little happy that I was getting a nice boy.

We decided on an October wedding and set the date on Dad's birthday, which was on the 26th. My Mother thought I was too young at 17 to get married, but I had a good foundation in cooking and helping around the home. Mother had boarders and I helped with the cooking as Myrtle had left home by then. Her friend Blanche tried to talk me out of getting married, but I just listened to and thought to myself that she was old and didn't know about love. She was all of 28 then! Anyway, we got a little anxious and set up the date to October 10th.

Taking my parents and his parents with us, we went to Ellensburg to get married. We came back as far as Cle Elum where we got the train to Seattle for a honeymoon trip. From there we went on to Bellingham and back to Seattle on the boat that ran a round trip every day.

We rented a small house in back of the Company Store. I think it was furnished, as I don't remember buying furniture for it. The first thing I did was get pregnant. Of course, we were happy about that. During the winter, we moved in with my parents. Our first piece of furniture was a leather davenport that made into a bed, which we bought to sleep on in Mother's front room, or parlor, as it was called in those days.

In the early spring I became very ill with the flu. The Doctor examined me and said that the baby was dead. I was taken to the hospital in Cle Elum. One morning after they had taken the baby I was hearing the most beautiful music and was in a beautiful place. When I woke up, the Doctor and nurses were around me. I asked where the music was coming from and they looked at me like I was crazy. Later I was told that the nurse couldn't find a pulse, and they thought they had lost me. I think that is as close as I'll ever get to Heaven.

Later that year I was pregnant and looking forward to a baby. We were in the middle of painting and getting ready for the baby in early April, when he decided to come early. Jim's sister came down to put the house in order, while I sat around laughing and thinking what a good joke it would be on them, if the baby decided to wait awhile. We lived across the street from the practical nurse that helped deliver most of the babies in Ronald, and had the only phone that was close.

The Doctor came in the evening and stayed with me until the baby came. Early in the morning, a little over 4 pounds baby boy was delivered! The Doctor had problems getting him to breathe, so swatted him and put him alternately in hot and cold water. So for the first day, he lay and whimpered. He also had yellow jaundice, so the nurse was reluctant to show him to me. Jim told our parents we had a bouncing baby boy, but the Doctor had told his Mom that he didn't think the baby would live and they should go see him right away.

MEMORIES OF ANOTHER TIME

Jimmy gained fast, and by the time he was 3 months old, weighed 15 pounds! Since the coalmines went on strike almost every spring, the first of April, there wasn't much work around Ronald. Jim went to Issaquah and found a job working on construction. Around the 4th of July, he came home and we moved back with him. We had a tent and camping equipment and moved into the public campground. We had a choice spot right by the water and one of the large stoves.

The first few days we were there it rained constantly and everything in the tent was soaked, including the baby. The sun came out eventually, and we put everything out to dry. It didn't seem to bother the baby. He gained in spite of it. I would give him his bath, sitting on the bench by the stove. My mother came to visit us and found me giving the baby his bath. She very near had a fit, but I told her I was sitting by the stove, so he wouldn't get cold. Anyway, it didn't hurt him.

After we had been there a few weeks, one of the park attendants came to see us and asked if my Dad was there. He thought we had been there long enough, as the time limit in the park was only a week. I don't think we moved right away but the miner's strike settled by the first of September and we could return to our little home in Ronald.

While we were still in Issaquah, we went to Seattle by bus and visited Mrs. Bell, the lady we bought the house from and gave her the final payment on the house. She saw us coming up the street and said we looked like a couple of kids carrying a baby. We also bought a car while we were there, so had transportation home. It wasn't much of a car but we were happy with it.

*   *   *

The winters were always quite cold and we had snow from November to March. It was quite cold around New Year's Eve, and we did the usual amount of first footing, the English custom of home visits welcoming the New Year. We had left the water running in the kitchen sink, to prevent it from freezing. We came home quite late and being young, we really slept soundly. Late in the morning when Jim got up to build a fire in the kitchen range, there was about an inch or more of ice on the floor. The sink had frozen and the water ran on until it froze, too! What a mess to get up to and company coming for dinner! Jim scraped and shoveled the ice out, and we mopped up the water. We had our company come for dinner and thought it was a lark!

Both of our parents lived in Ronald, so holidays were fun, as they both wanted us for the holiday dinner. That worked out fine as Jim's parents had their meal at five o'clock or later, while my parents had their dinner around two o'clock. Being young, we could really enjoy both meals.

When Jimmy was 16 months old I went with Jim to the lookout station on Jolly Mountain. It was a summer job, as the mines were on strike again as they were almost every summer. It was fun living there in a glass house, watching for fires.

While we were there we had to go downhill a mile every day for our water. Sometimes Jim would take some of the baby's clothes down and wash them in the spring.

Jimmy got hold of the Iodine from the first aid kit and drank some of it before we knew what was happening. We phoned the Doctor right away and he told us to give him canned mild and make him vomit. We were low on supplies but found our last can and he was fine, although it scared me so much that I wanted to leave that place.

In a couple days, I started down the mountain to the main ranger station with Jimmy on my hip, and a bundle of clothes. On the way, I met the Ranger taking the supplies to the lookout station. It was eight miles to the main station, all down hill. The Ranger said that a big bear had followed me all the way down. I spent the rest of the summer at the main station at Salmon La Sac.

Jim was with the forest service the next summer in another spot where we rode a horse to the station. I was very pregnant with Bud by that time. On the way in the horse got frightened by something and started to run with Jimmy and me on his back. We were on a hill trail with the river several hundred feet below us. I was afraid the horse would fall down. Jim finally caught him and we were both O.K.

We enjoyed our summer there and I stayed until a couple of weeks before Bud was born. The job usually ended by the 10th of September, or until the first good rain, so there was no more fire hazard.

Bud was born on the 29th of August 1925 in the same house that Jimmy was born in. I was all set to have a girl but when I saw him, I wouldn't have traded him for even twin girls. Jimmy gave him his

MEMORIES OF ANOTHER TIME   47

nickname of "Bud". He climbed on the bed and looked at the baby and said, "baby sister?" I told him "no, baby brother". He repeated "baby buddy".

Work was poor in the mines then. When Bud was a few weeks old, Jim went to Bellingham to get work in the mines there. After he had worked a couple of weeks, he found an apartment and came back for us. Frank and Myrtle took us to our new house and while Frank was there, he too got a job in the mines and they moved to Bellingham. That was nice for me as I had never been away from my parents and was very lonesome that first year.

We had never lived in the city before and shopping in the dime stores was really different than the Company Store in Roslyn. We could walk to town and shop at Kress's for a pound of candy kisses for 15 cents.

During the second winter there Jim was ill and old Doc Stimpson couldn't find the trouble. Jim got steadily worse. By Christmas time, he was so bad we decided to go back to our little home in Ronald. The Doctor there decided to put him in the Veteran's Hospital in Tacoma. In January of 1926, he went there on the train by himself.

In a short time Mother and I took the boys and went to see him. He was in serious condition. My Mom and I went knocking on doors in the neighborhood to find a place that I could stay to be near the hospital. A young couple with two little girls kindly took me in. Mother took the boys and returned home.

Jim lapsed into a coma. That last morning he didn't know me. Mary could see he was going so she took me for a walk. When we returned he was gone. I felt that was the end of the world for me. He was only 26 years old, and I was 22, with two little boys to raise.

I gave up my little home in Ronald and moved in with my parents. Since work in the mines wasn't very good, I talked Dad into coming to Bellingham to find work, which he did. We found a house for them and moved them over.

Work was scarce for me, only some housework, or snipping beans in the cannery, so I started to business college thinking that would help me get work. After a few months, I found there were students that had been going for eleven months and there was no work for them yet. I gave up as it was very expensive, and I didn't have much to go on.

Myrtle and Frank were living in Marietta by that time with Grandma and were trading some at Wanamaker's store. Through them, I had a chance to work in the store. I would have lunch with Myrtle, then stay until closing time.

It was while working in the store that I first met Carl. I was at a dance at Birch Bay when my dancing partner pointed him out to me and told me that he worked at the Co-op with him. I asked him not to introduce him to me, as I didn't like the looks of him. Anyway, he did. I wasn't very impressed but later in the week, he came to the store and bought gas from me and made a date to go to a show. That was in late August in 1931 and in December, we were married. We moved in the home in Marietta with his mother, who he was living with and supporting.

My mother begged me to let her keep Jimmy. She said, "We could have other children and she wanted him". That is one of the things I will never forgive myself for doing. It's hard to put in writing the way I feel about it. My Mother and Dad gave him a good home and I know he always thought a lot of them. I did keep Bud with me.

We moved into the little house next door after living a few months with Carl's mother. While we were living there the Marietta River overflowed and water came into the house. We stayed at my folks until the river went down, then cleaned up the mess and moved back in. Not long after we bought our first home, a neat little place with a large garden spot. Carl loved to garden so we always had a big garden.

We moved several times after that. During all that time I was hoping for more family. One day I was reading in a magazine about a lady who wanted a blue rug very much and she prayed for it. I thought if she could get a rug that way, why couldn't I get a baby if I prayed for one? That was how it all started. After a few months, I became pregnant. The first boy was premature. He was a beautiful blond boy, weighing about five pounds. He only lived for six days.

I was heartbroken but wanted another one right away. This time I changed Doctors and he built me up so I could have a healthy baby. To my relief and great pleasure, on December 17, 1939, Paul was born. The boys were so proud of their baby brother they wanted to buy him an electric train for Christmas.

MEMORIES OF ANOTHER TIME

Jerry was born in 28 April 1941. We were happy to have two little boys. In December when Jerry was 7 months old, the Japanese bombed Pearl Harbor and war was declared. Bud had enlisted in the Marines, so was shipped out before we had much word from him. Jim had graduated from high school and was in the Navy.

Those were rough times, not knowing where or how Bud was. Many a night was spent in prayer for his safe return or some word from him. He went to Guadalcanal with the first Marine Division and he was only seventeen. We finally had some letters from him and at one time he sent me $300.00 to buy Christmas gifts.

We got a letter from the Red Cross telling us he had been wounded on Guadalcanal. He was taken to a hospital in Australia and then sent home to Oak Knoll in Oakland. Along with his other trouble, he had attacks of the Malaria he had contacted on Guadalcanal. Finally we had some letters from him and learned that he had landed on Guadalcanal with the First Marine Division.

By that time I was pregnant with Alice. Just before Alice was born they let Bud come home on leave. He was so thin you could almost see through him. He wanted to go to the hospital with me for the birth but labor started in the middle of the night so we took off for the hospital and left him in bed at home.

After she was born, the nurse leaned over me and said, "You have a girl, what are you going to name her"? I was still half under and said, "Finish". I was so pleased and happy to finally have a little girl after six sons. I used to look at her and think how good God had been to me. He had given me such a beautiful little girl, and what had I done to deserve her. I thank God every day for my sons and daughter. They are all so special to me.

While I was still in the hospital Bud had to report back to the hospital in California where he spent several months more. Then he was sent to a convalescent center in Colorado Springs.

When Alice was a year old we started looking for a place in the country, as Carl wanted a small farm. We bought a home on Marine Drive. The children loved it there. The former owner lived across the street. He had horses and encouraged the boys to ride his horses. They became good at riding and wanted a horse of their own. After much saving and picking up beer bottles, they had enough money to buy one.

50   A STORY TO TELL

When we moved to Marietta, the war was going on and gas was rationed, so we joined the little church in Marietta. I was involved in Church work and took the children to church and Sunday school regularly.

After the War ended, Jim was sent to Oak Harbor, WA. Joy and he planned to be married in January 1946. At that time Bud was married to a girl in California. So Bud came up to be Jim's best man. On the eve of the wedding Jim was out for a last fling and was in an accident, so was married in St. Luke's hospital.

The following spring, Bud and his wife invited us to come to California to visit them. After school was out, we loaded the three children in the car and took off for California. I had just found out I was pregnant with David and was sick all the way down and coming home, too. David was born on the 23 January 1947.

While we were there, Joy and Jim, returning from their honeymoon in Mexico, stopped to see them too. Mom and Dad had been visiting in Illinois and they came too. Together as a family, we had a happy time.

On New Year's Day, Joy and Jim announced at dinner that they were expecting their baby and my first grandchild.

Carl was having trouble with his ulcer. While he was in the hospital that fall were busy times for me, what with four little ones to care for and a trip to the hospital every day, too.

Returned home, he was sick again with his ulcer. One morning his ulcer perforated and I rushed him to the hospital. He was a very sick man. At one point I was sure he wouldn't make it. Myrtle phoned and I started to cry and told her I was afraid that Carl wouldn't make it this time. She said, "Have faith". Most of the night I prayed for him to be spared until we could raise the children. After that he had a large part of his stomach removed and although he was very thin, he had no more problems with it.

I think that is another lesson in what prayer and faith can do.

*   *   *

Born Hazel Alice Thompson on the 15th of July 1904, she celebrated her 100th birthday in a large family and community gathering on the 15th of July 2004.

CHAPTER 7

DISEASE AND FAMILY SURVIVAL

By
Robert H. Wells

"YOU'LL BE carrying that big fellow out next" grandmother Lucy was told on arriving at the Fort Lewis army post during the dreaded influenza pandemic of 1918.

It was WW I and Dad was on active duty soldiering at Fort Lewis, WA. Among thousands of others, he became deathly ill during the influenza pandemic of the winter of 1918-1919.

Notified that her son was ill with the flu, his mother Lucy managed to travel, by train, from Weiser, ID to Fort Lewis, WA and arrive in time to provide the nursing care that saved his life.

It was touch and go for a time but eventually she nursed her first-born son back to health. In view of the large number of deaths attributed to that flu epidemic and the inadequate medical care offered to military personnel by an overburdened medical service, her nursing care was without doubt critical to his survival. In saving her first-born son she added to the many miracles of his survival of killer epidemics.

Fortunately for me, he was one of the survivors at a time when an estimated twenty million people worldwide died; 850,000 of those deaths occurring in the United States. We might note that the death toll from the flu pandemic was greater than the identified death toll of all wars to that time.

Since leaving Missouri her nursing skills had been honed fighting a series of killer epidemics that had attacked her family.

51

Of a total of seven sons, two were taken when disease struck the family and one was stillborn. She was determined not to lose another child.

The threat of death during the flu epidemic of 1918 was but a continuation of death threats by disease since leaving their farm in Missouri.

Coming West to homestead new land was a great adventure, made life threatening by exposure to a series of killer diseases not faced before on a Missouri farm the family had settled in 1837.

The homestead staked out on lava rock above the Snake River near Gooding, Idaho in 1908, was not the immediate challenge to the family. Instead the challenge proved to be a continuing exposure to a series of deadly diseases, including smallpox, membranous croup, scarlet fever, diphtheria and typhoid fever to which the family had no natural immunity or previous exposure. There were no known medications, antibiotics having not yet been discovered. This meant that these diseases were all life threatening.

While attempting to establish themselves that first year, all but Dad came down with the measles. Later that winter they all suffered from membranous croup and a life threatening attack of the smallpox. Dad had a few barely discernible scars on his face from the smallpox that in no way distracted from a very handsome appearance.

In August of 1909 three and one half year old Francis Neal, the youngest son, succumbed to diphtheria.

Even at this time father Jessie, described as "thin and sickly", suffered from the early stages of Bright's disease. As a result, much of the heavy labor fell on Dad's seventeen-year-old shoulders, including most of the plowing.

It became a calamitous situation made even more difficult with the discovery that the land staked out as a homestead consisted of 140 acres of lava rock.

Abandoning the homestead to share crop a farm in the Weiser, Idaho area the luck continued to be bad. In November of 1911 second born son Raymond died in a typhoid fever epidemic that attacked all the family.

What with the death of Raymond, the second oldest son from typhoid fever, and then the death of the father on 13 May 1913 from

MEMORIES OF ANOTHER TIME

Bright's disease, the tragic consequences of the move west from Missouri seemed unending.

Widowed and with four sons to raise the challenge and the struggle was continuous although as each son married and established homes of their own, her personal challenge was to make a living for herself. Experienced if not trained in nursing, she supported herself for years as a mother's helper, including assisting in the home birthing of her twelve grandchildren.

*   *   *

Mother's entire family was caught up in a Scarlet fever epidemic when she was about three. At that time, contagion was controlled by a legally enforced quarantine, a form of house arrest. No one was allowed to leave the house and yard area for almost six months as each family member came down in turn.

The story of that period as told by her sister Barbara, opens a small window on the problems of quarantine and disease in those times. A local handyman / drunk was their only tie to the community. He would come to the fence where some family member would give him their grocery order. Some weeks he wouldn't show up and food would be in short supply.

Although they did have a milk cow, oatmeal and potatoes were basic to all the meals. Aunt Barbara's gripe in her nineties was that Brother Jim, who apparently did the cooking when the parents were sick, "burned the potatoes and made the oatmeal lumpy, and then made the kids eat it".

One story told by Barbara was that during this time of isolation, Jim made a slide from the barn roof to the ground and covered it with snow. The children all played on the slide. Mother was given a turn but fell off and received a concussion that scared all of them. Apparently, it was a frightening experience as they thought for a time that they might have lost a baby sister.

As the baby of the family, mother seemed to have been favored by her father. As a result, she was not forced to find work, as the others had been when they reached their eleventh birthday. Possibly for that reason, she grew to be the tallest member of her family at five foot five inches in height.

She was fifteen and had completed the tenth grade or sophomore year of high school when she was stricken with rheumatic fever. Lying in bed, immobilized by the rheumatic fever, she developed bedsores. A Tetanus infection resulted from the bedsores. The Tetanus infection left her with a permanently locked jaw and the rheumatic fever left her with a damaged heart and a leaky heart valve.

As a result she was bedridden and still quite ill when her brother George died of a Tuberculosis infection.

The funeral services were held in the Episcopalian Church across the street from their house. She was propped up in bed by the front window so she could watch the funeral procession. Later in our home, she had a large studio picture of George that hung in our bedroom. His eyes always seemed to follow when we were in the room and contributed to a spooky feeling as if he were looking at us from the beyond.

In the course of the Tetanus infection her limbs became locked in place. When the doctor attempted to flex the limbs her own mother found her screams almost unendurable. Her sister Barbara's story of how she was asked to hold her screaming sister down while the doctor forced the locked limbs into stretching and movement is as vivid to this day as the trauma must have been at the time. And for the rest of her life mother's jaw remained semi-locked, allowing for less than a quarter inch opening.

Although suffering for the rest of her life from a damaged heart and frequent attacks of rheumatism, she went on to bear and raise six children before her heart finally gave out at age 72.

My own birth and survival depended on the good fortune of my parents surviving uncontrollable diseases and to a lesser extent to the good fortune that permitted me to survive many of the same diseases during my own growing up years.

For example, mumps, chicken pox, flu and other communicable diseases during my childhood each, without benefit of doctor, had a turn in our household. Perhaps most serious was being bedded in our cold, drafty upstairs bedroom with pneumonia. Treatment consisted of mustard plaster poultices prepared by mother and placed over my chest. Warm milk-toast meals were provided when I was able to sit up.

MEMORIES OF ANOTHER TIME

I believe Dr. Gilmore did visit but there was little he could do other than establish a diagnosis of pneumonia and support mother in the treatment she was providing.

In mentioning our cold, drafty bedroom it should be noted that the kitchen cook stove provided the major heat in the house. A pot-bellied heating stove provided heat to the living room in the evening. The upstairs bedrooms were entirely without heat. Worse, walls were one board thick. Paper on the inner wall was often torn where the boards joined, allowing the cold winter winds direct access to the room. Just surviving freezing winter temperatures in that bedroom was enough of a challenge without the additional problems presented by pneumonia.

Doctors were important in dealing with broken bones and amputating mangled or blood poisoned limbs but most surgeries now taken for granted were not performed, both due to lack of knowledge but more importantly, to lack of supportive medications.

Doctors did assist in delivering babies although the midwife or experienced family member more commonly provided that service. For example, my siblings and I were all born at home with the assistance of a doctor and in my case, my grandmother and aunt.

Disease, before the discovery and development of immunizations and the modern miracle drugs beginning with anti-biotics, was an on-going challenge to survival. My own birth and survival depended on the good fortune of my parents surviving killer diseases almost unknown nowadays and to a lesser extent to the good fortune that permitted me to survive many of the same diseases.

The drugs we now know and use were for the most part unknown even into the 1930's and only beginning to appear in the 1940's. Even the carriers and means of communicating these diseases were just beginning to be discovered as we moved into the mid-20th Century. Only since then have we seen the disappearance in this country of Tuberculosis, Smallpox, Polio, Malaria and other diseases born by Ticks, Mosquitoes, animals, and other humans.

We now know so much more about disease and the tools for treating disease that at times we almost feel as if we were in charge and immune to what in my years was considered a natural force for weeding out the weak and the unlucky.

As a survivor of the many forces of nature that kept man from overwhelming the checks and balances of nature, I am grateful. Whether that has been or is a good thing for man or the earth we inhabit only time will tell.

CHAPTER 8
A RURAL UPBRINGING

By
Harriet Gladys Wilkerson

BORN MAY 18, 1922 in Weiser, Idaho, to Harry M. Wells and Gladys Jones Wells, I was the first of three children who lived. We lived in Weiser and our home was there until we moved back up in the mountains in the forest area where we lived in a small cottage.

We didn't even have running water in the house. It was very primitive. We had to carry water to the house, usually from a creek that was close by. At that time the water wasn't all polluted. We had an old wood cook stove where we heated the water. The toilet was a little house at the end of a path down the way. Usually it was quite a ways to walk. There was a little fence around the cottage. I could climb anything. They couldn't keep me in that area because I could climb over it.

About the time I was two years old, we moved to Union, Oregon where Dad's older brother Robert lived. Brother Jimmy also moved to Union about the same time. Brother Glenn was born while we still lived in Union. There is 20 months difference in our ages. We spent several years there before we moved back to Weiser.

The house was small. I don't even remember whether we had running water. Possibly we did.

It was there that Glenn became seriously ill. It was discovered he had a kidney problem. He was treated in the Hot Lake Sanitarium Hospital for a while. Mother worried for years he was not that well. They didn't baby him but they sheltered him a little more because of that for quite a few years. That probably wasn't good for him.

Jimmy had a road-grading contract to grade sections of Highway 30 under construction in Pyles Canyon. All three brothers worked together on this project. When the road project was completed they used their equipment to haul logs from the mountain area near Union. The story goes that my father and his brothers Jimmy and Robert could bring out the logs. They used nothing but teams of horses. They had these big horses that would haul the biggest loads of logs of anyone. Many commented about that.

It was soon after that we moved back to Weiser. Moving back and forth was by horse drawn wagon. It would take several days to get back and forth. We didn't think anything about it but what furniture you had was all on the wagon. You camped out on the way. We didn't think of it at the time but the route we followed was the old Oregon Trail developed by the earliest pioneers coming to Oregon by wagon. We probably used many of their same campsites.

*　　　　　*　　　　　*

After we moved back to Weiser, we lived near the old high school.

My ninety-year-old gr/grandmother Emily Jones lived with us until she died. She would walk around with a cane and we always rode her cane for a pony. She had some neat stories. In the spring she said everybody should have Sassafras tea because it was good for the blood. Oh, we hated that. It was terrible tasting stuff. It made quite an impression on me. The same day she died her daughter also died in Vale, Oregon.

Later we moved over on Butterfield Street. That is where my sister Donna Mae was born in 1929. My father was working in the creamery. At that time, ice cream was a real treat. We didn't have much of that. Once in a while he would bring a little bit of ice cream home. At that time there was no refrigeration at all. It would be late when he got home but believe me, that ice cream was a treat.

*　　　　　*　　　　　*

The Depression hit about that time and it was rough going. One summer the folks farmed for Dad's brother Jimmy. We were there only about a year before we moved to a farm in Thousand Springs Valley about

MEMORIES OF ANOTHER TIME

seventeen miles out of Weiser. It was strictly a rugged farming area. I think Dad was leasing it from his brother, Jimmy.

The banks were closing. My grandfather J. Jones was working in Weiser as a custodian for the school. He was interested in the farm and helped Dad a lot. I think quite a bit of his money went into that operation. We were there for four years until we moved to a farm on Pine Crick eight miles out of Cambridge.

At that time I would have been ready to start the third grade. Brother Glenn was in the first grade. It was a hardship because of the long trek to school. We rode three miles on horseback to school.

We had a black saddle horse that liked home better than it liked traveling. It would balk and we would have to get it going again.

Three miles in all kinds of weather is really something. We wore sheepskin coats in all types of weather. Going to school from Thousand Springs Valley, Brother Glenn and I rode the same horse. We had a saddle and he rode behind me. We went for about a half mile or so to pick up George and Francis Bane. It was another mile to my Uncle Jimmy's place. There we would pick up my two cousins Buddy and Shirley. All of us were on horseback. We went on another mile to school. There were at least six of us on horseback going to this small school. The others rode horseback too. The school had a barn where we put the horses.

I had to be a horseman. A lot of people rode for fun, I rode because I had to. My sister Donna loved to ride. She was on one from the time she was four years old. She would carry water to the men when they were haying while she was still just a small child. Later, when they were stacking the hay she drove the derrick horse that pulled the hay to the top of the stack.

She liked the outdoors. I liked the outdoors too but I had to be inside helping mother. I was the oldest. I didn't get the fun chores but I wasn't deprived. We had lots of fun times. We were fortunate because our cousins were close. We grew up with them.

I do remember one year when Glenn was ill and couldn't go to school. We had a blizzard and I stayed with the schoolteacher where she was boarding. I thought staying with her was a great experience. It was only about three-quarters of a mile or so from the school so we didn't have so far to walk. I think she walked a lot of the time.

I remember her as an especially good teacher. The schoolhouse was small with about twelve students. The teacher taught all eight grades. She did her own janitor work. She had to be there early enough to start the fire in the old pot bellied stove. They used coal to heat the school. It was a hard life but an interesting experience. We certainly didn't feel deprived. We had a very happy home.

*   *   *

Our clothes washing was just done on the washboard. We had to hang the clothes out on the line. For meat, Dad would butcher the pigs or a calf, mostly pigs because then he could smoke the meat. We had a smokehouse out there. Dad cut and hauled the wood used for smoking this meat and for the cook stove as well as heating for our home.

After a time, Dad did pipe water into the house so at least we had water in the house. That was a treat. It was a home with a porch around two sides of the house. We liked that. One porch was even used as a bedroom.

Dad built a big chicken house and we raised Leghorn chickens. We also had a lot of milk cows. From the time I was very small I learned to milk and believe me I was pretty good at it. We had to herd the cows. He had quite a bit of land that he farmed. We had lots of alfalfa and were able to stack enough of the hay to feed the cattle through the winter.

Up in Thousand Springs Valley my uncle Jimmy and Aunt Temperance lived two miles from us. I have fond memories of cousins Shirley and Buddy. We spent a lot of time with them. I was always envious of Shirley because I thought she was just a lot prettier than I was. Also, she was more outgoing. I think Buddy was about two years younger than Shirley.

We all had horses. I remember so well it would frighten Uncle Jimmy when we would stand up on the horses bareback and while holding the reins, gallop down the road. I don't remember Glenn doing it.

Uncle Jimmy was soft hearted. He was always giving you a hug. I just loved my Uncle Jimmy. He was good a looking man and very kindly to the children.

MEMORIES OF ANOTHER TIME

In growing up we were very fortunate to be so close to our cousins, Shirley and Buddy and my other cousins Cecil, Delmar, Lena, and Ethelene. Our families spent a lot of our time together. Every Fourth of July my Uncle Ken and Aunt Mina and their four children would come up. We would all take turns cranking the old ice cream freezer.

We had to get the ice in town because we had no refrigeration. To bring the ice home, we wrapped the block of ice in gunnysacks. We made one freezer of ice cream after another. Mother always had her chickens that were ready to butcher about that time. It was fried chicken, mashed potatoes and gravy, home made ice cream, cream pies. We had so many good times with our cousins there.

I remember that for Thanksgiving they would have goose instead of turkey. My folks did not think goose was as good as turkey.

*   *   *

We lived in Thousand Springs Valley for four years. Then Dad bought a 5,000-acre ranch that was mostly grazing land but with some land that could be farmed. Once again he had milk cows and pigs and chickens; you name it. We raised just about everything that was used. Mother always had a big garden. We canned all of our fruits and vegetables. Each summer we put up about 400 quarts of vegetables as well as fruit. We had a cellar where it would be half way cool. Everything was put down in the cellar.

Here again we had to carry water into the house from Pine Crick, which was downhill from the house. We had to bring in every drop of water that was used in the house. Let me tell you, those buckets were heavy. We heated the water on the stove to do the laundry. When it was done we had to hang it out on the clothesline, rain or shine. We had to get them dry some way.

We had a crick above the house with which we irrigated the garden and the fields. Later, there was enough flow in the crick we could use it in doing the laundry. Keeping the milk and butter and things like that cool during the warm weather wasn't easy. We had to take it down a hill to the spring and then go after it when we needed it.

Dad was always good with horses. I think Jimmy and Robert and Dad just grew up with horses. They were good with them and good at training them. I always thought it was cruel the way he would manage those horses. He would whip them and so forth, I don't remember exactly how he did it.

Both Dad and Jimmy would break their own saddle horses and bucking horses. First thing you know the horse would settle down and do what was wanted like being able to lead them around. It took a lot of patience, a lot of time.

In the Pine Crick area we had to go a little over two miles back up and over a mountain to school; rain, shine or whatever.

One winter during the Christmas vacation we had quite a snowstorm. I went with my Dad with a string of horses up this one pass where the snow would drift in. We had to shovel through 12-foot drifts and then use the string of horses to break trail in order that we could go back to school after Christmas vacation.

Later that winter we had so much snow that we were snowbound over on the other side of the mountain. Glenn and I boarded with a family for a month. Mother got so lonesome to come see us that she rode on horseback about seventeen miles around by a road they kept open in winter time.

On weekend's brother Glenn could take the skis and ski over the fences to get home. He walked up to the top of the mountain and then skied down the side. This time we were in a small school in Advent gulch.

We had a Seventh Day Adventist teacher. She was a very patient teacher. I believe there were only about twelve of us in eight grades there. She had to bring in her own wood to fuel the pot bellied stove and do her own janitor work. To help her we would do the erasers and do the board and the boys brought in the firewood and kept the fire stoked.

Many, many times I helped with the first graders. I would take them into what we called the clothes closet and would drill them on reading and on phonics.

It was quite a life. We had our sleds and toboggans and so forth. On the weekends we would get together with other children to come down the mountain on the toboggan and the sleds. You had to pull them back up the hill and make a trail in order to come down.

MEMORIES OF ANOTHER TIME

*   *   *

I do want to tell more about my Dad, Harry and my mother, Gladys. Harry was such fun to be around because he had such a wonderful sense of humor. He kept us laughing as well as working all the time. My dad was so good at whistling. If Dad was worried, that was the only time he would be real quiet, he would whistle. I knew he was thinking it out. He whistled all the time and he sang quite a bit. Songs I remember were The Bucket in the Well and School Days, School Days. I remember that quite a bit. He was good at construction or building, he was good at farming, and he was good with the horses. At that time you had to do absolutely everything yourself and he did it.

Often, when we were there in Thousand Springs Valley like on a Sunday people would come from all around, the young men especially, and we would have a rodeo right there at our house. We would ride the calves and there would be bucking horses and so forth. I was good at riding the steers or the calves. In fact they all commented on it. I think I got throwed off a time or two.

We would have a big Sunday dinner. Mother would fry a chicken served with mashed potatoes and gravy. She always made the best cream pies. Dad loved cream pies. It seemed like about every Sunday she would have a cream pie for Dad.

Mother and Dad were always on the school board when we were in Thousand Springs valley as well as when we were in Pine Creek. Mother was a very good secretary. Dad would always have the leading role and hold the meetings.

One other thing I really liked about him, his education was only to the eighth grade but he was an avid reader. He brought us up reading everything. He told me when I started to high school "the one thing I want you to take is Public Speaking". Believe me, I had to take public speaking in high school. That was good because I was very shy. I enjoyed it. I also took debating. We would go to the Grange Hall and the Masonic Masons for programs and so forth. It was a good education but a hard way too.

When we were in Thousand Springs Valley, Mother would be in plays. They had a little literary building where the talent around there would put on the program.

64   A STORY TO TELL

Mother actually had a very good education. Her health was not that good. From the time I was little I had a lot of responsibility for cooking and laundry and gardening and keeping house and taking care of my little seven years younger sister. She was born just four days after my birthday, the 22 of May 1929. I thought she was the nicest birthday present I ever had. And I still feel that to this day.

I remember when mother was in this one play they thought that it was so good we had to give it at another place. They thought I could sing. I didn't think that. I did a couple solos. I sang without a piano or any other accompaniment. It was well received. It was just a way of life. You made your own entertainment. You had to do everything for yourself. I think that was good for everybody. In high school it was the same way. There I sang with a quartet. Two boys and two girls.

*   *   *

After Aunt Elsie's death during childbirth, Uncle Tommy came back to Weiser in about 1931, I'm not absolutely certain about the date. Grandma Lucy was taking care of and raising Tommy's son Neal. I spent many times in the summer with Grandma Lucy and played with Neal when he was little. He was very artistic. His mother was an artist as far as that goes. He would make match airplanes and all sorts of things like that. He was good at it. He was more a less a loner. I had some happy times with him there.

*   *   *

When I graduated from grade school it was eight miles into Cambridge to high school. To go to high school I boarded with a lady in Cambridge the first two years. I think there were seventeen of us in my high school class. After going to the small grade school that seemed like a lot of kids. I was very shy that first year. In two years my brother graduated from grade school. He was able to drive the pickup in the good weather so we were able to drive back and forth to school.

In the winter, we had an apartment that Dad rented for us. I was taking piano lessons. Dad had bought a piano for me when I was about thirteen years old. We were in an upstairs apartment without running

MEMORIES OF ANOTHER TIME

water. They had to bring the piano into the hallway of the apartment and I practiced right there in the hallway.

My brother and sister were there with us. I had to cook for them and do the laundry. I remember there was one of our friends who lived up there on Pine Crick. Her father couldn't afford to have her enter high school. Dad said, "stay with my children". We made room for Rita to stay with us for all of that year. It worked out fine. Nowadays you would never think of such a thing. The next year her father built a little house for her. But then she got married.

High school was very good for me. I did a lot of things. In a small school you take part in everything. It was a good education there. I was in the senior play when I was a sophomore. A girl got sick and dropped out. The Principal came to me and asked if I would take over. I had a very short time to learn the leading part. It worked out fine.

At the time I was a senior in high school I was home when our house burned to the ground. Dad had started the fire in the kitchen and had gone on to the barn to do the milking. He returned to the house in time to alert us. We were asleep in bed when the house caught afire. You could see the curtains burning when we got out.

The first two things mother thought to save was the twenty-two rifle they had bought for my brother and my formal. The only formal I ever had. The Prom was coming up. Those two things she rescued. That and the business papers in the drawer. Those were the only things we got out of that house. That was a terrible thing. There was no one around to even help and even if there had been, the fire was just too far along. That was an experience that I hope to never see again.

Then Dad brought in a small trailer. We got by in it for a while. He had a tent set up for sleeping. It was about that time things were getting really tough for him.

He got out of farming and went to build a sawmill up on the Salmon River. He built that sawmill from scratch. He even had to build a bridge across the little Salmon River. He built a cook shack and had several people working for him including Uncle Jimmy, my cousin Buddy and two or three others. He still had horses at home but was using trucks up there.

At the time they were cutting logs quite a ways up this road they had built into where the timber was located. Eighteen-year-old Cousin

Buddy was logging with his father and my Dad when a falling log killed him. Buddy had cut down the tree. They yelled for him to get out of the way. Something happened and he didn't. The tree fell and crushed him. That was a terrible, terrible thing. I think that was the main thing that discouraged my Dad and Uncle Jimmy about the logging business.

That kind of put a damper on the logging business. Dad went on down to Portland. Virgil and I were already there. He rented a house and went right to work on construction. That worked out very well for him.

Uncle Jimmy took his son's death very hard. Within a year he had a heart attack and died. I can't remember how old he was [48] but he was a young man.

*   *   *

On the thousand spring's farm, Aunt Temperance parents lived fairly close to them. Their daughter Lottie had been a schoolteacher. She had had a stroke so was in a wheel chair there at home. Shirley, Buddy, Glenn and I spent some time with her because of her being a schoolteacher. She was interested in us learning a lot of things.

In fact, she worked with Shirley to where she made two grades in one year in school. We found out later it was a mistake. When she got to high school it was very difficult for her. More so than it was for me. She just fell behind in her classes. She couldn't keep up with her studies there.

She was married when she was fifteen, maybe sixteen. That was the end of her high school. She had two boys and then a little girl later. Tyrone, her oldest one, was a remarkable young man. He knew from the time he was small he was going to be a pilot. He was a wonderful student all the way through school. He realized his dream and ended up a Colonel in the Air Force. He has done very, very well.

Her second son, called Buddy in honor of her brother, was killed in a logging truck accident in Wyoming when he was only 22. He was logging some place in Wyoming. Shirley's daughter Tempy Anne was nine years younger than Buddy.

In 1958 Shirley and husband Howard had gone to a dance in Cambridge during rodeo time. While at the dance she had a heart at-

MEMORIES OF ANOTHER TIME

tack and died on the dance floor. She was just 35 years old. The terrible part was Shirley died when Tempy Ann was just nine years old. At that time her youngest son John was just seven-eight years old or so. Aunt Temp, Shirley's mother, pretty much raised Tempy Anne and John. It was kind of rough going. There was a lot of tragedy in their lives.

*　　　　　　　*　　　　　　　*

Virgil's sister is the same age as I am. We were in high school together. I spent many weekends out at their farm. It was one of the nicest farms in the Cambridge area. Velma had a sister and three brothers. I thought each one of them was about the finest people you could imagine but I never dreamed about going with Virgil until after I graduated from high school. Virgil kept calling me for a date. I finally gave in. I was going with two others at the time. I started going with him and soon after I knew we were serious. On our dates we would usually go to a movie or to a dance out at the Cove out of Cambridge. He would always have to wait until I was through working which was late.

*　　　　　　　*　　　　　　　*

When I started working at the telephone office I was just out of high school. At the time I was working for a family out of town about three miles. We were right in the middle of canning. I was doing peaches on the old wood stove using open kettles canning. About that time there was a knock on the door. It was the owner of the Telephone Company in Cambridge. He had come out there to see me to ask if I would go to work for him as a telephone operator. He was going to pay me fifteen cents an hour but my board was furnished there and he paid my room. He put in a telephone where I stayed so he could call me if they had an emergency and needed me at the telephone office.

It wasn't just telephone work. I did the cooking and the laundry most of the time for the family of the owner, his wife and their three-year-old girl. I thought the world of her. I worked on the switchboard where we had both long distance and local calls. You knew every voice and every number on the switchboard.

At one time I operated it for twenty-four hours a day while the owner and his wife were having marriage problems. It was quite an experience. At night you turned on the big bell and went to bed. If there were an emergency I would get up and take care of it. If I was alone I always had a friend of mine there with me. She was able to operate the board also.

When I put in my application at the department store they immediately hired me. Once again it was a tremendous experience. I worked in the office, did the office work, billings, and when they were busy in the store I worked in yardage, in the grocery department, any place in the store and they had everything. People would come in and hand you a list of groceries. You would put up the groceries; total it up and they would either pay for it or charge it. The rice would be in a bin; the beans would be in a bin. They did have a meat counter.

The part I really didn't like was slicing lunchmeat and bacon and things like that. It was a good education, believe me. They had shoes, Levi's, yardage, and pants, just about everything you could think of. They heated the building with a wood-burning stove. Many people would come in to sit around that stove and visit.

When I started they paid me $60.00 a month. I had to pay my own board and room. I boarded with the same lady I had boarded with when I was in high school. A lovely lady. I was there even when I was working at the telephone office.

$*$ $*$ $*$

I was at the telephone office when I started going with Virgil. I always had to work until seven anyway. When I worked at Jewell's department store in Cambridge I always had to work until nine on Saturday night. Virgil's family had one car. There were three sons and two daughters. We all, including the boy's dates, would be in that car to go to the dance. It was about in April Virgil asked me to marry him. My engagement ring was in September. Those were tough times.

Virgil was very good with horses. When Virgil and I were going together he had a real good team of horses. There was a pulling contest in the Cambridge rodeo. All summer, after working all day, he spent his evening training and conditioning his team of horses by gradu-

MEMORIES OF ANOTHER TIME

ally increasing weight on a pulling slip. Of course, he won the pulling contest and the prize provided enough money to buy my engagement ring. The funny part was I was working so I didn't get to see him win. Somebody came in and said, "Oh, Virgil won the contest". About that time he came in and asked the owner if he could take me out to lunch. So it was really kind of special.

At that very time WW II broke out we were engaged. By this time we had gone together for over a year. It was soon after that on January 3rd 1942 that Virgil and I was married.

I still had a saddle horse when I was married. The joke of it was I had to have foot surgery and my tonsils and adenoids removed. While I was in the hospital, I sold my horse to pay for the hospital and doctor bill. Of course, I didn't need the horse. We were getting married and going to Portland.

Soon after that we loaded our meager belongings in his Chevrolet car and went to Portland. He worked in the shipyards for a while, then in construction and then was called into service. I went to work in Portland for one of the war agencies as a PBX operator.

Virgil was sent to Camp Roberts in California for basic training and when he returned on leave, he wanted me to go back with him. We had to go to the ration board for approval of gasoline to make the return trip to Camp Roberts.

The trip was uneventful but the search for housing, with so many soldiers living in the area, was very difficult. We had to take an upstairs room with a hot plate and no running water. Later, we moved to a small cottage. Even so, to do this we had to live in Atascadero, 30 miles from the base at Camp Roberts.

*   *   *

In September of 1943 he received an honorable discharge because of a back injury. We returned to Boise and later were blessed with two daughters. We had a wonderful life together for 61 years.

*   *   *

Post Script: 89-year-old Virgil died in December of 2003.

CHAPTER 9
A WILL TO LIVE

By
John Van Beekum

M<small>Y NAME</small> is Cornelius John Van Beekum. This is my story. My parents immigrated to the United States. They met on the boat. My father and mother were unmarried at that time. They came to Salt Lake City in 1922. My father didn't like the sponsors who had helped my mother come over. She came over by herself. He came by himself and later managed to get her an apartment. For the next little while they managed to get better and better acquainted. They didn't know each other well except on the boat. They had seen each other in branches in Holland but that's all. They courted for a while before they got married.

Father had gone to school in England to become a certified fitter so he could speak English quite well. Mother did not do very well with English so it was convenient to have him around. He worked in town as a fitter and tailor for Anderson Tailor's Company who fit fine clothes. Of course, it was difficult to find good fitters. He proved to be very good in his profession over the years he worked for Anderson. When they went out of business he went to work for W. E. Fife and Co., a fine clothier.

Well, I don't know how long they lived in this apartment. Mother's parents, John and Cora Vanderunnd came over a year later. They brought their younger daughter Cory. They lived together in this apartment a little while. Grandfather went to work for the Hotel Utah. Grandmother went out cleaning homes and so forth. That's how they started their stay in Utah.

Grandfather had been a teamster in Holland and got a job as a teamster on the Calhoon Ranch. They moved out to a little farmhouse on a dirt road in Holiday at 4800 south and just below Highland Drive. It was quite a beautiful farm area. Calvin's ran sheep out in the west desert. Grandfather was hired to go out and work on all the wagons and harnesses for the teams. That plus take care of a five-acre razzberry farm there in Holiday.

I was born in my grandmother's house because my mother went to her mother at her time. They had a Doctor in attendance. In fact, my grandmother's story is she was so shocked when Doctor Jack came to take care of the delivery. He came in and examined my mother and said, "This is going to be about six hours". To my grandmother he said, "I think I will go sleep". He went to bed on their bed and that really shocked her. She had never had someone do that, especially a Doctor. I guess the Doctor was there when I was ready to come. That's her story. I was there but I don't remember all of it. My mother never did tell me the story.

So that is where my life started. My grandparents stayed pretty well in that home for almost 14-15 years, I'm not exactly sure. It was a nice home -- it wasn't lavish or large but it was comfortable. Their home in Holiday was red brick, well built because the owners were the owners of the brick company. It was two bedroom, living room and large kitchen, and had a cellar where Grandmother kept all her canned goods.

I visited my grandmother every week. She worked in town and would come pick me up during the time my mother was pregnant with my sister. I spent as much time with her as my grandmother would be home. I don't know whether that was because my mother was having difficulty with my sister's pregnancy or just why. Apparently something of that nature was going on. I was two, going on to three by that time. After my sister came I was still farmed out to my grandmother on the farm. I enjoyed that. That was my most pleasurable place.

Father spent long hours working so we didn't see much of him. I enjoyed the farm work, living out there in the country, and grandfather seemed to like having me around. He had neighbors to the west of their home, the Nichols. They were an old pioneer family and owned quite a lot of land in that area in conjunction with the Calhoons. West of

MEMORIES OF ANOTHER TIME

there was the Wenter dairy. They were a big concern at the time. There weren't an awful lot of homes in that area

Grandmother would sell the raspberries on the street and make them ready for whoever ordered them. Aunt Cory and whomever they employed picked them from time to time. That's how they made their living for a long time. Of course I enjoyed going out there and watching them run the irrigation water and whatever else was out there. That was my youth.

I spent a lot of time there. My grandfather took care of me a great deal of the time. The way he would take care of me would be to sit me on the back of his horse he was harrowing with all day long. I would hold on to the halter and play like I was running the horse although I was just sitting up there keeping out of trouble. That was for my first three, four, five years that I spent a great deal of time there.

On one occasion after a harvest of hay, I was three or four years old, they had just brought in a bunch of hay and had it stacked next to the barn. A neighbor friend named Royce and his older, somewhat mentally retarded sister who became a very good friend came over. She couldn't speak rapidly but was a very alert lady in many, many ways.

We were playing on this haystack that was stacked alongside the barn. While sliding down near one of the posts near the barn, I hit a nail and tore my arm severely. They didn't have any way to call a Doctor so my grandmother and grandfather took care of the rather large tear in my arm. The way they did it was to wash it well. Grandfather chewed tobacco. He took a big gob of tobacco and put it on there and bandaged it up. I still have the scar but it is minor. That was home first aid.

During that time period my father was apparently doing quite well. He bought us an Essex car. It had a wooden steering wheel. The only reason I remember that steering wheel is right after my father bought it my grandfather did some private work and the man couldn't pay him. To pay my grandfather he paid him off in land. So we acquired 180 acres of dry farm and rocks out west. We went out there to see that farm.

I'll never forget the old mechanical brakes on the car. You had to hang on to the steering wheel to get enough pressure on the brakes to slow it down. When we were out gunning over those hills on the dry farm Dad was pulling back so hard he pulled the steering wheel off. That was a thrill. That's how come I remember that car. I was still

74   A STORY TO TELL

young then but I remember grandfather and grandmother all excited
about that.

*   *   *

In July I turned six and started to school that fall. Sometime that fall
I went down to watch some boys who had built a fire to cook some
weenies in their back yard. I guess I had been sort of a plague to them.
They were twelve years old and I was only six. I sort of followed them
around.

You can't get rid of a young kid that age that thinks they are doing
interesting things. So they thought they would scare me with a quart
bottle of gas they had drained out of their Dad's car. They thought it
would just flame up and frighten me and I would go home. Instead, it
caught my clothes on fire.

That's where I got the burns. They didn't throw it on me; it just came
up out of the bottle in front of my clothes. I had a half a block to run.
They ran into the house frightened to death and I ran home, burning
all the way and of course it burned more and more. My mother caught
me and put out the fire.

With the fire out I was taken to the LDS hospital. I believe I was
conscious all the time. I don't remember ever being unconscious. I don't
have an awful lot of memories. They get blurred out with time. I know
that after I got into the LDS hospital I had third degree burns over
my chest and neck. In those days that was pretty terminal as far as the
hospital was concerned. So the first little while I was in the hospital all
they did was try to keep me comfortable.

I remember that my mother was there just about every day; my
father would come in the evenings. They didn't dope you in those
days; you just had the pain. Pain was continuous but seemed worse
when the crust and puss formed. I don't remember how extensive the
pain was. I've had so much pain over the years I don't remember how
bad it was during that particular period of time. Mother would tell my
Grandmother that it was quite bad. Grandmother took care of my sister
when Mother came to the hospital

Eventually, as the scars started to heal somewhat the contraction
in my muscles got so fierce I couldn't keep my arms or my head up.

MEMORIES OF ANOTHER TIME

Muscles started pulling together and my arms started pulling to my chest. They tried everything from strapping me down to boards to keep it from happening but I would break the gauze with the contractions so that didn't work very well.

During that time period I got a rather bad kidney infection, which is generally the case with burns because the body can't get rid of the poisons. They thought I was going to pass away so my father thought it would be nice if I would come home. They agreed. They thought it would be a few days and I would be gone.

Once I was home my grandmother who had been a European Herbalist decided she was just not going to let me die. She administered an herbal wash to my burns, which reduced the fever and also made teas that flushed my kidneys out. Eventually she won. The hospital was amazed. It didn't change what had happened beforehand. The arms had just contracted more to my body. My chin was pulled down. The arm was grown together; the pit of the arm had grown in together. I hadn't walked for I'm not sure how long, about a year, maybe two years.

When they saw I wasn't going to pass away and the doctor saw how healthy I had become they then decided they would try to do some surgery to modify at least the skin so I could eat better. They wanted to open one arm up. The first operation they were going to do after I got back in the hospital was to work on the arm and get both arms loose. That was their main concern. The second operation was to relieve the pulling down of my chin. My father attended most of my operations.

During those days the operating rooms weren't that fancy. They were rather large rooms and some lighting but not very good lights either. The operating table was just a hard old table they could strap you down to. Of course, ether was their only way of putting you away.

That first operation they started putting me down with ether. The doctor administering the ether flooded the mask. I strangled. They cut off all my air. I died on the table. . .

My father said they worked furiously. They didn't have oxygen standing by or hypos to stimulate the heart. He said they were frantic. They didn't know what to do. They took the mask off and tried to get me to breathe. For about six minutes . . . the only thing I remember and I don't tell this very often. . . I could see my body . . . I could see the doctors administering anesthesia. The other doctor was standing off to the side trying to get me to breathe by pressing my chest. I could see my Dad . . . and about the only question that came to my mind was how could I see when my eyes were in my head down there? I don't know why that thought has stayed in my mind all these years. It was very vivid. How can I see? I didn't have any other big experience except that I was above it.

My father said when I came to, revived sufficiently, I somehow pulled loose from the straps that held me down, of course they had loosened them some to work on me, but I got off that table and ran down the hall. Mrs. Black, who was the head nurse there, had to really hustle to catch up with me and bring me back.

That started them off. That was my first operation. They brought me back, put me under, and did the operation.

Well, time passed. I spent most of the time in the hospital after that for about two years. As the scars healed they would find another good operation to make me functional. There was no physical therapy, no drugs administered, no pain drugs. I was confined to bed most of that period of time.

Just before I got out of the hospital my brother Bob was born. There is three years difference between us. They brought him to the hospital to show him to me through the window. It was not long after that I went home. It had been about three and one half years between my burn and the time that he was born. During all that time I was in the hospital except for the time I went home when they didn't think I was going to survive. Once it looked like I was going to make it, I went back. I don't know how much time elapsed while I was home.

I know my grandparents had to take care of me during that Christmas period of time. I can remember the pretty southwest bedroom. In the hospital there was a children's ward that was sort of an added room up on top of the east wing of the LDS hospital. It was just roof and the sky.

Somewhere during the second stage of my being in the hospital I was placed with the other young kids. I guess all of them were under twelve in the Children's ward. One of the lasting impressions made on my mind occurred when a pretty little girl was put in the hospital. She was pretty bad. She would go into seizures and lose control and carry on

MEMORIES OF ANOTHER TIME

for a little while. They would get her down and tie her to the bed. She wasn't there much more than a week or so when she passed away.

That was my first encounter with death. I liked her. She was a pleasant little girl when she was fine. Her folks were very kind people. They visited her quite a lot. We didn't have little rooms; we just had curtains around the beds so you knew everything that was going on with the patient next to you. It was one of those startling experiences to me, having a friend dying.

Well, to shorten up my story about the hospital, we didn't go to school at that time because they didn't have a tutor.

It wasn't until sometime after my tenth or eleventh year of age they began to sequence the operations. For most grafts they did them in stages. It usually took three operations to do them. They didn't dare do them quickly. Until I was eighteen I would stay in the hospital sometimes for a 3 to 4 month period, sometimes for a month.

When I was eleven years old my mother passed away as a result of what had been termed a ruptured appendix. It hadn't really ruptured. When they operated the doctor apparently nicked the bowel. My father was there. He saw the doctors were startled at what had gone wrong. They sewed her up. My father asked what was going on. One of the nurses told him they had had an accident. I forget what they call that infection that takes place inside. Peritonitis, that's what happened to her.

When they sewed her up they could see she wasn't recovering. Her death caused quite a stir in my family. It certainly angered my father and caused quite a ferment in the family that the Doctors would not admit they had made an error at the time even though he was standing in the operating room and saw what happened. My brother was just going on two so I was about eleven then.

I don't how the death of my mother effected me or impacted me emotionally. By that time I had gone through so many pain filled years, I don't know that death really bothered me that much. Knowing what had caused it and knowing they were not capable of repairing it . . . I don't know. I really don't remember it as being an emotional time. Death seemed a normal experience.

I know it impacted my sister far more than it did me. The passing of my mother really hit her hard. She would come to me more often than she would go to my Dad. The result was that I became her anchor. Later, she came to me more often than she would go to my stepmother. Brother Bob, he could go to my stepmother very comfortably. That worked out well for them.

From the time my mother passed away my grandmother and Aunt Cory, mother's younger sister, took care of us most of the time. Either Aunt Cory or grandmother was at the house for the next two and one half to three years. Father, to keep up with things, worked not only his first job with W. E. Fifer and Co., a clothing store but also worked at DCMI in the evenings where he would fit and sew clothes. He was busy but didn't get very much pay for the work there. Half the time father was trading for bonds or something, anything to get paid. Of course, they couldn't cash them in, neither could he for a long time. I still have some of these old bonds they paid him off with. It was tough times for them.

It was there that he met my stepmother who was also a tailor in the DCMI tailor shop. The two of them were very industrious. He married Hilda perhaps three years after my mother passed away.

She was a good lady. She treated us well, was very conscientious in training and helping us in all that we needed over the years. She took good care of us. She took a real shine to my baby brother Robert. She didn't give the older kids the kind of love and affection that she did to my younger brother Bob. As a little older children we had a harder time finding it comfortable to give her the motherly hug that she needed. Maybe it was because we didn't let her. I got along with her just fine. Anyhow she took good care of all of us.

We had moved into a rented home in town just north of where the new Church office building is. The house was at the end of an alley that doesn't exist anymore. The home was broken into several times and robbed. It didn't take too many of those experiences for my folks to want to get out. They decided to go out in the country where that kind of problem was minimized.

We bought a home out on 2700 South and 3rd East. It had 3 1/2 acres, 200 chickens in coops and a calf that went with the house. I believe they paid less than $3,000 for the whole works. It was a little two-bedroom home with small kitchen and living room. The chicken coop was actually bigger than the house. The chicken coop was income; the

MEMORIES OF ANOTHER TIME

house was just shelter. We did add on to that home eventually, putting in a nice big kitchen, added a couple of bedrooms and increased the size of living room so that it became a very comfortable home.

We burned coal in that home. We had a big Heatrola stove in the living room that we would light on the weekends. In the kitchen we had a coal stove with an oven to cook on. It took the chill out of the bedroom sections in the winter months. The doors to the bedrooms would stay closed until we went to bed, then we opened them up. We lived in the kitchen most of the time. Bath water was heated on that stove. We had our own well and running water. It was a good four-inch well with good water. We irrigated that piece of land with it.

*　　　　　*　　　　　*

I started going to school at Garfield Elementary just a half block down the road from where we lived. When not in the hospital I went to school there sufficiently to get through sixth grade. I had had some private tutoring. I had a private tutor in the hospital that helped me learn to read but I never did learn to read well. I couldn't concentrate. Too many painful distractions. I remember I started in the fourth grade. Around Christmas I got out of the hospital and went to school. The kids were just starting to read these little Christmas things.

Of course the teacher didn't know too much about what had been going on when I was put in her class. All I remember was those Christmas stories we were reading in the history class. She called on me to read and I couldn't read the story. My sister was very uncomfortable. I had been set back, in fact I hadn't been in school. I remember that was extremely embarrassing to get back in the middle of the school year and I couldn't compete or do as well as the other students. I was good at math and slowly and steadily I have improved in my reading but I'm still not a very good reader, what I consider a good reader.

Coming back to school, I remember some of the kids would protect me because I was bandaged part of the time and others didn't know whether to make fun of it or how to handle it. Both were going on. I made some good friends, actually the Patterson boys. They were a big family of boys, nine of them, each of them a rough, tough kid to survive in their family. They took a shine to me. If anybody picked on me they were there. In the sixth grade I became a traffic cop. The school selected a number of young men to be traffic police. They gave us badges and banderoles. We walked out with little flags to stop the cars. We raised the flag in the morning and took it down in the evening. I became lieutenant of our squad. I thought that was pretty big stuff. I don't know how I got it but I did get it.

I tried to learn how to play the trumpet. We bought a trumpet because Dad said you should do more than one thing with it. I practiced when I went out to milk by blowing it to my cow with a tune to get the milk to come. Neighbors didn't always appreciate my early morning practices.

It was at this time that, with a little assistance from mother and Dad, I worked to buy my first bicycle. That was quite a feat. It was about that time the WPA started putting the sewers in. When that job was completed the road was paved with blacktop clear out to 33rd St.

I went to school on and off, missed part of the year in fifth grade and stayed the full year in sixth grade.

I went to the hospital in the summers. During sixth grade I played soccer and did a lot of other things with the kids. At this time my scars were all hidden. Also, my chin had been relieved of pulling down and my arms were fairly functional by then although I still had quite a few operations ahead of me. Most of those were done during the off school season after sixth grade.

One of our neighbors and I got to be good buddies when I was just starting junior high. At one time he was an infantryman in the Army, which probably had something to do with the fact he always favored horses. Now he was a cook in the Hotel Utah and he had burros. He let me ride his burros all the time.

My friend Tubby Nelson rode with me. He was a fairly heavy little guy. When we got on the burro he would sit backward and hold onto the tail and we would tie our belts together so he wouldn't slide over the tail while we rode around the neighborhood. Burros don't have shoulders, if you don't have a saddle and a rump strap, you don't stay on them.

One of those Burros didn't like dogs. If a dog came out after us the burro would take after the dog and if he caught him would bite the dog and break him in half by beating them against the ground. Fortunately,

MEMORIES OF ANOTHER TIME

it was as gentle as could be with people. We had some interesting experiences with that burro.

About then I heard you could get mustangs from Skull valley for $3.00 to $10.00. You could pick them up in North Salt Lake at that time. I saved up enough money one summer doing lawns and one thing and another. I didn't tell my Dad that I was going with my neighbor to buy a mustang. When we were bringing it home and unloading it from the trailer my father was just walking up from work. The mustang came out of the trailer like a bolt of lightening. We had a rope on it but it was bucking and kicking up quite a fuss. I can still remember the bewildered look on my father's face. We finally got it in to the old cow corral where it calmed down.

My father used to go out and milk in the morning because he said that made him patient enough to do his tailoring but now he wasn't too sure about that horse so I got the full assignment of milking morning and night for about a year.

That horse became quite an enterprise. My father had a barn for the old cow and a hayloft above it, which we had built out of old road signs. I didn't have a place for my horse. My friends told me I had to get a barn for my horse. We found a lot with a partially built garage on it that had been vacant for a long time. I got the name and address of the man that owned it and my friends and I bicycled up to his place to see if we could buy that old shed. We dickered and I bought it for three dollars. No one had any idea how I could get it home.

Another neighbor had just cut down an old car with low gears in it to make a little tractor to plow his piece of land. He gave me permission to use it to tow the shed home. We boys figured that if we could get pipes under it we could drag that old shed to my house with that old car. My neighbors had fences for their cows so we had to take all the fences down to tow that shed to our home. We negotiated with the neighbors and they agreed that if we restored everything we could do that. We finally devised a way to frame that shed so we could drag it on pipes a half a block down to my house where we pushed it in place. Then we fixed all the fences for the neighbors, maybe a little better than they were, by stringing the old barbwire tighter.

It was the second day when we finished the work. We still had this man's tractor. We decided to go swimming in the Jordan River about three miles to the west of us. We knew a good place that had a rope hanging from a tree above the swimming hole. We all climbed on the old tractor and drove it down there. On the way back it got a flat tire. We had no way to fix that tire. I had to tell my neighbor that we had taken his tractor down to go swimming, a no, no really. He was pretty good about it. He didn't turn us over to the police. He got the tire fixed and the tractor home. I sure felt bad about doing that for a long, long time.

I finally got that horse trained. To buy oats and some hay each year I took on a paper route. I delivered the papers on my horse. That way I could take a double paper route carrying a load I couldn't do on my bike. I did that for one summer and one winter before I quit. I didn't think I made enough on that job. That horse was a good horse. He knew just when I was going to come to work and would be standing ready. He was just as patient as he could be with me. Grandfather helped me train him and of course, my friends all helped.

I liked my junior high years. Each summer operations sometimes going into the fall took place.

When I was eighteen I received my draft notice. I was excited to go serve Uncle Sam and went up to Fort Douglas where they had the physical exam. It happened that when I got up there Doctor Collister, my longtime burn surgeon, was head of the department. He pulled me off and got me regraded before my physical exam. He said, "This man has done so much work that is vital to this war he will be going with me".

So, for the next year I traveled with him to seminars. He would show pictures of the operations, step by step, processes reached in operations in each graft, he was teaching doctors. It was sorta fun. I didn't mind it. In fact, I thought it was better than working at Hill Field. I got paid leave, plus I got paid to go with him. I didn't mind that a bit.

I was classified 4F in the draft. They were never going to take me. I don't know how he did it or what he {Doctor Collister} did but I never talked to my draft board again.

After that I worked at Hill Field and when the war ended, the GI's started coming home of course. Civil Service work was open to them and with a priority for the good job positions. We felt it was good. Of course, a lot of them never got out of the country and still had the privi-

MEMORIES OF ANOTHER TIME

leges. It didn't designate whether they had been serving overseas or not. They started coming up to Hill Field and bumping the better jobs.

At that time I was on the emergency crew. We would go out and pick up the planes that had come in from the Pacific. We would canvas them and bring them into Hill Field. Canvassing means we would stretch canvas over them and heat it. It would stretch as tight as aluminum skin. It made it possible to fly them in without patching all the holes. I was on that crew. We had to learn how to parachute to be on that crew. I didn't think I would make that because I thought the harnesses might cut my scars. I did get to jump.

On that crew I knew that a lot of those men were far more qualified than I was. For sure when you are working out there in the field you learn all the tricks of the trade to keep planes flying.

Well, I thought we aren't going to have any more terrible wars like this. In about a year, year and a half after they started coming in, I thought I would go to school. So I took a pre exam at the University of Utah to see if I could get in. I was a non-credited student because I hadn't finished my high school. I hoped to get my high school credits completed while getting some classes in at the U. I thought that would stimulate me enough to go back to school. I spent one quarter at the University of Utah and finished my high school.

One of my friends who had been in the Army Air Force came home. He wanted to go to Utah State. We decided we would do that. I thought I would become a veterinarian because I had been taking care of some animals, especially horses which my grandfather helped train and I thought being a veterinarian might be interesting.

My uncle trained at Boswitch's riding academy where he trained trotters and jumpers. I got to ride some of them. So I went with my friend Willard Erickson to Utah State. We found a room and boarded together.

My friend got married and something with the stress and one thing or another he suddenly for some unknown reason got amnesia. During the war he was a gunner on one of the planes. Something had happened to him during the time he was in gunnery. He was off to the hospital for quite a little while.

I finished that quarter of school and stayed for winter quarter. He was in the Veteran's hospital. His wife would call me and say come on up, he doesn't remember me but he might remember you. Bring some pictures. So I would come down to visit him.

On one of those occasions when I came home from school I hadn't been in my LDS ward for almost a year, and certainly not often enough for any one to know me. We had a new Bishop, a man who had just moved up from California. The European war was over but we were still struggling with Japan.

With the end of the war in Europe, the Church wanted to put people in there during the first part of the occupation. The American government had asked for help for Europe from other sources besides the Red Cross and had pushed all the churches to gather blankets, clothes, and food.

The LDS Church had already practiced that to some extent. Church President George Smith asked the President of the United States if the LDS could participate. We had quite a lot we could contribute to that kind of effort. This was all going on while I was still in school and I didn't pay much attention to it until I got caught up in it.

I came home this particular weekend to see my friend and see my folks. I had never met this Bishop. He didn't know me. He knew my previous Bishop, Bob Shepherd. On Sunday morning he saw me in church. That afternoon he called up and said to my father " I would like to see your son this afternoon in my home." My father said, "This Bishop doesn't even know you are coming." I said "no, I've only seen him a few times a short time prior to coming home from school".

As we were eating lunch, my father said, "You're going to go on a Mission." He said, "he's made that decision fast, he doesn't know you that well and they haven't opened the European Mission yet." They hadn't actually called missionaries during the last part of the war.

That afternoon I went down to see the Bishop. I can't remember his name. He didn't stay there very long before he went back to California. He offered a mission saying "you'll be going to Europe with a welfare mission with the Red Cross." He said, "You'll probably start off in Belgium but will go on to Holland. That's where we would like to assign you because you have the Dutch language due to your grand-parents. You will probably pick it up very quickly." They had always spoken in Dutch. I had picked up some of it by that process. My father

MEMORIES OF ANOTHER TIME

spoke English very well so he didn't have to rely on partial Dutch. Sure enough, the Bishop made the recommendation so I left school.

Actually, I was pleased to be going on mission and the thought of going to Europe excited me so I looked forward to getting started.

CHAPTER 10
A CHILD'S MEMORIES OF THE 1920'S

By
MaryBelle Preston Wells

THE BREEZES blew cool in the bustling young city of Seattle, where I was born on October 4, 1920, and where later my first memories began. Those breezes brought the smells of nearby forest and sea, for Seattle was then a much smaller city.

Let me share with you the Seattle of the 1920's. The city was young, founded only in 1852, so it was less than seventy years old when I was born. That meant that Princess Angeline, daughter of the respected Indian leader, Chief Seattle, for whom the town had been named, was still living and a respected social leader. Also that the first white child born in Seattle, during the pioneers' first hard winter, Reginald Denny, was not only still alive but still active. (I was told the story that his mother couldn't nurse her newborn, and of course there was no cow closer than San Francisco, five hundred miles away, so the baby's parents dug desperately for clams. They squeezed clam juice, rigged some sort of baby bottle, and got the baby to suckle it. The claim was that you could have heard that colicky baby cry—between suckles--as far as you could see the tiny settlement, but Reginald Denny, like his new little city, survived.)

In the Seattle of the 1920's some men wore suits in their public dealings—along with dark felt hats, and the high stiff collars of the time, above their starched white shirts. (The collars were washed separately,

87

and heavily starched; fresh collars were attached to the fresh white shirt each day by fancy collar buttons, matching the ones that pulled together all four layers of starched cuff on each of the owner's wrists.) Such men's shoes were shiny and their hands uncallused. They were richer and more respected than most, and our (underpaid professor) Daddy was one of them.

Most men did hard physical work. They wore darker shirts, work pants, and thick wool-plaid jackets every day but Sundays. Other men owned or worked in stores, such as Mr. Jamieson who owned the drugstore, Mr. Ernst who owned the hardware store, or the grocers who waited on us at Augustine and Kyer, the best grocery store on busy Fourteenth Avenue in our University District. They wore tie-on jackets or aprons over their white shirts and ties. They were very polite and humble toward their housewife-customers, and sometimes threw in a given-away weenie or a piece of candy to us small, wistful tagalongs.

Seattle's horizon was everywhere jagged, edged by the dark pointed tops of the evergreen trees that surrounded us. Evergreen forests had held undisputed reign from time immemorial around Puget Sound, and still seemed ready to close in on the town at any moment, to reclaim the land for themselves, particularly on dark, wintry days.

Above those dark, tree-covered hills loomed spectacular, brilliantly snow-covered mountain chains--visible in clear weather only. East of the city the rugged Cascades were backlit at sunrise, while to the west, the Olympics, beyond the wide waters of Puget Sound, outlined themselves against the long sunsets. To the south and slightly east of Seattle rose that glory of the Northwest, Mt. Rainier, a fourteen-thousand-foot dome always covered with white glaciers, rivers of ice that guarded its crown. Rainier was as beautiful as carved porcelain when it was "out," and was our most loved symbol throughout western Washington. But the mountain was temperamental; when winter hid our horizons behind lowering clouds or rain, months could go by without our seeing that proud totem.

Even during the spring and summer, our skies were a constantly changing parade of great sailing clouds: white ones, black ones, sunrise and sunset clouds tinged with rose tones, that alternately obscured and revealed our mountains. We were constantly reminded that ours was a land in which great mountain ranges encircled an inland arm of the sea,

MEMORIES OF ANOTHER TIME

Puget Sound, and our moist air always blew hints that we were never far from that sea.

Brawny men were creating riches from a wilderness in those days. Few men worked behind a desk, and those were both respected (more powerful, richer) and regarded somewhat as sissies. Men made their living in lumbering and saw-milling, fishing, mining coal or iron, in local manufacturing, and importantly, in loading and unloading the great freighters that docked in Elliott Bay, our deep harbor on Puget Sound. Seattle's harbor--out of sight of our home--was constantly busy with the trucks, railroad boxcars and loading cranes that filled or emptied ships from around the world. We could hear, even in our inland, residential part of town, the long exciting whistles of the loaded trains that carried those goods to and from the city.

Because we lived in the city, we children also heard sirens. Firemen rode exciting, screaming red trucks, and they waved! We admired firemen. Policemen were a more serious matter. They wore navy double-breasted suits with gold buttons, and Navy Officer-style visored hats. Policemen had whistles, and we were a little afraid of them, because, of course, they knew every bad thing we had ever done and might any moment decide to arrest us. Traffic officers, friendlier, rode horses; they used long sticks to make chalk marks on the tires of cars to be checked an hour later, to tell if we had parked too long. They kept people back on the sidewalk during parades, but they liked kids and would let you pet their horses.

The sounds of hammering, and the growls of steam shovels were in the air of the University District when my brother Frank, two years older, and I were small. We were two of the "baby boom" children born after World War I, and in our north-end suburb, new houses were going up all around us. At the south end of our own block, when I was two and he four, three houses were going up simultaneously, so picking up short wooden "curls", shavings left by the carpenters, and sticking them in my red, curly hair to make myself more beautiful, was important to me. We watched, awestruck, as the grown men walked house-beams high in the air, hammered noisily, and yelled at each other.

After the men quit each late afternoon and drove their trucks away, we (my brother, his also-four-year-old buddy Jack Ayer, and little Mary Belle) tried to imitate them, walking boards or beams the men had left behind on the rough ground. "Boys can do that," I was told sternly by my four-year-old elders; "girls can't!" Girls could sneak a try--and I did. "Girls can SO!" was a big issue in my two-year-old life.

Weekdays we also heard the resonant bell tones of the University Chimes, played by blind musician George Bailey in the Chimes Tower, at the edge of the University of Washington campus. He played beautifully for fifteen minutes, first from seven forty-five each school morning to bustle students and professors alike into their eight o'clock classrooms, and again at noon to celebrate the whole campus' joy at dismissal for lunch. Last he played at five in the evening to signal suppertime to the entire University District. The wooden, two-story Chimes Tower was only two and a half blocks southeast of our house, and my young, serious father was one of those the Chimes summoned.

Howard Hall Preston was a newly minted Associate Professor of Economics, who had moved his small family from Oberlin College, in Ohio, to this remote corner of the United States because, by that move, he had the chance to advance quickly in professional rank. Both my parents were ambitious, and expected then that the next jump would take them back to the Midwest, where both their families lived, or even to the east, to teach at the most prestigious colleges in the country.

Since my mother, Lucy Helen Steele Preston, had been born in Greencastle, Indiana, she was a "Hoosier" (their sports teams still carry that name), while my father and my brother Frank Steele Preston, were both "Buckeyes," born in Iowa.

As the first member of my family born in the far-off State of Washington, where the University team was then known as the "Sun Dodgers," I was proudly designated the family's "Sun Dodger." Since neither Frank nor I could say anything closer to that than "Wodger," I probably learned my name was "Wodger" before I learned anything else.

Brother Frank was my constant playmate, of course; my hero and model, my instructor and protector. He is quoted by my parents as having said sternly in my defense one time, "Her name not "Fuzzy" any more! Her name Murray Bull!" He was correct, for I had been named--properly, according to American and British tradition--for my mother's mother. Which translated to being "Mary" for her next-older sister, who had recently died and had been her closest emotional mother,

MEMORIES OF ANOTHER TIME

and "Belle" for her actual mother, hard-working Arabelle Garner Steele. The resulting name, "Mary Belle" has been very special, but has also been difficult for people to remember or spell, and therefore a lifetime embarrassment.

Other sounds enlivened our 1920's urban world. Horns "ah-OO-ged" from the high, noisy cars that rattled up and down our street. (There were fewer cars then, but they honked a lot.) Church bells sounded on Sundays; by the time we were in grade school, we could see seven church buildings from the Fiftieth Street end of our own block. Newsboys called "Extra, Extra!" up the middle of the street when there was breaking news; radios were not yet available, and boys prized jobs we'd call child labor today. The traffic light on University Way (and two blocks south) sounded a loud, long alarm bell each time the signal changed from red to green, bragging to the drivers about how up-to-date our city was. (Those bells drove people who lived nearby absolutely wild, until all cities silenced the noise.)

The clatter of Seattle's electric trolley cars carried up to us from busy Fourteenth Avenue, one block below the hill on which most of our homes sat. (The trolleys' metal-on-metal rattling seemed especially distinct during the quiet of the night.) Jouncing along loudly most of the time, clickity-clack on the rails, they squealed their brakes loudly as they stopped, before we heard the "jing, jing" of the conductor's warning bell clang as they lurched on again, clanking slowly away.

From farther away, to remind us of the out-of-sight sea and harbor which were the center of the city's existence, came the sounds of commerce: factory whistles, and the trains switching on the tracks at the south end of the University District, bringing coal and firewood, lumber and milk cans. On foggy nights, from even farther away, we could hear the deep bleating foghorns of each of the ships in the harbor, signaling where they were all night long, to ward off collisions, sounding as lonely and afraid as children lost in the dark. . . .

Behind our house there was a concrete paved alley all through the block. (We were in a really modern new district; the better homes had alleys.) That alley allowed all tradesmen to make their deliveries to our back doors, properly and respectfully. (No tradesman or hired help ever came in the front door, or kept his hat on, or sat down, in the presence of the Lady of the House. Front doors were only for company and being dressed up.)

Women worked long hours then, as almost all cooking and laundry, sewing, bread baking, canning, and so on was done in each home, and "from scratch." So the honored Lady of the House was in most cases actually a drudge from morning to night, a dependant who never knew what her husband's income was, nor had any realistic hope of earning an adequate living if she were widowed or deserted. Still, because the women were regarded as Respectability itself, and since as a group they determined much feared Public Opinion, they were deferred to as no one is today.)

To dare buy that fine house near the University, our young parents had undertaken much hard extra work. Our father had volunteered to teach the correspondence courses in his department, on top of his daytime courses, and our mother was doing all the hands-on work involved in boarding "co-eds" attending the "U". They had invited mother's younger sister Kathryn to move from the Middle West to help, and in return, they were putting her through the University, to fulfill her dream of becoming a high school music teacher. Ours was therefore a busy household; our father, Aunt Kathryn, the student girls, and we kids all needed a hot "dinner' at noon as well as a hot "supper" at night. Mother even felt guilty about not baking our own bread—desserts were all home created, of course, as well as all canned fruit. And much sewing. Her day was from six in the morning to eleven at night.

But I was telling you about the lively, noisy scene of the alley. We--and everyone else in the block--had an icebox (always kept unlocked, on an honor system) and a supply of colored cards to put up in a rear window, printed in colors as "25 lbs." "50 lbs." or "100 lbs." The toot of the iceman's arrival in the alley brought all us little kids running. He got out and walked toward the house of his first customer in the block, first to read the colored card placed in the rear window. Then he marched back to the rear of his truck to chip off the appropriate sized block of ice from the wet-burlap-bag-covered iceberg in the rear of his truck, sending chips of ice flying. He pitched his huge black tongs into the block he'd cut, swung it onto his leather-protected shoulders, and hurried it into that first back-porch icebox. While he was doing that, we little kids rushed his truck, crowding each other to grab the fresh, melting chips he had made. Big boys--old enough to go to school--bravely climbed up for the biggest chunks, but even the littlest kid--at first little Mary Belle--could reach for some ice at the edge of the truck if she stood on tiptoe.

Other trucks came down the alley: the egg man, calling out. The milkman, who delivered the milk bottles directly into the icebox, also picked up the carefully washed empties. If Mother called in her order before nine in the morning, the grocery boy would come running in before noon to put the grocery crate on the kitchen table. Some deliveries were still made by horse-drawn wagons, although that was rare; perhaps the coal came by wagon, or the firewood, or a farmer with vegetables. Cars, many of them Model-T's, came home at night, of course, turning into the small, one car garages lining the alley. What family could possibly afford—or need—two cars?

This—and the "Bacant Lot" at the north end of the block—was where we played. We collected bee-stings and skinned knees as kids will, but were pretty independent. There were few backyard fences, so we ran through other people's yards, climbed other people's trees (or fell out of them), collected other people's iris stalks to use as swords, stroked other people's pets. Neither kids nor dogs were on leashes, but we all got along. And the kids' world insisted on a strong basic morality. "That's not fair!" or "I'll tell!" stopped everything. The big kids would have to see that the littler one got his turn, or got his ball back, before the adult world intervened, with unpredictable results. It was a pretty good system to teach us a lot about the natural world-- and about self-reliance and being fair.

Our busy mother taught us to stay out of the street, out front, but did let us play in front sometimes with the older children

Some special angel must have been protecting near-sighted Mary Belle, because I thought I could do everything the bigger ones did. For instance, I had been carefully taught that I should "Look up the street and down the street, before starting across." I did so faithfully--until my mother saw me looking straight up into the sky, then straight down by my shoes, before running across the street regardless of what the cars were doing.

When I was perhaps four, it was the fad in our block for us kids to wait until a car was coming (cars were high, usually black, noisy contraptions with narrow tires, seldom more than one to a block at a time.) Just when the car got about 15-20 feet away, six to ten kids all ran across the street just across its path. We might get "Ah-Oooga'd" by the outraged driver, but we got away with it, so we thought we were hot stuff. Of course, as one of the youngest, I had to do just what the big kids did, even though I might be the last as the fender passed. Then the braver ones started showing off by patting the passing fender just behind them, so I did that too. There were no accidents, but someone's parents must have been tipped off, because suddenly the big kids told us not to do that anymore.

(I can remember my sense of outrage and betrayal just a few years later, when the first car with balloon tires and quieter motor passed by without a warning racket. "Those things could be dangerous!")

And how did we cope, as children, with rainy Seattle? To begin with, the city was almost always overcast in the winter, but rain, if it did come, could be only what adults called a "Scotch mist," very light. Mother outfitted us with raincoats and hats--often-bright yellow, like New England fisherman's gear--and we simply did whatever we wanted to do.

But really *rainy* rain could spoil the fun. On days when it actually poured, my brother and I were encouraged to take out toys that were kept in the basement, and play there. The basement was not a finished "rumpus room," as people called them then, as cozy as any room upstairs. Our basement was mainly one big room, concrete floored and walled, topped with ground level windows all around for ventilation. It was dominated and warmed by the big furnace in the center, which supported an octopus of great asbestos-gray-white pipes that carried heat to the floor registers in the rooms above. Around the walls were wooden shelves holding Mother's canning, two stoneware pickle crocks, my parents' trunks and those of the "student girls," Dad's fishing gear, and wooden frames called "curtain stretchers" on which the lace curtains would be dried after washing.

Near the bottom of the basement stairs stood a clothes-sorting table, the wringer washer and stationary tubs with its large copper clothes boiler. ("Whites" were boiled at that time, before today's better detergents and stain removers.) Strong wire clotheslines were strung from the

MEMORIES OF ANOTHER TIME

ceiling, full, on rainy days, of the day's wet washing. The basement was always warm, and always a little dusty and furnace smelling.

We children had a large, thick old rug to play on in one part of the basement. That was the place to push toy trucks or march metal soldiers. Both of us used my dolls a lot. Though I was the tender mother, doing all the traditional doll dressing and feeding, Frank also needed them. When he was the surgeon, a doll was the patient; when we did a play, they were lined up as the audience. They rode in the red steel wagon when we Indians attacked the settlers, and of course were the Huns when we were victorious soldiers.

Since kids need big muscle play even on rainy days, we had one big rag-doll I had been given that Frank chose to be our kick-ball. So we also kicked and re-kicked that doll, all around the furnace and into and out of the basement corners, as a kind of rag-doll soccer.

Or I rode my kiddy-car while Frank peddled his tricycle or foot-pushed scooter, around and around the big furnace. Which brings me to two kiddy-car adventures.

Frank's occurred before my memories begin, when I was new and he was about two. He managed to ride his kiddy-car not just along our front sidewalk, where Mother thought he was, but all the way to the end of our block, down the steep hill of 50th to Fourteenth Avenue ("University Way") and south a block or so into the shopping district. He had got himself safely through traffic and was sight-seeing happily by the time our desperate Mother had called our father to come home from the University to help search. But it was the police who actually found little Frank.

My own adventure I remember well. I was at the top of the basement stairs on my kiddy-car, and found that someone had left the basement stair door open, against house rules. I studied the new vista carefully from the top, and decided I could make it. As I passed the edge of the first step, that proved to be a mistake. Next came a lot of falling, hitting and banging before the kiddy-car and I came to rest most of the way down the second flight of steps. I did a lot of yelling during all that, before Mother was carrying me back upstairs and started the bandaging . . .I still carry a scar under my chin from that mishap.

Much later my sister Anne, born in 1925, another adventurer though on foot, got as far east as 20th Avenue, over the top of the hill behind

96   A STORY TO TELL

our house and down the other side as far as residential streets could reach. Jeanne, born in 1932, was found almost at the far end of the campus, about three miles from home, also exploring but also safe.

*   *   *

One of the most significant events I got to witness early took place one afternoon in 1924, when I had just turned four. Lots of people were going to remember that day, we were told. My father, who owned a car, had made a point of taking little Frank and me with him on this historical occasion. Two men had flown two small Army airplanes on the first around the world flight, an unbelievable 26,103 miles. Those little planes had started in Seattle and were now returning to Seattle. The men would land at Sand Point, a bare sand spit on Lake Washington, north of Seattle.

We drove north through tall virgin forest until we came out onto an open, sandy point jutting into the lake. Daddy found a place to park on the edge of a big crowd, mostly of young men, and we started to walk across a gritty sand spit broken only by streamers of long, narrow beach grass.

As the crowd got thicker Daddy picked me up, keeping Frank close beside him. Then the waiting men began to cheer and shout, and we could see the first of two tiny single-wing airplanes high in the air, circling down. Men yelled to "step back," the plane roared to a landing, and the crowd surged noisily forward, Daddy included.

From high on Daddy's shoulder I could see two men in brown leather helmets and jackets, brown pants flaring out at the thighs, and high boots. Men on the ground nearest the plane helped the aviators get up out of their two open cockpits and climb down, using footholds on the outside of their plane. Cheering men and boys immediately hoisted the two pilots onto their shoulders to carry them off to a waiting car. We watched from a distance, then as the heroes were driven away, before we slogged back through the sand to our car.

Those men had flown south that day from Alaska, were late getting in and they were anxiously expected. But what a tiny plane they had in which to venture that risky trip! They did have hand-cranked radios,

MEMORIES OF ANOTHER TIME

but were missing today's navigational aids, emergency landing fields, and precision instruments.

In 1927 when I was already in first grade we shared another great moment in flying history. Charles Lindberg had flown the Atlantic from New York to Paris May 20-21, 1927, and immediately everyone in the world was excited about the possibilities--and their handsome new hero. Our whole school (University Heights School on Fourteenth, now called University Way) was excused to the playground, to wave to Mr. Lindberg when his motorcade was to pass by. First came the motorcycles, then the other cars, and then there he was: sitting atop the back of the rear seat of an open touring car, young and blond, waving to us school kids and all the grownups crowding the other side of the Avenue.

*   *   *

Independence was sometimes expected by our mother. When I was five, Mother learned that low-cost swimming lessons were to be given by the YWCA downtown, and saw my chance. She took me once on the streetcar, carefully pointing out the place on University Way where I was to catch the streetcar, and how I was to put my nickel into the cash jingler beside the trolley motorman. She showed me how to ask him to call out "Union Avenue," and how to get off, walk up the steep hill two blocks to the Y Building, and then use the elevator to get up to the top floor where the pool and dressing rooms were. After my lesson with all the other kids, she showed me how to reverse the process, turning in my metal tag to get my bag of clothes, dressing myself, and turning in my suit and towel. I had to take the elevator down, walk downhill in the right direction, and then find the different spot, to take the return trolley. I had to read its number, "7," and pay my token, which had been carefully tied in the corner of my handkerchief up to that time. (Neither she nor I realized that I was quite near-sighted. At five I couldn't have read the street signs even if I could have seen them, so I memorized the storefronts.) After that one trip I did successfully get myself to my lessons alone, downtown and back, for at least half a year. The Seattle School System wouldn't let me start kindergarten yet, until the February term when I was five and a half, but I *could* go downtown on my own.

*   *   *

Keeping children amused on a long trip was a problem then as now, of course. We saw small towns and farms, threshing crews, orchards and haystacks, learned from our parents the names of the crops, not only the obvious corn but also alfalfa, barley and oats. Farms then had livestock, down to ducks, chickens and geese, and a variety of crops instead of endless rows of corn and soybeans.

We played "Roadside cribbage", pitting children on one side of the car against those on the other, one point for a chicken, three for a duck, more for a horse or cow etc. up to a mythical 100 points—and game!—for an elephant. In one small town Dad spotted a poster advertising a coming circus, featuring a brightly over colored elephant. "100 points!" he shouted, "I win!" Great uproar from the back seat—"that was just a picture, Daddy!" But it did reward sharp observation, fast counting as we passed a farmyard, a lot of learning.

Frank and I counted the cars on the freight trains, and often saw trains with over a hundred, up to 120 cars in tow that prosperous summer of 1928. A few years later, during the Depression, trains of ten or fewer cars, loaded with "bums," was more the rule.

We drove through to Virginia and did a lot of sightseeing in the Civil War areas.

Our parents, of course, knew the history of the area and told us stories all the way, explaining what we were seeing. Going through the poor country of small farms I asked about a rail fence, and learned what it was like not to be able to afford nails. The houses were often unpainted; Dad quoted "too poor to paint and too proud to whitewash" and told us what it meant. The poverty left from the Civil War was still, 63 years after that War, heavy on the south.

In Virginia, we were taken to the remains of the small brick church at Jamestown, not then a restored national monument, and learned about the starvation and Indian raids that killed the first settlers there. In Williamsburg we were taken to a kind of wide pit, and learned that

MEMORIES OF ANOTHER TIME

the Rockefeller family had bought the land, and were planning to re-build Colonial Williamsburg.

In parts of northern Virginia, Mother marveled that billboards—the present system of national monuments and restoration not yet being in place—could be seen, sometimes marking the sites of battles in the French and Indian wars, the Revolution, and the Civil War, all in sight from the same place.

We visited Monticello, and were awed by Jefferson's chosen obituary on his tombstone. Only three achievements were named there: "Author of the Statute for Religious Freedom, Author of the Declaration of Independence, and Founder of the University of Virginia." Nothing, as our parents told us, of his being a legislator, Ambassador to France during the Revolution, the first Secretary of State, or third President of the United States—for just those three accomplishments he wanted to be remembered.

We saw the University of Virginia with its famous serpentine wall, then drove north to another battlefield to the accompaniment of Dad's reciting of Thomas Buchanan Read's Civil War epic poem titled Sheridan's Ride: and beginning:

Up from the South at break of day,
Bringing to Winchester fresh dismay,
The affrighted air with a shudder bore,
Like a herald in haste, to the chieftain's door,
The terrible grumble, and rumble, and roar,
Telling the battle was on once more,
And Sheridan twenty miles away.

And when we drove through the narrow streets of Fredericksburg, Maryland, we were regaled, in stentorian tones, with all 30 verses of John Greenleaf Whittier's "Barbara Frietche". Beginning with the lines "Up from the meadows rich with corn, Clear in the cool September morn" to the verse that has stayed with me to his date "Shoot if you must, this old gray head, But spare your country's flag, she said!"

It was history, it was family togetherness, and it was a remarkable example of our father's photographic memory, all at once.

Our stop in Washington D.C. was also memorable. The weather was brutally hot, and we had had a day of seeing all the postcard sights of the Capitol, before we settled into our rented tent along the shore of the Potomac.

I suspect the location is now part of the beautiful Mall, with its reflecting ponds and broad lawns; then it was part of a kind of lake-shore swamp. As darkness deepened and we tried to sleep on our rented narrow cots, the mosquitoes descended in hordes. We slapped, we itched, we cringed from the ever-growing shrill hum, we hid as much of ourselves as we could under the sheet despite the muggy heat—and we swatted.

"Settle down, children!" came crossly from our parents. Until we noticed that outside, all the electric lights in the camp were on high above us, and crowds were out, walking about in various kinds of night-gowns and pajamas. Everyone was miserable, everyone, adult and child alike, was out walking and swatting, pacing up and down the paved promenade between the tent city and the Potomac. Sometime before morning we all straggled back to out cots, but we knew what it would be like to live permanently in the tropics. People today, who can have ice and air conditioning at will, may not understand what summers could be like then.

From there we drove to the New York area where we stayed about a week with Dad's cousin, Irwin Smith. While there, although it was a Sunday, we drove down deserted Wall Street, to stare reverently at the outside of the Stock Market, the heart and source, our father told us respectfully, of the prosperity and progress of the whole country. That was September of 1928 at the height of the investment bubble.

After a winter in Dartmouth College where Dad taught as an exchange professor, he determined to drive us home over a more northern route that took us through South Dakota, Montana and Idaho before reaching home. Caught in a rainstorm somewhere out on the prairie, we struggled out of the car and up the farmland to a lonely shack on the prairie.

The farmer welcomed us all into his one room home; company was company, including bedraggled kids. For us, just being out of the wet and cold and sitting or standing around his black stove with its very welcome fire while we dried out was a joy.

He and Dad started talking farming. It seems he had moved west from Iowa, lured by cheap land and high hopes, but hadn't earned

MEMORIES OF ANOTHER TIME

enough to move back and couldn't sell out. Best remembered was his statement, "No sir, I bin here ten years and I ain't made enough to buy a necktie for a mosquito!"

Going west through the Big Sky country was a new, different experience for us. We could tell where any farmhouse was, in the distance, by the silvery glint of the windmill towering far above the house. Redwing blackbirds and meadowlarks sang from the fence tops; the land was empty except for distant bands of sheep, or herds of grazing cattle.

Nearer the road, we began to see whole large "towns" of prairie dogs. A few animals stood stiff upright, on picket duty, as the others moved about. Then when the watcher whistled, all the others dove out of sight, the last one down being the duty-bound sentry.

By the time we got to Spokane, Washington, Dad was low on money. He and Mother talked apart between themselves; we didn't know why. We learned later he was worried he wouldn't have enough money for gasoline if we stayed in a hotel, even the cheapest. He drove to the railroad station and talked to the stationmaster. So we had a special adventure; we slept on the floor of the waiting room that night. By the time we got to Seattle, Dad said he had exactly $1.37 left at the end of a cross-country trip that had lasted about a month.

One last example of our independence, and our living up to our parents' trust, has to be added. In the summer of 1936, when my sister Anne was eleven and little Jeanne was four, my father's sister Winifred and husband Asahel Moore brought their sons and Grandpa Moore from Minneapolis to visit us. Grandpa Moore was going home separately by train, and my father got an inspiration. Anne could travel for half-fare, and Jeanne free, at those ages. Why not send the little girls back to Minneapolis by train in the care of Grandpa Moore, and after a visit with their girl cousins there, have them put on the train for the three-day return trip to Seattle? He would meet them at the King Street Station to drive them home.

So that was exactly what was done. Two little girls got a cross country train trip to Minneapolis, including a berth for three days each way, for a chance to know their little-girl cousins, all for the price of one half fare rail ticket. (Today children travel by air alone routinely, but then it was probably unheard of. Even then, the conductor was probably well tipped to see that they got back aboard after each of the souvenir-and-leg-stretching stops, and were getting their meals all right in the dining car.) Anne handled their money, and the trip went fine.

Money was hard to get in the 1920's, and was therefore respected in a very unequal world. Those years were later looked back on as "prosperity" from the vantage-point of the Great Depression, but at the time, they were called "Back to Normalcy" after the Great War. Few people could afford to travel, but our parents were ambitious and ingenious. And little Preston's could do that.

CHAPTER 11

REACHING FOR A COLLEGE EDUCATION

By
Patricia Murphy Burns

MY NAME is Patricia Murphy Burns. I was born in August 1918 in Seattle, WA just prior to the end of WW I. An early memory is of my parents relating that on November 11, 1918 my father phoned Mother and said excitedly, "The War is over! Bring the baby and come downtown. Everybody is celebrating."

There was no radio or TV then, only a newspaper extra, a Fox Movietone News or word of mouth to spread the news.

Father was selling insurance in Seattle at that time. He and my mother had both attended the University of Washington where they met. They saw each other off and on for a couple of years. In September of 1917 he persuaded her to elope.

He had all the Irish charm, loved social things, parties and so forth and he could charm anybody, especially the women. He charmed my mother but also he was a "big man" on campus. It surprised me in a way that he went after mother because she was certainly the antithesis of him in personality. She wasn't a party girl by any means.

To elope was totally out of character for her, but he prevailed and they were married in Toppenish, WA. Her parents were quite upset about their getting married in that way. Dad was a big football star at the University of Washington, Captain of the team and voted the most inspirational player. He promised mother he would not go back

103

to school, but would get a job and they would start their life together if she married him.

When they got back to Seattle in September school was about to start. Football coach Gil Dobie was very upset and angry that Dad was not planning to play football that fall. The only way Dad had been able to attend the University in the first place was with almost complete support by the school given in whatever way was available then.

I have the original recruiting letter the coach sent him which assures "You come over here to Seattle and everything will be fine. We'll take care of you." Gil Dobie was a famous coach at the U of W. He had one winning streak of nine years without losing a game.

Coach Dobie was both persistent and persuasive so Dad did go back to the University and played his final year of football. Consequently, he and mother were not able to have a place of their own, but lived with Grandmother Murphy for a year.

They had married in September 1917 and I came along eleven months later when they were living with Grandma Murphy. By then school was out and Dad immediately started selling insurance for a Seattle company. His sports ability, reputation and outgoing personality undoubtedly were helpful in securing this job. They were then able to rent their own apartment. Sadly, Dad was just two or three credits short of graduation.

Dad was born in Colfax, WA in 1895. He grew up in Wallace, Idaho, a very small silver mining town. His father died in December 1904 when Dad was nine years old. While still quite young he worked part time in the silver mines to help out at home.

In high school he had been a four sports man. He lettered in baseball, track, basketball and football. When Dad died in 1977 we found about a dozen silver medals, which had been awarded to him for his prowess in the various sports. He was an outstanding athlete, big, handsome, a wonderful example of his Irish-German descent. That was why Coach Dobie recruited him, of course.

My Dad hated to be alone. He had to have people around. He had a strong, analytical mind. He was sort of a dual personality in a way, socially charming but very controlling and one who carried a grudge forever. Not surprisingly, he was an alcoholic as was his father. On the

MEMORIES OF ANOTHER TIME

German side he was the stubbornist man who ever lived. He could be pretty mean.

Cullen and I were never close to Dad because he was so strict and so stern. Dad's punishment was always more mental and emotional than physical, although he did use a leather strap when we were young. He was his own worst enemy because of his having to be in control in every situation. In more social situations at home, he could be so much fun. He liked card games like Rummy and the family played a lot of Pinochle.

Mother was born in Jackson, Michigan in 1893. When she was ten years old the family moved to Spokane, WA. That remained her home until she was married. She attended and graduated from North Central High School. In the 1912 yearbook she is described as "formal". She was the class secretary; writer of the class Will; in the cast of the Senior Play; and one of four members in charge of the Senior Reception.

At the University Mother was very active in her sorority, and remained so as an Alum for the rest of her life. Rather than "formal". I would describe her as "reserved", "dignified" but very friendly and kind, intelligent, capable and resourceful.

After a couple years selling insurance, Dad left that business and went to work for Bryant Lumber Company in Seattle. His first job was piling lumber in stacks, which was probably the lowest position. It was hard work but he was big, strong, and able to do that very well. Before too long he became the manager of the yard, and then general manager of the company.

My brother Cullen was born in October of 1921. It was good to have a little brother. He is the only sibling I have. Soon Grandmother Murphy came to live with us to help care for Cullen and me as Mother had gone to work at the McDougal Southwick department store in the stationery department. Eventually she became head of the department.

She was a very supportive parent, and when we entered school was always keenly interested in our progress and activities. She was active in PTA and in her Alpha Xi Delta alumni group, serving as Vice President and President.

She was a lovely lady in every sense of the word as well as a fine homemaker and cook. One of her PTA responsibilities was to see that cakes were donated for refreshments at each meeting. If any cake was left over she could bring it home. That was a big treat.

I recall very well the evening she was to be the honoree at her sorority banquet. Grandmother had made her a formal lace dress, and she looked so pretty.

I should say that in all my school years I rarely had any clothing purchased ready made. My two grandmothers' and my mother were fine seamstresses. One or the other of them made all of my clothing, even the coats or jackets, p.j's and undies.

During the years we lived in Seattle there are pleasant memories of friends, schools, lots of picnics at various parks and lakes, especially Lake Washington. Often we went swimming there or at Green Lake.

School was easy for me at Latona elementary. We lived in the University District within easy walking distance of the campus. Each morning and evening we could hear the chimes being played, at the entrance to the University campus, by George Bailey, the blind man who rang them for many years.

Often I went to the campus to roller skate on the smooth blacktop roads. It was so interesting looking at the buildings and learning the names of many of them. Occasionally we went to football games. On the fourth of July we usually went to the hill above the stadium to watch the fireworks and wave our sparklers. Cullen and I thought this was all great fun. Children did not have expensive games or toys in the 1920's.

Mother and Dad remained active with their campus friends. The University was a part of our lives. I planned to attend it one day.

In 1930 I was twelve years old and had completed one semester of 7th grade at Hamilton Jr. High when Dad was offered a position as a salesman with a very fine wholesale lumber company, the W. D. Davis Lumber Co. in Portland, Oregon. This was really a bonanza for our family because they supplied him with a Buick automobile, a much nicer car than the Ford we had, and a salary of $250.00 per month. That was a lot of money to us. Mother could quit working.

We moved to Portland, Oregon and everything seemed to be going along fine except for the gathering economic clouds worldwide. Soon, businesses started failing. Of course, the stock-market crash of 1929 had occurred prior to this, and that really started the economic downturn.

MEMORIES OF ANOTHER TIME

As the Depression deepened the W. D. Davis Company went bankrupt and closed. As did many, many companies then, and in the following years.

Shantytowns sprang up, soup kitchens opened, some people were trying to sell apples on the streets, and many men were riding the rails, going from place to place looking for work. There was a veteran's march on Washington D.C. and there was a Federal three-day closing of all banks, as I recall.

I had started high school in 1932 and I guestimate that W.D. Davis closed in 1933. Rent was $35.00 a month for the three-bedroom house in which we lived. And of course Dad wanted to take care of his family. So he tried various things including selling Electrolux Vacuum cleaners door to door. Electrolux had just been developed and put on the market. The company convinced him Electrolux was the best vacuum on the market and he wouldn't have much trouble selling them. Until the day he died the only vacuum cleaner in his home was an Electrolux. I always hated them. Dad had very little success selling vacuum cleaners, thus had to find another way to try to make a living.

These were pretty difficult times. There was no such thing as an allowance. Cullen got a paper route, and I did a lot of baby-sitting. Over a period of time Cullen managed to save $5.00 with which to buy a used bicycle so he would no longer have to walk the paper route.

With the baby sitting money I could get some school supplies, personal items, and go to a movie occasionally—admission .25 cents. Most of the sitting was done for a neighbor who had an only child. For four to five hours they paid me .50 cents.

Cullen and I were both good students, and both aspired to attend college. Cullen had no athletic inclination even though he was 6"3" tall. He hoped to get to a college or university via his brain, and so did I. Cullen's interests were in his Boy Scout activities, school friends and projects, his bulldog Lindy, and the paper route. Lindy, named for Charles Lindberg, the world famous flyer we heard speak at Volunteer Park in Seattle, was also a lovable family pet.

Somehow there was always food provided, and the rent paid. I remember a Christmas when my father gave mother five dollars. That was to be for her Christmas shopping. With that five dollars she purchased a piece of yardage in order to make a skirt for me. She gave it to me

Christmas morning as the piece of yardage. She purchased a pair of mittens for Cullen, a little pink glass candy dish or jam dish for grandmother and some candles and a little holder for her sister, my aunt.

Mother and I were very close. These were anxious times for her. She didn't go to work again, probably because there were no jobs. I have no recollection of her ever complaining about the difficulties of the situation, or of Dad's need to control. However, I understood that it was often hard and unpleasant for her, as well as worrisome.

Dad had an Irish temper and German stubbornness so could be very difficult to live with at times. All the financial worries exacerbated this. Mother always seemed to remain calm, even though anxious.

My grandparents were living with us at this time. They had had a little Mom and Pop grocery store in Portland had had lost it and the investment in purchasing it. They just couldn't sell enough groceries to support it.

During these years, in the early thirties when my Dad was struggling, he was also helping some of his friends who were out of work. I remember two different gentlemen coming to live with us for a while on a temporary basis while they looked for work. They were college friends of his. There were quite a few people in our three-bedroom home. Doubling up was required. Cullen and I slept in the basement.

In 1935 my father and a friend, with experience in the lumber business, formed a small wholesale lumber company with borrowed money—from whom I do no know. They worked hard trying to make a success of it, and did well enough that we were fed and the rent paid.

In January 1936 I graduated mid-year from high school but stayed on as a postgraduate student.

In the middle of February father and mother were coming home from the little mill town of Glendale in southern Oregon. He had gone there to see about purchasing some lumber. He had received an order for a particular type and he wanted to check to see how good their grades were.

About thirty miles from Roseburg, Oregon a man coming toward them, going south as they were going north. His car slid off the road on his own side. In trying to get back on the icy road on that cold February night h e skidded across the road and hit Dad's car. Mother was thrown out of the car. Her spinal cord was severed. One arm and her jaw were

MEMORIES OF ANOTHER TIME

broken. There may have been other internal injuries as well. My father sustained a broken arm and a broken leg.

Being a cold wintry night on a highway in a rural area, there wasn't much traffic. Help was not available. It was quite a long time before they were rescued. Eventually, they were taken into the little town of Roseburg and admitted to the hospital. It was a very, very small hospital with poor facilities. They were there for three days.

One of our good friends was a fine doctor in Portland. He went to Roseburg, did what he could for them with the facilities available, and arranged to have a wooden frame made for my mother. She was not able to lie in a bed. She was paralyzed from her arms down and could only move her arms and her head. She could talk, but it was very difficult with the broken jaw.

The only way they could transport her back to Portland was in a freight car. My father's leg and arm had been set. He was also able to return at that time. The doctor decided that mother's prognosis was very, very poor. They didn't want to put her through what would be involved in setting her jaw. I don't believe they set her arm either but did put it in a sling. All of this was a terrible shock to the family.

After about a week in the hospital she wanted to come home. The Doctor kept her on the wooden frame that had been constructed in Roseburg. They brought her home on that and put it on her bed. Dad, my grandparents, Cullen and I were there as well as my mother's younger sister Alma, who lived in Southern California. With the help of a nurse, who came frequently, we were doing our best to take care of her.

Mother died the 3rd of March 1936.

Our world was really shaken with the sudden loss of Mother. Grandma and Grandpa continued to live with us. Their presence was most helpful. It gave stability and continuity to our lives

I was attending Grant High school taking typing, shorthand and bookkeeping as a postgraduate. All this time my father hadn't been able to work. I really don't know how he managed to pay the bills.

In June, when classes ended, I started looking for a job. I had a friend who was working in a law firm. She told me she was quitting her job and suggested I apply for the position. This was one of the finest law firms in Portland. They hired me to be their receptionist, typist and to operate the five-line switchboard. The salary for working five days a week and 9 to 12:00 on Saturday was $35.00 per month. The hope was to be able to save some money toward going to college, but, after paying bus fare and personal expenses, there wasn't much left to save. A brown bag for lunch sufficed each day.

Being only seventeen, the job afforded the opportunity for experience in office work and procedures, which was quite valuable. It also helped me to mature and gain confidence.

When Dad's injuries were healed, he rejoined his partner in their small business. This man had been working to keep things going through this period, but there was little success.

Consequently, these were very troubling times for Dad, as he was also grieving the loss of Mother. He kept wondering if there was anyway he could have avoided the accident. Always the authoritarian and stern disciplinarian, he now seemed more so to Cullen and me. This was hard for us.

All that spring and summer of 1936 I was wishing to go to college. My dreams were focused on the University of Washington. I was determined to go there one day. My best friend, Ann, left in September to go to Whitman College. I kept working at the law firm, and the months went by.

In May of 1937 I visited my friend at Whitman College for a weekend. It was a wonderful occasion. Everyone was so friendly and welcoming. The two blind dates Ann had arranged turned out well. An interview with the Dean of Women, Thelma Mills, provided lots of information about the college.

The campus was beautiful. I fell in love with the college and decided, "This is where I want to go. It seems just right for me."

The months kept going by and before long it was September of 1937. Ann had been home all summer and was again preparing to go to Whitman. Dad and his partner were still struggling to succeed with their business.

Things just went from bad to worse financially that summer so there was no way for me to go to college. It was so disappointing.

In September, suddenly my life was changed. Dad was in downtown Portland late in the morning. He heard a voice saying, "Murph, Murph, is that you?" He looked and recognized a man who had been a fraternity

MEMORIES OF ANOTHER TIME   111

brother at the University of Washington as well as a teammate on the football team. They had been fairly good friends. They decided to go to lunch and catch up on the intervening years. In the course of conversation Dad told this man about mother and his son and his daughter who very much wanted to go to college.

This gentleman was in the oil business in Houston, Texas, and was not feeling the Depression. He had no children. He said to my Dad, "Well, Murph, I'm going to help her get started in college." A little later that day my father called me at the office and said, "Pat, quit your job, you are going to college."

Coming out of the clear blue sky that was an unbelievable surprise to me. When I calmed down I told the lawyer, who was head of the law firm, what was happening. He immediately had one of the young lawyers go out and get cookies. Somebody else made coffee and we had a party. They were all so kind and so happy. Everybody knew I wanted to go to college. By then I was nineteen years old.

I went home that afternoon to start preparing to leave. We didn't do any shopping for clothing. I went to Grant High school for my transcripts. They called Whitman and gave them the records. I'm not positive I filled out an application until arriving in Walla Walla.

I had a good high school record. Whitman, as a private liberal arts school found it harder to get students than the public schools. Even if I hadn't been a good student they probably would have accepted me. Of course, they didn't know how poor I was.

On the train to Walla Walla, a nighttime trip, it was hard to sleep. I still could not believe all this had happened. Ann and some of her friends picked me up at the Walla Walla depot. At the college a room in Prentiss Hall was assigned, registration was completed, and I was indeed a college student!

I was able to attend that first year in those Depression years of 1937-1938 with the help of the gentleman from Texas who contributed $50.00 per month. Fortunately, I was able to get some work on campus to supplement that. With my dream of college now realized, the school year proved to be a happy and very successful.

In the spring of 1938, father and his partner ended their partnership. Dad moved to Eugene, Oregon where he hoped to establish a lumber business.

Not having the money to pay the freight, he sold quite a few of our things including my mother's beautiful piano purchased by her father at the 1896 Chicago World's Fair. It was an oversized red mahogany upright piano with a lot of hand carving decorating it. He sold it for $50.00. I had thought of the piano as being mine so his selling it has always been a very disappointing thing in my life.

I wanted to take piano lessons but there never seemed enough money to do so. Mother taught me the little playing I learned. She was not a very good player herself. The one favorite song I did master was "Star Dust" by Hoagie Carmichael. That was an accomplishment for me and the song remains a favorite to this day.

Dad sold a lot of things and then moved into a small rental house in Eugene. He started all over again trying to get a wholesale lumber business going.

Cullen was a senior in high school that spring of 1938. Moving to Eugene meant that he could not finish at Grant High School. He entered Eugene High School and graduated from there in June at age sixteen. That September he entered the University of Oregon a month prior to his seventeenth birthday and soon joined the R.O.T.C. program.

I came home to Eugene in the summer of 1938. I tried, unsuccessfully, to find a job Eugene is in an agricultural area. I heard that the people who grew green beans were hiring pickers. I was taken on as a picker and picked beans that summer. We were paid one cent for every pound of beans that we picked. We started at seven o' clock in the morning and usually finished between four and five o clock in the afternoon. The most I ever picked in one day was ninety pounds for which I received ninety cents. Most days I averaged around .70 to .75 cents. I did that as long as the beans were producing.

One good thing about it, we got beautiful tans. I worked with some of the migrant workers and have tried to imagine my children doing that type of work.

The migrant workers were very friendly, but we could not communicate, as they did not speak English. We smiled and they smiled. Being experienced they picked more quickly. I surely learned how difficult it is to be an agriculture worker. I also picked the summer of 1939.

The summer went by and I don't believe I saved anything. Dad's fledgling business was not doing very well so there was no money to go

MEMORIES OF ANOTHER TIME

back to college. That made me very, very unhappy but I was determined I would get back there some day. Dad wanted me to stay in Eugene and attend the University of Oregon, but stubbornly, I wanted to return to Walla Walla and Whitman.

My paternal grandmother was living with us now. Grandpa had passed away during the winter. My maternal grandmother had gone to California to live with her daughter, my Aunt Alma.

That fall a good friend of my father's who had three children and lived out of Eugene in a quite rural area, needed some help. His wife was having some surgery. Their little girl was eight and their boy was ten. There was also a grandfather living in the home. Father volunteered my help to work for them while she was recovering from her surgery.

I went to live with and work for them. It was not a modern home. There were six of us. The washing machine was kept out on the back porch. With a little help I brought it into the kitchen to connect it to the kitchen faucet in order to wash.

I did everything for the family. The house was heated with a wood-coal stove. I started the fire at about 4:30 to 5:00 o´ clock in the morning and did all of the cooking, cleaning, laundry, etc. For this they paid my room and board and me $5.00 per week. I did have a home with my father so wasn't in need of the room and board. It was not a pleasant or happy experience.

Shortly before Christmas I went home. I was longing and longing to go back to Whitman. My grandmother was very supportive and encouraging. She wrote and asked her bachelor brother in Canada if he could possibly loan or give me $200.00. He very kindly sent me $200.00 as a gift. Once again, in January, I got on the train and went back to Walla Walla, Washington to start my sophomore year.

Dad became angry with me because I went back to Whitman after we got the money from my great uncle. He remained angry with me for years. When he got angry with someone he was angry forever.

The first day in Walla Walla a good friend of mine with whom I had gone to high school, was delivering the campus mail. While doing that he looked me up in the dorm. With him he had a gentleman named Bruce 'Sandy' Burns. Within a week Sandy asked me out. He became a great part of my life, so much so that in July 2003 we celebrated our 61st wedding anniversary.

This time, having been at Whitman a year and returning the spring of the next year, I had established that I was a good student and college material. I had become very well acquainted with the dean of women. She helped me get some scholarships and saw to it that I was able to have work in the dormitory. I also borrowed money from a Kappa Alum, which helped greatly. During my junior year I was awarded a Kappa Kappa Gamma undergraduate scholarship of $250.00, which enable me to complete that year.

For the rest of my college days I had jobs on the campus cleaning the infirmary, cleaning the huge living room we called Great Hall, and all of the little side rooms. I dried dishes in the kitchen, was secretary to the Physics Professor, and ended up the last year as secretary to the Director of Admissions and Registrar, Douglas McClane. I worked for him from 9:00 to 5:00 every day of the week and 9:00 to 12:00 Saturdays. For that I was paid $75.00 per month.

I took all 8:00 o'clock classes. As an English major I had to write a thesis. English majors had to take two four hour written examinations and a one-hour oral examination with all the professors in the department. I managed to graduate Cum Laude in June of 1942. Although Dad was unhappy that I went back to Whitman and did it on my own to finish and graduate, when I was elected to Phi Beta Kappa it was in the newspapers and he showed it to all of his friends.

That is how I got through college during the Depression years.

Sandy and I were married a month later in July of 1942. Dad was still angry with me and wouldn't even come to our wedding to give me away. We reconciled after our two boys were born and were good friends the rest of his life. My brother, now 1st Lieutenant Cullen Murphy, escorted me down the aisle, and gave me away. He was very handsome in full dress uniform.

WW II had started December 7th 1941 at Pearl Harbor. The country had been helping the allied countries of Britain and France and supplying them so the economy was picking up. Sandy graduated from Whitman College in 1941. He was a graduate of the Civilian Pilot training program at Whitman but he was unable to get in the Army Air Corps or the Navy Air Service due to heart problems.

In the fall of 1941 at age 20, Cullen was called up from the R.O.T.C. as a second Lieutenant in the infantry. In the European Theater he

MEMORIES OF ANOTHER TIME

fought in the Battle of the Bulge and all across France. He was a company commander and received promotions quickly, which is unusual in the infantry.

The rapidity of his promotions reflected both his leadership skills and the frequent battle action that decimated the troops and senior officers in his group. As a Captain he was awarded two Bronze medals and the Silver Star for gallantry in action.

By war's end he was a major, one of the youngest in the infantry. He remained in Wiesbaden, Germany at the US Headquarters for some time after the war. Upon returning home, he entered the U of California from which he graduated. We remained close, good friends until his death in June 2001.

In 1941 Air bases were in dire need of Controllers. With the background of his flying experience and his college education, in December 1941 Sandy was accepted into the Airport Traffic Control program. He was sent to Boeing in Seattle for a crash-training course and then sent in February 1942 to the airbase in Pendleton, Oregon for his first job as a Controller.

The pay for a Traffic Controller was about $260.00 per month. Relatively speaking, that was not nearly as big as the $250.00 per month my Dad had made in 1930, 31 & 32.

While in Pendleton I worked for the Sergeant Major as his secretary at the airbase headquarters. He had been in the service for 25 years. Not surprisingly, he was quite contemptuous of all the very young pilots, who were officers, and especially of the older officers who were reservists and were quite ignorant of the "real army" [quoting the Sergeant]. In spite of being an alcoholic, the Sergeant really ran the Base. For my part and among other things, I learned a great many words never known to me before!

We lived for a year in Pendleton. After a year Sandy was transferred to Gowan Field in Boise, Idaho. Boise had been his hometown. At Gowan they were training B-17 and B-24 bomber crews. He stayed there for the duration of the war.

I worked as a secretary for a company called Boise-Winnemucca Stage's. We had a son born in 1944. Seventeen months later our second son was born. I never worked again. No matter how poor one was, in those days mother's stayed home and took care of the children.

Though I did not pursue a business or professional career, the Whitman College experience has nevertheless had a determining and most beneficial effect on my life for over sixty years, i.e., from the day of matriculation until the present.

The Liberal Arts education offered was informative, stimulating and inspiring. The many friendships formed with both students and faculty has been an enduring gift. My husband, Bruce (Sandy) Burns and I met there. We have returned frequently for reunions and Alumni Colleges. Intellectually, socially and personally my life has been shaped and enriched by those years at the college.

CHAPTER 12
*W*ESTWARD MIGRATION

By
Alexander J. Sharp

I WAS BORN; home delivered, on May 17, 1921, the first and only child of my parents union. This history making birth took place in a small, ramshackle, old even then, house located on a quarter section of land [160 acres] twenty two miles north of Frankfort, Kansas, on which my father scratched out a living farming grain, feeding out livestock, and taking an occasional small gamble in grain futures.

Even in the early twenties with boom times afoot, the area was economically depressed. Much of the land had been homesteaded just after the Civil War. After the Dust Bowl of the '30's agronomists belatedly told the world that this was "land that should never have felt the bite of the plow". The topsoil was thin, and crops were poor. For Farm families, there was no electricity, and no inside plumbing. Outside the small towns, roads were plain dirt - - innocent of even a touch of gravel. In wintertime, you got where you were going by keeping your Model "T" equipped with chains.

My father scratched out a living on this quarter section, and we moved to, and farmed at, two other "places" before moving to Big Town — Frankfort. My Dad, who was a competent person, was able to brighten this rather bleak economic picture by operating a corn sheller in the winter and a thrashing machine in the fall. During the season, he went from farm to farm, shelling corn for a percentage. These people farmed wheat, oats and corn, with emphasis on corn. This was "horse farming"; very few farmers owned tractors, although we had an old,

117

rattletrap, Fordson that furnished the "power-takeoff" powering the corn sheller and/or a thrashing machine. I recall watching Dad lie on his back beneath our old Fordson tractor, and lighting a fire under the Magneto to start the motor on that thing.

Corn shucking took place in late fall, in freezing temperatures, and I recall Dad's hands cracking across the fingers and palm, with blood oozing therefrom. I find this sort of memory horrifying even in retrospect, but it seemed to be accepted by everyone as simply part of a lifestyle. I don't remember hearing anyone complain.

Everyone milked a few cows. A cream separator, centrifugal and hand-cranked, separated the cream from what is now known as "No fat" milk, which went to the hogs. A creamery truck came by twice a week to take the cream to market, from which a small check — hard money — found its way out to our RFD mailbox. In 1928, I believe, my father guessed, correctly, that corn was not going to bring a very good price, and so he, with a number of other farmers in the area, decided to "feed it out".

This was done by acquiring a number of shoats, little pigs, then feeding the corn into the shoats for a period of time. If you got the shoats to market, properly prepared by feeding slightly saline water, which led them to drink lots and lots of water, the entrepreneur occasionally made some money. Please note that, in terms of money, I speak comparatively.

This little vignette has an unhappy ending. The dread Hog Cholera intervened. I remember wondering why my mother was crying while she watched my father and my uncle, using a blade hooked to the front of the aforesaid Fordson tractor, push a hundred seventy-nine shoats into two old well shafts.

Frankfort served an area, which was, and is, very rural. The natives of the area were predominantly Scottish in origin, with a liberal (only in a quantitative sense) sprinkling of Swede, Germans, and Danes. Protestants of some kind were in the overwhelming majority. The morals, ethics and lifestyle of these people remain what might be expected of a region located squarely in the middle of the "Bible belt". It was, and is, a veritable hotbed of Protestant Fundamentalist ethos. Kansas remained a "Dry" state for more than two decades after the repeal of Prohibition,

MEMORIES OF ANOTHER TIME

and then only grudgingly, and unwillingly, extended to the general population some sort of slop, which was 3.2 in alcohol content.

The farm people "visited around" on Sundays, weather permitting. In 1928, at age seven, I sat on various living room floors, or lurked around the corner in the kitchen with the other kids, listening to some of my elders hold forth concerning the threat to our way of life posed by Al Smith, the "radical" Catholic Democrat who was running against Herbert Hoover for President. The kids heard all about the direct telephone line that would link Smith to the Vatican from whence he would receive detailed instructions from His Holiness, the Pope.

There were also the stories, told as Gospel -- no play on words is particularly intended here -- concerning tunnels which had been burrowed between the living quarters of priests and nuns in various Catholic enclaves in Topeka and Kansas City.

More tales were told of the babies spawned among and between these befrocked and begowned fiends from Hell, which were buried beneath the floors and into the sides of these tunnels.

My mother was "raised" Catholic but was quite ecumenical in her thinking. She listened to this stuff, said nothing, or very little, except that she occasionally emitted a small giggle. My Dad knew better, too, but then, he had the advantage of being something of a cosmopolitan person, having traveled as far away as the Gulf Coast, and even upstate New York. It was even bruited about that my parents had, in an earlier election, voted for a Democrat, Woodrow Wilson. So far as I know, this base canard was never proven.

I might have had my feet set firmly on this straight, narrow and religious path had it not been for the fact that my parents, who shared only ten years of education between them, were pretty bright people. My father was blessed with an inquiring mind, which he undertook to impart to me. As a matter of fact, I learned to read sitting on Dad's lap, while he read the Kansas City Star and the Midwest Farmer to me. At age five, before entering school, I could handle the reading text from the first through the fourth grade.

My father was born in Marshall County, Kansas, a few miles from where I was born, in February of 1884. He was of Scottish/Presbyterian ancestry, which ancestry, in a collective sense, lost at Culloden in 1758.

My father and his brother, Reno Sharp, named after Major Reno, who was one of those who got away from the Cheyenne and the Sioux at or near Custer's Last Stand, both secured -- endured? -- seven years or so of the schooling provided nearby. Both boys were "farmed out" to other farmers in the area at age twelve. There were four girls. Two of them were also "farmed out" in the foregoing fashion.

There would undoubtedly have been regular and frequent additions to the six kids already in existence, except for the fact that my grandfather was caught in a cold spring rain in '92. The situation involved driving home a spanking new team, and he was not about to hurry that team. His death, of course, created a serious problem for the widow and the kids. The concept of or even a phrase for, anything like "Social Programs" was nonexistent. The neighbors did what they could to help, but it wasn't much, except for the "farming out" situation set forth above.

It should be noted that the story as to how and why my parents ended up on the Kansas prairie farming on of those 160-acre "knobs," as they were called, is a tale too complex and involved to recount here. Suffice to say my father had been a kind of peripatetic union organizer, among both coal miners and copper miners during the industrial wars shortly after the turn of the century, and was twice seriously injured in the strikes of the day.

My mother was born in 1887 on another quarter section of land located near La Grange, Texas. As with the birth of my father and all his siblings, a midwife officiated. La Grange is a small town of less than 5,000 souls, and is the Fayette County seat. The courthouse was built in 1860, just before the Civil War wiped out any possibility of any public building in the Southern states for a couple of generations. The Fayette County fathers have undertaken to maintain this building as a functioning courthouse, a historical site, and have succeeded in putting together a bit of old Americana. It is a truly marvelous place to visit.

My mother's parents were Czechs who immigrated to the United States through Galveston, Texas, rather than Ellis Island. When they hit Galveston and by the time the I.N.S. office finished with them, their name was Samohyl. From there they went to their quarter section of land as sharecroppers, and began to raise cotton and kids. They took advantage of the Homestead Act a few years later.

MEMORIES OF ANOTHER TIME

Only eight children — six girls, and two boys, blessed their union. This was pretty low production for people of their religious and cultural background, with thirteen to sixteen offspring being quite common. Confronted by the same distaff-side numerical disadvantage as my widowed grandmother in Kansas — too many girls and not enough boys — my Texas grandfather met the problem in much the same way; i.e., he "farmed out" both boys, and three of the girls. Thus, at age 14, having absorbed a total of slightly more than three years of that "book larnin" offered by the small parochial school in La Grange, my mother was "hired out" to the County Sheriff and his wife. Mom cooked, did general housework, and took food to the prisoners in the county jail, which was adjacent to the Sheriff's residence. She was well treated. The Sheriff was the legendary Will , made somewhat famous in song and story by Burt Reynolds, Alexis Smith, and others in the play and movie entitled "The Greatest Little Whorehouse in the World."

After several years, my mother graduated to a boarding house situation in Beaumont, Texas, where my father boarded. He worked as an oil field roustabout for the Texas Company [now Texaco], and played a few games at shortstop and outfielder for Beaumont in the old Texas league.

They married in 1910 and lived in and around the Beaumont-Port Arthur-Galveston area for several years. They were in Galveston for the "Big Flood."

Memories, some quite clear, and some rather fuzzy, which indicate the "culture, demographics, politics, and the impact of 'religion' on our way of life in general, and on A.J. in particular, will be recounted below:

At age six, I matriculated at a tiny prairie school where there were seventeen other kids, ranging from first to the eighth grade, the little Timber and Brooks Schools. I personally comprised the entire second grade.

The teachers came out and "boarded around" with the various members of the School Board, usually three in number. The teachers were required to be High School Graduates, and furthermore, were required to attend "Normal School"; a six-week course offered such girls in places like Hastings or Wichita. This led to a situation in which every school district could claim at least one High School Graduate. These schools were one-room jobs -- if you've seen the Little Red schoolhouse at Knotts Berry farm, you've seen them.

When I was seven years old, my Dad leased the pool hall in Frankfort, and we moved to town. I "skipped" the third grade. It was the school principal's decision, and probably a bad one, a decision that I still regret. Thenceforth, I was a year younger than most of my classmates through both elementary and high school.

Frankfort, Kansas, with its population of slightly over 1,200 souls, offered a considerable contrast to what I had experienced as a little kid on the prairie. I was amazed to find that there were so many other little kids in the world, and to learn that I liked them and that they seemed to like me. And I discovered two business locations, which were to have considerable impact on my life: one was Litel's Drugstore, and the magazine rack contained therein, and the other was Dad's pool hall.

Simultaneously I found the tiny, seldom used public telephone booth beside that magazine rack. I straight-a-way became that "quiet little Sharp kid" who spent many of his waking hours huddled in that telephone booth, reading periodicals, such as "Wild West", Western Stories", and the various pulp magazines which had spun off World War I — "Wings", "Battle Stories", and "Combat".

Litel's Drugstore, and that telephone booth, furnished an escape into a fantasy world that looked infinitely better than did reality in and around Frankfort, Kansas. I have compared that magazine rack to Alice's looking glass. Starting in the phone booth, I became a voracious, insatiable reader of anything and everything I could lay my hands on. And while this material and a lot of that which followed it, might be a bit trashy by classic standards, I did acquire considerable familiarity with written words.

But it was Dad's pool hall, and its impact on its patrons, and the surrounding area, which left a vivid and lasting impression on me. It was of course, a totally masculine establishment staffed and patronized by men only. There was no television and very little radio during the day. In the evening, the radio came through in reasonably good shape. I don't believe there was a golf course nearer than Topeka, the State Capitol. Even the "professional people", like the local doctors, two lawyers and the dentist frequented the pool hall on a regular basis.

MEMORIES OF ANOTHER TIME

Roads were poor. Cars were rather primitive. Fifty miles was a long way. Frankfort had a very good baseball team, which beat everyone around. Its radius was perhaps a hundred miles. This baseball team headquartered at the pool hall. Where else? This bunch of small town jocks was touted, I think accurately, as the best "Townie" team in the state. Those games, played at Frankfort, and occasionally at Marysville, the County Seat, drew amazing crowds at 25 cents admission.

This team could even beat the traveling teams from places like Topeka, and Wichita. However, they could not handle the Kansas City Monarchs, who came through to Marysville, the County Seat, once a year and whipped our town team, and the half dozen ringers whom it pulled in from such places as Waterville and Blue Rapids. I saw Satchel Paige and Josh Gibson play. Dad, by this time in his mid-40's, could still play a little short stop and pinch hit. I saw him scratch a weak ground ball to second base off Satchel Paige. His young son sat, and watched, and glowed.

Some quiet bootlegging went on, an activity in which I'm afraid my sire participated. Some pretty fast poker was played in "the room up above" the pool hall. This room was adjacent to the dance hall, which furnished the Saturday night activity for a good part of the surrounding community. I was allowed to watch these poker games, sitting in an elevated spot a few feet behind and above the table. This situation was allowed to continue on condition that I kept my mouth shut. I complied with any and all conditions, and watched those sharks play poker by the hour. And I plugged into some amazing conversations (to be evaluated much later), which reflected the seamier side of life as it was lived thereabouts, and perhaps everywhere else.

I remember very well the incident, which earned my first major eyeball-to-eyeball, man-to-man compliment from my father. I noticed one of the participants of the poker game placing one of the cards — just one — under his foot. The knowledge of the location of one card — just one card — gives the knowledgeable one quite an advantage over a few hours of poker. This is particularly true when the Joker is counted in "Aces", "Straights", and "Flushes".

I told my father, and no one else. He didn't tell anyone else. Years later, he told me that he had used the situation to his advantage when he sat in the game.

The St. Louis Cardinals were taken quite seriously, and the World Series was taken very seriously indeed. Because of the lack of TV and daytime radio, no night games, the pool hall came into play. The off-duty telegrapher for the Atchison, Topeka, and Santa Fe rigged a wire from the train depot to the pool hall. This telegrapher assumed the duties of a radio announcer. He would report to another man, who operated a large blackboard, with a baseball diamond laid out upon it, and the infield and outfield positions. Upon reports of offensive activity — single, double, or triple — a small round marker was moved to the appropriate base, or bases. A home run was celebrated by a blinking red light, and the blackboard operator also worked a scoreboard. In terms of entertainment, the thing worked amazingly well. The "fans" from town and the surrounding countryside really got in the game.

The move to town had been predicated on a lucky break: Dad had scored on a gamble in wheat futures, and had invested in King Gillette stock, which had rocketed upward with the rest of the Wall Street market. In October of '29, the boom went bust; the Gillette stock was close to worthless. Trade at the pool hall (and everywhere else) fell off. The Depression came down upon us, the revenuers got both numerous and watchful, which all added up to trouble in Paradise. We moved on.

My parents and I left Frankfort, Kansas during the late fall of 1930. The stock market crash of October 29, 1929, had occurred just a year earlier. Moving on involved Route 66 in Oklahoma City, and was to end in San Bernardino, like Johnny Mercer's song. Enroute we stayed on it to Amarillo, and then detoured to South Texas to visit my mother's people, and for my father and mother to locate old friends in and around Port Arthur and Beaumont.

My memories of the trip West, which are amazingly clear, entail watching, both the flatcars and the boxcars carrying many "Depression casualties" — unemployed men moving aimlessly from place to place. We waved at all of these men we saw. They invariably waved back.

There were no motels. The concepts of "autels" and "motels" were to come some years down the line. It cost one dollar per night to stay at these places. The one-dollar was negotiable. Often, "accommodations" were limited to a bedstead, a straw tick and an outhouse.

In Gallup, New Mexico, where we picked up route 66 again — Dad commented on the fact that gasoline had dropped from eleven cents a

MEMORIES OF ANOTHER TIME

gallon to nine cents. This was also negotiable — you could barter food, or any of your other possessions for gas, oil or parts.

The "Dust Bowl" had yet to happen. We were just ahead of the first wave of Okies and Arkies going west to California. The "picket line" of Riverside County Deputy Sheriffs, of whom Steinbeck wrote in The Grapes of Wrath, had not yet set up shop. However, the Border Patrol was very much in evidence at the California - Arizona line. My parents endured a rather searching hour's worth of interrogation just over the California border. I didn't hear it, but they got back into the car very angry, indeed, and talked about that particular encounter for years afterward.

We landed in San Bernardino in the spring of '31. "EmmyGrants" were not particularly welcome. The residents, some of whom might be second or third generation Anglos, vocalized their opinion of us on the street, and some wrote "letters to the Editor" voicing their concern about the fact that "cheap labor" was coming into the state in vast quantities, and they were obviously concerned that the new arrivals represented a real threat to their settled way of life.

I do recall that because we lived next door to the man who had the sewer contract for the city, Dad got 16 days worth of down - in - the - ditch day labor during our 16 months there. I came home one day to find Dad sitting at the kitchen table, white as a sheet, with a vein having popped out on his temple, which remained there until his death. It was a simple case of heat stroke. My father, who should have known better, listened to his Anglo compatriots and refrained from drinking water in quantity. Several Anglos got knocked off the job that way.

San Bernardino was the County Seat, and there were a number of city and county employees, along with people like schoolteachers, who remained employed all through the bad years. They were paid off in scrip. It worked this way: One week, they would get three day's pay in script, [good with the local merchants] and two days in cash. The next week, it went the other way — two days paid in scrip and three days in cash.

There were seven primary schools in San Bernardino, and each year the schools held a Spelling Bee for the fifth and sixth grades. I won this thing in the fifth grade, and received a "Gold" medal for my efforts. That was the zenith of my career — It's been all downhill since.

126   A STORY TO TELL

The overall atmosphere in Southern California was not a pleasant one. We packed up and went north to a rural area near Salem, Oregon.

Oregon represented a move back to a rural area. My father's sister lived in a small Parsonage next to a United Brethren Church about eight miles out of Salem, Oregon. The plan, which was followed reasonably closely for the next few years, was to follow the itinerant fruit harvest trail, which consisted of strawberries, loganberries, orchard crops, and hops. We followed this trail for a couple of years, and then my parents began sharecropping. This went reasonably well. Dad was an excellent farmer, and my mother helped, as she had on the farms in Kansas. Today, we would probably be categorized as 'working poor". In the late '30's', we sold the Gillette stock -- it had increased a bit in value -- and made a down payment on a small farm.

This time, farming went well. My parents were good at it and, gambling a bit on borrowed money, committed to relatively high plantings of both strawberries and Boysenberries. Meanwhile, their son and heir was at last beginning to help out.

While attending school, I worked the farm -- part-time in the spring, all the time in summer, and again part-time in the fall.

The "grade school" was staged in a rural setting. There were two rooms, with four grades; the other teacher, usually the 'Principal', taught grades five through eight. We did all right. When we went on to high school, a rather high percentage did so; we were ready for what they had to offer in town. I graduated from Salem High with the Class of '38 after a totally undistinguished career as a scholar, athlete, student leader, or anything else worthy of note.

We farm kids rode the bus into school and back. This service cost thirty-five dollars per kid. We had the farm chores to do before we left, and those chores were waiting for us after we came home, which left little time for anything else. I was a good swimmer, and in my sophomore year, I was able to swim the dashes faster than a couple of kids who went on to be three-year lettermen. And as a Lightweight, believe it or not, I could whip the kid who later became State Champ as a Welterweight. The "city kids" were able to "go out" for athletics, while the country kids stood still.

MEMORIES OF ANOTHER TIME

In '39, '40, and '41, employment off the farm began to loosen up. I could do the farm work in the spring and summer, and caught on with a labeling crew in a cannery warehouse, California Packing Company, Del Monte to you, during the winter. In 1940, three Kaiser shipyards opened up in Portland, and I bluffed my way into an I.B.M. tab installation at St. Johns as a Tab Operator.

When the Japanese struck Pearl Harbor, we had 28 acres in small fruit -- strawberries and Boysenberries -- a respectable small fruit operation at that time. However, there was a sizable fly in the ointment. By the late thirties, Dad had been hit with severe rheumatoid arthritis.

With the war under way, prices were ready to take off, and did. We were ready to cash in. But a bad thing happened. As a consensus among neighboring farm families put it, "That goddamn goofy Sharp kid, who always has his nose in a book, has finally gone completely out of his mind."

They were right. That goddamn goofy kid had indeed become imbued with the strange notion that Roosevelt, Churchill, and Stalin could never win this thing unless, and until, the last of the Sharps stood straight and tall beside and among them.

I talked with my parents about my decision to enlist in the Navy. They agreed that they could handle the farm with the help of a couple of prospective "deferrees". I could have been deferred with no strain whatsoever.

I should have known my folks couldn't maintain the farm operation. They sold out and the people who bought the farm cleaned up during the war years. That decision -- to leave my folks in the lurch -- is the major regret of my life. I ended up enlisting V-6 in the United States Naval Reserve. At this point, I need to follow the lead of an infinitely better-known lawyer, and "make one thing perfectly clear". The decision to enlist was not based on super patriotism, or lust for combat, or anything of that nature. I simply knew the farm was not for me, and I was utterly bored with being a Tab Operator. I had to enlist.

A buddy and I enlisted in Portland and, soon after, found ourselves taking boot camp at Camp Decatur in San Diego.

CHAPTER 13
RELIEF CHECKS KEPT OUR FAMILY GOING

By
Harold E. "Sam" Haight

I WAS BORN on December 1, 1923 in Edmonton, Alberta, Canada, third of six children. An older brother died in infancy, leaving me as the oldest son of a Canadian schoolteacher {and ex-flyer in the Canadian Royal Air Force-WW I} and a Canadian pianist/organist.

By age two, I found myself, with family, in St. Petersburg, Florida, immigrants to the United States. My father became assistant manager of the municipal pier and yacht basin; my mother became a well-known local church musician. The "Haight Family Orchestra"—six of us—was born and during the winters, we entertained tourists from up north. This paid for our music lessons.

I played first violin in this marvelous collection of musicians. My father, never into music, learned bass fiddle. We were great, simply great! And we did hilarious skits too!

When not fiddling, I sold the St. Petersburg Times and Evening Independent, the Saturday Evening Post, Ladies Home Journal, Colliers, Liberty and Country Gentlemen to the tourists at my Dad's pier out on Tampa Bay.

Afternoons at the pier, the tourists and I followed the Yankees and the Boston Red Socks; evenings, we listened to Amos and Andy. These miraculous broadcasts to pier goers came courtesy of an outdoors loud-speaker system connected to the NBC radio network.

129

In 1927 I have the vaguest memory of the news that "Lindberg Flies Across the Atlantic". I think I remember the newspaper headlines in St. Petersburg, the sense of wonder in the adults around me and the hero worship in which I participated. What a miracle, that a person in an airplane could fly from the U.S. to Paris, France.

I started pre-school where my mother was teaching at the Cilley Foundation School, then went to Roser Park Grammar School and South Junior High. What I do remember about those days has to do with wondrous feats on swings, parallel bars, teeter totters, etc, playing soccer, cutting a small part of my thumb off on a jig saw and breaking up my face and two teeth on a runaway tricycle down a steep hill.

My particular memory does not go back in any meaningful way to the Great Market Crash in 1929. All that I do recall is the general sense of panic and anguish in our town when banks failed all over America in the early 30's. My father and mother must have been Democrats as I saw Franklin Delano Roosevelt as a special hero and doubt that would have been the case unless they had also cherished him.

I remember the tragedy of the kidnapping so vividly, as I ran through the streets of St. Petersburg after dark one evening, selling the Evening Independent, screaming, "Extra, Extra; Read all about it; Lindberg baby kidnapped." I sold a lot of papers, and I followed the trial of Haupmann for weeks, fully accepting the popular certainty that he was guilty and deserved to be executed. But there was always some doubt...

I spent the better part of my days at Virgil Junior High School, where my main claim to fame was playing first violin in the school orchestra.

A special memory came on May 6, 1937 with the crash of the Dirigible Hindenberg during its landing at Lakehurst, New Jersey. It had just crossed the Atlantic from Germany. Loaded with scores of wealthy passengers, the event was being covered by newspaper photographers, a nation wide radio hookup and by a newsreel company planning to show the arrival of this great airship in the nation's movie houses.

The images in newsreels and newsprint of the dirigible on fire, falling helplessly, disintegrating, killing all onboard, caused me great wonderment and horror. But there was also a trace of developing hostility towards German leaders in my reactions. I knew they were becoming a threat in Europe and had heard that the dirigibles they were building

MEMORIES OF ANOTHER TIME   131

were part of their military build-up. As a paperboy I made money on this event.

Our family was not seriously affected by the depression until 1937-38. By that time, we were living in Los Angeles. In the earlier depression years, Dad had been regularly employed. We always had sufficient, if modest, income from his salary, mother's piano lessons and our family orchestra.

In 1936, politics removed my father from his job at the pier. The family moved to Asheville, North Carolina where my Dad got into the health and the chiropractic field.

We lived about six months in Asheville, North Carolina, where Dad's new business, Gravatonic Life Ray kept us comfortable enough to buy a new Chevrolet.

By December of that year, after only six months in North Carolina [Lord, what a beautiful place it was], we moved to Los Angeles in time for Christmas and temporary poverty. Shortly after moving us to Los Angeles to take over the health franchise there, Dad abandoned it, having finally decided that it was fraudulent.

We were shocked to find ourselves on "relief" within a matter of weeks. As I recall, "Relief" in Los Angeles consisted of a check and perhaps also some excess agricultural products. But Dad and Mom never discussed anything about that with us; at least, I don't remember them doing so

*   *   *

Dad was assigned as a crossing guard at a nearby school. For two years, most of my Dad's time was spent in Chiropractic College instead of on some job. During that period, he studied nights and became a chiropractor.

I sold newspapers in front of the Brown Derby on Wilshire Blvd., across the street from the famous, old Ambassador Hotel, and also at a nearby Vons Market on 7th Street, and contributed to family income.

I remember quite well a day in 1938 when there was no food in the house for the seven of us. I had a dime in my pocket and went to the market on the corner of Vermont and 6th streets. The manager sold me a large bunch of spoiling bananas for ten cents. That was our supper.

We went off relief in less than a year upon moving from Los Angeles to Montrose. Dad had graduated from Chiropractic College and had become an assistant to a Dr. Cutler, a chiropractor with an established practice in Montrose.

I was finishing highschool at Glendale High, delivering the Southern California Bowling News throughout the greater L.A. area and reveling in the ownership of my first car, a Model B Ford coupe.

My "teens" were spent happily in the Montrose-LaCresenta-LaCanada crescent, north of Los Angeles, mostly within a LaCanada teenage church group, dating girls, participating in drag races and making numerous gourmet stops at the very first Bob's Big Boy drive-ins. All these things, I think, made my life unusually wonderful.

From there on our economic situation gradually improved. But my parents were still too poor in the 1940's to send me—or any of my sisters or brother—to college.

A half scholarship and my own work on the campus saw me through the University of Redlands. And I remember occasional money gifts ($25, $50, etc) from my mother while I was there (she earned some money—a pittance—giving piano lesson to children in Montrose).

I volunteered for navy service in June of 1942 and was returned to Redlands as a V-12 officer candidate in June 1943. After three months of trig, calculus, bus-ad, close order drill, obstacle courses and romance, I found myself assigned to Mare Island Navy Yard. There I learned the basics of the navy supply system, while making great weekend liberty in San Francisco.

CHAPTER 14
MY FATHER WORKED

By
Theodore 'Ted' Lumpkin

MY FATHER worked as a custodian for Goose Shoe store. He was employed constantly throughout the Depression. He was in good shape from that standpoint. Even so, we had a hard time making ends meet. Even to this day I eat everything and enjoy cleaning my plate. I make sure that what I have is what I can eat. If I don't think I can eat it then I don't want it ahead of time. That's just built in.

We had chickens and rabbits and a dog. Every Sat. my father would go out and wring a chicken's neck. We would have a big old pot of steamy, boiling water to put on, then pluck the feathers out. I never did care for that. I never did care for chicken. I'm just beginning to like chicken now. It wasn't so much I didn't like it; I just didn't care for it.

Clothes would be hand-me-downs. Had to use them in whatever way we could.

We had a house that had a lot of rooms in it. Seemed like it was a real large house at that time but you go over and look at it now and it isn't very large. It only had one bathroom. We took baths every Sat.

We had coal and wood stoves to keep warm with. You could keep warm if you were close to the stove. In my opinion it still got cold here in Los Angeles. And I'm still of that opinion after having gone to other places.

My uncle and my father both worked at Goose Shoe store. My uncle came home one day, one evening from the store complaining of stomachache. Without any warning he died. I remember how devastated my aunt was. They had three sons. She had to work in service. Mother did not work. So the boys were always over to our house.

I have three brothers and two sisters. I'm first. My other brothers and sister were born the same way except there was a six year interval between them and the first three of us. I was always a half a generation ahead. When I was in the service they were going to school so their experiences were a little bit different. We had a good family.

Mother really raised my cousins. She believed in spanking and stuff like that. Occasionally we would get so bad we had to wait for Daddy to come home. That was one of the toughest deals in the world. That belt or that switch, oh boy.

Many times the cousins were on welfare. Occasionally they would get some beans, some money I guess and a lot of in-kind things, dried beans, dried lima beans because we had a lot of lima beans, dried apples, dried fruit, mother did a lot of canning too.

Father used to get up early, get to work about 5:30 and take me to the Red car stop three doors from our house and get the car up to his place. I worked there from the time I was about ten years old all through junior high school, high school and college.

I cut a lot of lawns. I remember Mrs. Randall now; she was a good friend of my mother. She had a big rough yard to cut. She did pay well. I used to run a lot of errands for the lady across the street. A real stout lady. She always wanted aspirin. Whenever I was completely out of money I would go over there and ask if I could get some aspirin for her. She would say yes and I would get a nickel or dime or so.

I remember when I got that NYA [National Youth Administration] job at Jefferson high school. Boy, that was big, big thing. The job as I remember it was sweeping the sidewalk around the school. I used to take pride in having the sidewalk clean.

Then I sold the Post Record, a newspaper at that time. We used to deliver it and you could win trips getting subscriptions. I got a lot of that and I got a bicycle.

My father worked long hours so he wasn't around home much. He would come home at dinnertime.

We always had dinner together. That was a very rich time as far as I'm concerned. In fact throughout my life now I try to be present for dinner. I think that dinnertime is very, very important.

MEMORIES OF ANOTHER TIME

We had closeness during the Depression that caused we to appreciate what we got and what we had. We realized what a penny meant, what it was worth. I found not having things during the depression was difficult but in terms of our family being together it was good. I thought it was a time this country really did not appreciate what we did have and emphasized the wrong parts rather than the important parts.

CHAPTER 15
GROWING UP POOR

By
Robert H. Wells

I WAS EIGHT years old in 1929, the beginning of the "Great Depression" and seventeen in 1939 with the Depression finally beginning to ease up. Even so, it wasn't until 1941 with the beginning buildup to WW II that work became plentiful and wages slowly rose.

For me, those critical preadolescent through adolescent ten years of my development, living in the shadow of our grinding poverty that seemed to foreshadow a hopeless future, left the soul searing scars and a psychic imprint felt to this day. There is no question in my mind that those critical shaping years of my adolescence, a shaping that for better or worse over time left a sense of caution and self doubt seemingly deeply imbedded in the man I became.

In our community in the best of times, poverty was no stranger to our way of life or for that matter, for a large portion of the community. Being poor was relative and largely a matter of degree. The rule appeared to be, the larger the family, the greater the degree of poverty and ours, with an eventual six children, was one of the larger family's in town.

Poverty, we called it "being poor", was the basic condition to our way of life all my growing up years. As there wasn't anything Dad could do about it, the burden of our poverty was a condition to be tolerated and to the extent possible, ignored. While always a burden, it was most heavily felt on the occasions when any kind of purchase was called for. Money, "cash" in any form, was without fail, inadequate to lacking. To

137

make any purchase, it was always a matter of scraping for the last few pennies and making choices among essential items.

Recreational money for movies was so rare, even at ten cents for the junior admission that I remember the few movies I saw to this day. They were Westerns, starring Tom Mix, Bob Steele and Ken Maynard, names well remembered because I saw one of each. About 1930 the movie "Wings", starring Richard Arlen and a bit actor named Gary Cooper, came to town heavily promoted and costing twenty-five cents for a junior admission. Somehow, at this early stage of the depression, I managed to scrape up the admission price. It was the last movie I saw for several years but scenes from it stay with me to this day.

Movie going stopped entirely sometime before my twelfth birthday. Because of my size, I was thought to be twelve and no longer eligible for the ten-cent admission. The fact was, I didn't even have ten cents to spend so the fact the theater now wanted twenty-five cents in actuality made no difference to my movie attendance.

For recreational reading the town had a Carnegie Library. It was a wonderful resource that provided me the opportunity to know something of the world and its peoples. A newspaper was out of the question and we weren't able to purchase a radio, on credit, until 1937.

I don't know how he did it but Dad usually provided some kind of income, if only in kind, as when he took his wages out in trade when working for a local store owner. Mother managed the limited resources available to her so that we always had enough to eat. Still, money income of any kind was far short of the family's needs.

In addition to cash income, Dad always managed to provide an adequate supply of fuel for our two stoves, whether of logs or slashings, slashings being the discarded limbs of the tree downed when logged. This wood was harvested in logging areas within ten miles or so of our home. Dad drove his team of horses to the area and worked all day to cut and load the available wood. Several trips were required to furnish our household for the winter. The cost of course consisted of his labor.

We also used slabwood, waste material recovered when logs were squared up in the milling process. When we had money the slabwood was purchased from the sawmill by the truckload.

On occasion and when Dad had the opportunity, he traded his labor to the farmer for hay for his horses. At a rate of $2.00 a day it took

MEMORIES OF ANOTHER TIME

five workdays to purchase a ton of hay. Of course, if he used his team of horses on the job the pay was $4.00 a day so for the same five days of work, he got two tons of hay.

As a general rule, anything other than basic necessities requiring cash to purchase was added to the list of the things we could do without.

Clothing was always a problem as the dry goods store required cash. Traditionally, we were taken on a fall shopping trip when Dad's summer wages had cleared off the previous winter's debts and it was time to prepare for school. In our earlier years, Dad often worked for the owner of the pony farm who also owned a small grocery, dry goods store. In lieu of wages, we were outfitted from this store.

Our typical fall outfitting consisted of one pair of shoes, two sets of underwear, two pairs of socks and for the boys, two blue denim shirts and two pairs of overalls or waist overalls, now called jeans. On alternate years and if Dad had a reasonably good year we got a jacket. A jacket was essential to deal with the cold, windy winters where daytime temperatures remained in the thirties and low forties.

I lost my jacket when I was thirteen and had no jacket for fall school term. My Aunt Edie sent the outgrown sports jacket of my cousin. It was skimpy for me and did little to protect against the cold but that was all I had that winter.

Caps, sweaters, gloves, woolens of any kind, came as Christmas gifts to us, if they came at all. As a result of the meager clothing winter weather was not just uncomfortable, it was dreaded. Not surprisingly, by fall outfitting time the clothes of the previous year were essentially rags held together by patches.

Shoes were a problem as the cold, wet winters and mucking about in the barn tended to both wear out the soles and deteriorate the upper leather. Three sets of half soles by spring was par for the winter. By the end of winter, the leather would be so rotten; it would scarcely hold the third set of half soles.

As soon as school was out, the shoes were thrown away and we all went barefoot. As a result, by fall our feet were so tough we could run on the gravel roads without flinching although in point of fact, most of the streets were of dirt. As they were seldom graded, they were rutted and rough. Adaptation being the soul of survival, we looked forward to what we thought of as the "barefoot" season, a time when we could throw away our worn out shoes.

The family's small hoard of cash usually ran out shortly after Christmas so any purchases thereafter were managed by credit. In the early years, coal oil for the lamps was a necessity as was lard for cooking. Stored potatoes, flour and sugar also ran out and become part of the store bill.

A winter's grocery bill seldom exceeded twenty-five dollars but that would be a struggle to pay off in the spring. The grocery bill was paid before any new purchases were made. Credit had to be honored but it was also a matter of family honor that these debts be cleared up as quickly as possible.

Later of course, the electric bill substituted for coal oil but the problem of a cash payment remained the same.

The most telling example of the role of poverty came one winter when Mother was unable to leave the house because she had no shoes to wear. She did have a pair of worn out shoes she could wear in the summer when they weren't required to keep out the cold and wet but in the winter, without any kind of overshoes, the shoes just couldn't be worn outside.

To further illustrate the problem, I recall one year, possibly the previous year, when our water was turned off for failure to pay a $50.00 water bill, accumulated at the rate of two dollars per month. For several months, our household water was obtained from a nearby irrigation ditch and our drinking water from a neighbor's well a block away.

Our children have drunk the ditch water and became very sick. The well, when tested some years later, was condemned as unfit.

The city eventually relented after working out some kind of a promise to pay, accomplished many years later. Incidentally, the city water itself was potable only because it was heavily treated with chlorine.

Although having little or no money with which to purchase clothes was typical of our family life, going without running water was perhaps the most devastating period in my memory.

The lack of money had a marked effect on a number of activities other than attending a movie or going to the local fountain. No money to put in the collection plate and no decent clothes i.e. unpatched clothes meant no church going. Candy and chewing gum were unavailable to

MEMORIES OF ANOTHER TIME   141

us; we used hot tar from the streets as chewing gum in the summer and in the winter wax from honey when comb honey was available. Ice cream was fresh snow flavored with a sprinkle of sugar and vanilla.

Christmas was a time of preparation, anticipation, hope and inevitable disappointment. The renewal of hope was to deny previous experience and may be seen as a testament to the role of hope over experience. We always hoped for snow for Christmas to make it easier for Santa Claus and occasionally did have snow starting a few nights before. By the time I was seven, I confirmed with Mother there was no Santa Claus but played the game of the myth for the benefit of the younger ones. They gladly went along with it although I'm sure they were aware of the myth long before it was given in to, hope could not be denied.

We seldom had any money to buy gifts. Sometime in early December, we began our Christmas preparation by planning for and making presents for each other. Presents were usually homemade or represented a long period of saving for the pennies or nickel to buy a gift. Embroidered handkerchiefs and dishtowels, made from flour sacks, are best remembered. Whittled items had a place and a saved nickel and dime managed other presents.

Gifts represented sacrifice on the part of the giver and the sacrifice has come to represent for me a true gift of love.

Dad usually went to the woods to get us a tree, at least in the early years, and decorations were often hand made. These were achieved by stringing popcorn and cutting out paper ornaments consisting of Stars and Angels. Some hard candies were purchased and Mother usually made some fudge. Other small gifts such as handkerchiefs, stockings and gloves were wrapped and a card made for them.

It should be noted that the hard times we endured were not that much different than the hard times great numbers of the people of the country were enduring. How it was dealt with depended in part on circumstance and perhaps to a lesser extent, on character and experience.

Close neighbors of ours received relief at the height of the depression because the head of the household was crippled and had been from youth. He was a good worker, if somewhat handicapped due to his crippled hip. He was handy at doing many things. Best remembered was the time he wired our house for electricity. Wires were strung from the ceiling and provided an outlet for three downstairs rooms.

Nevertheless, with a final total of eleven mouths to feed and paying jobs few and far between at best, and also, frequently being totally incapacitated during many of the winter months, it was not just necessary but considered acceptable that he "go on relief".

"Relief", to the best of my knowledge, consisted of a hundred-pound sack of beans and a barrel of flower once a month. The bean pot was always on at their house and served with them was a tough, sourdough type biscuit that we kids were quite fond of. The biscuits were made with the usual ingredients but were leavened with both baking powder and baking soda.

During the summer months, a large garden supplemented this diet and a root cellar stored potatoes, onions, apples and pears for winter eating. Occasionally, they were fortunate enough to butcher a hog for some winter meat.

Even with supplementary foods from the garden and barter, the emphasis on beans and bread was thought to have had something to do with the boils the family was plagued with, but the choice was to complain or grin and bear it. Complaints were a waste of time, grin and bear it the accepted mode.

Obviously, our chances for survival depended in great part on Mother's ability to grow a garden, forage and barter for fruits and vegetables to can or store and above all, to manage the few cash resources effectively.

Dad plowed and dragged the garden area level each spring, working in some of our readily available horse manure while doing so. We all pitched in to help plant but he was usually gone before any crop appeared. Under mother's supervision and nagging, I took care of the garden, mostly by doing the weeding and watering. In time of course, all of us participated in the gardening activity.

My services were loaned out to whoever had fruit to pick on shares or anything else mother could barter for. One year, probably 1933, she managed to purchase a cow for $25.00, whether that was in cash I don't remember, and the cow, while being a good milk producer, had to have hay for the winter months. Hay was almost impossible to obtain

MEMORIES OF ANOTHER TIME

on credit so the winters were often thin going for the cow although we always managed some hay.

Possession of a cow became an important part of our food supply. I had full responsibility for taking care of the cow and originally was the only one in the family who could milk her. I was taught by old Bud, Dad's teamster friend. I don't think Dad knew how to milk, for sure he never demonstrated that ability.

During the summer I found pasture for the cow by staking her to grass patches alongside the streets. Some enclosed pasturage was also arranged for most summers, what form of payment given, if any, I don't know.

On a more practical level, the daily chores were represented by chopping and carrying firewood in for cooking and heating, twice daily feeding and milking a cow, summer gardening and working on shares for fruit among other jobs. This developed in me a life long respect not just for the importance of work but also for the opportunity to have work.

Canning all available fruit, berries and vegetables was a summer long job, done as fast as we could locate and pick. It was an ongoing disappointment to me that I was never able to get a job picking fruit for pay in the several orchards in the town That was because the migrant workers would camp in the orchards while the whole family picked.

Townspeople, especially the younger ones, were never allowed these jobs. Occasionally I would get a day or two picking for people with a few trees at something like one half cent a pound for cherries. Prunes paid even less but a pound could be picked faster so the daily take of fifty to seventy five cents was about the same.

Meat was harder to come by. Occasionally we shared in a butchered hog or a chunk of venison. Stew meat was relatively cheap, when we had money. A ten- cent soup-bone was the most common meat purchase.

As might be guessed, meals were generally light on meats. For the most part they were organized around oatmeal mush or hotcakes for breakfast with an occasional fried egg. Without the egg it was a meal guaranteed to leave a burning hole in the gut by eleven and an hour of tension until lunch.

For lunch it was hot breads, baked by Mother, and jam with chili beans, Boston baked beans, navy beans or in the summer, string beans.

Supper usually came with fried or mashed potatoes and gravy, or stews that included some form of meat, biscuits or hot rolls, canned fruit and often, home made cinnamon rolls.

Meat was a sometime thing. When no meat was available for the evening meal, a very tasty and satisfactory gravy would be made using lard, flour, water or milk and pepper and salt.

Life had never been easy for my parents. Dad was born and raised on a Missouri farm. Much of his school time had been spent helping his father on the farm and a few years after migrating to Idaho, his father died, leaving him the "Man of the house" and sole support of his mother and three brothers.

Mother, the eleventh and last child, was the daughter of a coal miner who had lost a leg in a mine accident and who himself had been put to work in the English coal mines at age eleven. She had known the struggle to survive all her life. From their harsh and demanding childhood's, both my parents were prepared, by experience and by character, to deal with the problems of unemployment and poverty, the continuing circumstance marking The Great Depression.

The fact we were often faced with a sense of helplessness and even hopelessness was never allowed to become crippling, mostly, I believe, because we were expected to keep trying, to neither give up or to quit. As a result, we were usually able to control or deny those feelings and even point to achievements to deny both the sense of helplessness and hopelessness, feelings we might otherwise might have been tempted to give in to. Above all, Mother set us an example of courage under duress. All her adult life she suffered the pain of her rheumatism, which at times was also quite disabling. Even so, she encouraged and helped us to have fun and enjoy what life did have to offer us. Her fortitude and strength in an adverse situation provides mental and moral support to this day.

Without welfare, unemployment insurance, medical insurance, the unionization of the worker and the many other protections built into the system now taken for granted, life in those Depression years seemed, and in fact for our family was, just one long struggle for survival.

As a formative experience, those challenging and difficult years growing up during The Great Depression offered certain positives. Without question, learning through experience never to give up was

MEMORIES OF ANOTHER TIME

undoubtedly the most important lesson of the time, however painfully that lesson was learned.

In retrospect, the best that can be said for those years is that we remained a cohesive family. All meals were taken together as a family although when there was work, Dad might be away from home months at a time. Mother was not only our spiritual leader; she led us in a sense of fun. Without other distractions, we all had a library card and became lifetime readers. And on the positive side, we all developed the kind of work habits and sense of personal responsibility that when the opportunity presented itself enabled us to establish responsible, useful, successful adult lives that couldn't have been dreamed of in the years of the Great Depression.

CHAPTER 16
MALNUTRITION AND OTHER THINGS

By
Robert Martens

I REMEMBER ALMOST nothing of my first five years. My earliest memory is of going to the hospital to see my mother and new sister when Beverly was born. I attended first grade in a two-room Lutheran school at age five and then at Faxon Public School. I don't remember whether the latter was first grade or second but the combination and skipping kindergarten put me a grade ahead for the rest of my public school career. As a result, I was always the youngest in the class.

I remember listening on an early radio to heavyweight fights involving Max Baer and Jimmy Braddock on the eve of the Joe Louis age. On one occasion I saw an angel standing silent by my bed and was convinced of this as a reality for some years before I became a skeptic. I played ball, was in a juvenile "gang" that erected a huge cave in a vacant lot and defended it against the rival Sixth Street gang. These gangs were not vicious although we did have some rock throwing battles with garbage can lids as shields. I also remember the proliferation of NRA stickers in the first year of the Roosevelt administration.

Dad had worked for the Jewel Tea Company and Allen Filter Service but lost one job and then the other. As I understand it, the depression began in 1929 at the beginning of the Hoover administration and lasted into the first year or two of the Second World War. Massive unemployment and severe malnutrition for the unfortunate continued throughout the 1930's. Dad was not unemployed until 1933 but he remained largely unemployed thereafter until he got into war production work in 1942.

The depression was on and only now beginning to affect us severely. We left Kansas City in an old beat-up car for Indiana in search of a new beginning and to visit some relatives of mother. The first stop was in Bippus, a tiny village of a hundred inhabitants or less in northeastern Indiana. Uncle Byron had an elaborate workshop including a lathe in his basement and this impressed Beverly and me. Also impressive was a large barn on fire across the street that brought in fire wagons from around the county—too late to save the barn but dousing water on the nearby houses.

A week in Fort Wayne devoted to unsuccessful job-hunting found my lying sick in our cheap hotel room with a bad case of influenza or something. A stay with relatives in Huntington, Indiana, a short visit with relatives in Kokomo, Indiana, another job-hunts in Terre Haute and back to Kansas City, destitute.

On our return from Indiana, we moved into a very large, ancient mansion. It had become a run-down rooming house owned by an elderly lady. Initially, we occupied the front two rooms on the second floor. We must have gotten a little money somehow for Christmas because we had presents. Dad and I worked all night putting together my present which was some kind of model galleon of the Christopher Columbus variety.

Poverty subsequently forced us into one room "apartments" in two-second floor locations. We had no Christmas presents the next year. Here for the first time we faced sheer hunger. On one occasion we went three days without any food whatsoever—only water. On another occasion our family of four survived one week on a single jar of mayonnaise, nothing else.

Two memories stand out. One was a fight between Dad and a drunken neighbor whom Dad easily whipped. I don't know what the man's beef was but he burst into our room and charged Dad. The other was my Mother teaching my sister and me pinochle, which became a great enjoyment in our lives. Mother continued to be the rock that held our family together. She always sacrificed herself to ensure that Beverly and I got enough of whatever we had.

MEMORIES OF ANOTHER TIME

In the second one room apartment, my only strong memory is lying next to a paper-thin wall to listen to a neighbor's radio play-by-play coverage of Kansas City Blues baseball. We could not afford a radio ourselves.

Two years later we moved two blocks away to an apartment building. I was probably eleven at the time or possibly twelve and Beverly, of course, was three years younger. This was a three-story building with two long corridors down each side. We lived there from around 1936 to 1946, the latter being for the first two months after I was discharged form the United States Army. The building leaves some fond memories too but it was a slum. It was infested with bed bugs and cockroaches which were consistently fought but which could never be subdued.

We lived in five or six different apartments during those years, at least one of one room only but most of two room—a living room/bedroom and a kitchen/bedroom. The rent for the two-room apartments was five dollars a week. During one one-year period, mother managed the building in exchange for a rent-free two-room apartment. I stoked the furnace. We may have gotten some other breaks on occasion as I remember Dad paper-hanging the central halls.

As for bedbugs, each apartment had a gas torch apparatus and we regularly stripped the beds and burned the springs, which resulted in, loud popping sounds as the bugs exploded. But they were undoubtedly in the mattresses and the walls and would drop from the ceilings at night.

The worst period was in the back apartment. It was at this location that I remember a number of occasions when I woke up in the middle of the night with a half dozen bed bugs visibly chewing on my body. Ugh! I also remember us coming home at night and turning on the lights suddenly to see literally hundreds of cockroaches scurrying across the floor in every direction. Management finally agreed to a thorough fumigation of the entire building. We moved for several days to a "cabin" on the outskirts of the city. These early "cabins" were the precursors of the motel industry that was yet to come.

We were there in 1939 when World War II began with the German invasion of Poland. I ran out at dawn to buy an "extra", the only time I can remember a newsboy coming down a neighborhood street selling extras.

This building, my home during the years of childhood and youth that I best remember, including all of high school and the year of work before the Army, was popularly known as the "Bucket of Blood". That was not because of the bed bugs but because it was reputed to be a place sometimes used by criminals on the run. Residents were decent, if poor and included both singles and families that included several memorable girls of my age or my sister's age. There were also a couple of boys who were, however marginal, members of the local "gang. I was generally considered the number two in this gang, the leader being a kid in another apartment building who was later killed in action with the Marines in the Pacific.

This reputation as a residence for hard cases was brought home more directly during the period when my mother was the manager. She evicted a man recently out of prison for manslaughter and obviously a hard case. He threatened to get even and he did.

I was in highschool at the time. One afternoon as I passed through a large vacant lot that was a short cut on my regular two-mile hike homeward two bigger boys jumped me. I was badly beaten. One held me while the other, a son of the evicted jailbird, kept punching me in the stomach even as I retched convulsively.

Dad was too proud to go on relief but mother did so against his wishes. We were able to get cans of food from time to time from some central relief authority. The cans had no labels and we often spoke, only half-jokingly, that they consisted of dog food. We also ate a lot of navy beans, the cheapest food available.

There were ups and downs of course, and occasional inputs of money from odd jobs. I walked the alleys looking for metal scrap, sometimes with other kids and sometimes not. Our local "gang" tore out pipes and window weights of a vacant house and stripped copper telephone wires over much of city block on one occasion. We were pretty desperate and egged each other on, I suppose.

A year or so later Dad made me a shoeshine box and I walked about ten miles a day the length of 15th street and back on 12th street, offering shines for five cents. The most I ever made, a really good day, was eighty cents. Still later, I sold newspapers on the corner of 12th and Walnut one summer, but could not continue as I was replacing the regular paperboy who returned. During the last two years of highschool, I worked for a

MEMORIES OF ANOTHER TIME

local grocer after school and for 14 hours on Saturday. I was initially paid five dollars per week but was raised to seven. After graduating from high school, I worked full time for fifteen dollars a week for this grocery but soon got a better job.

At one point my sister became very ill and was taken to Mercy Hospital, a public hospital for children. She was said to have severe malnutrition and might die without treatment. This was in the day of Kansas City's infamous Pendergast machine. The control of the machine was such that she could not be admitted to the hospital without the authorization of the Democratic precinct captain. Mother went to the captain and was told that she and my father were the only two Republican votes in the precinct. He said he would sign the authorization only if both she and her husband agreed to vote the machine ticket in the upcoming election. Mother was dubious whether Dad would agree. In fact, this was during one of his periods of extreme rage and depression and he wouldn't agree. Mother told the captain that she would vote for the machine but that Dad was too stubborn to agree. She pleaded that her vote be enough. The captain relented.

When he had work, Dad worked hard but more or less went to pieces when he could find no work at all. He moped, pouted and treated his family to fits of bitterness and verbal abuse. On one occasion when I was about sixteen he sharply criticized me for reading too much. I responded that he was the one that should feel ashamed for the way he treated his family. He leaped to his feet and lunged for me. He was a physically powerful man and I saw myself as an undernourished weakling. I was scared and ran. Dad chased me around the table. Mother grabbed a knife and warned Dad to stop or else. Mother, Sister Beverly and I left. We wandered for hours, visited the minister of our church and were prevailed upon to return.

I'll never forget looking through a window and seeing Dad with his head in his hands, the image of dejection. We all made up with much weeping and apologizing, especially by Dad.

There was a brighter side of those years. Sometimes we did all right, especially after Dad started painting and paper hanging. He developed a reputation for good work and low prices. If he bid a contract well, which sometimes happened, we would be in clover for a while.

I remember going with my Dad to Kansas City Blues baseball games two or three times a year when we had some money. The Blues were a triple A minor league team. Until they became a New York Yankee farm team in 1938 or 1939. After that they regularly had outstanding teams of young players en-route to the majors, players like Phil Rizzuto, Eddie Joost, Hank Bauer, Al Rosen, Moose Skowron, Mickey Mantle and many others. One day, probably in 1939, Dad and I were sitting behind first base and watched a young Minneapolis Millers outfielder named Ted Williams hit two home runs out of the Kansas City Park.

Mother always found a way to save us from catastrophe when things got bad. She maintained our morale and taught us character. What a giant she was in those times. She was a wonderful cook. I can still remember the wonderful Sunday roast beef prepared in her own unique manner. On lovely summer evenings when we sat on the large communal front porch I would jump on my bicycle and ride around until I found a hot tamale vendor and bring back hot tamales for all.

School was important to me. I seem to have been born with an unusually good mind and an excellent memory. I knew the alphabet before I was two and could read before I was five. I learned all the states and state capitals before they were taught in the first grade. At nine I knew all the countries of the world and I could draw rough but accurate maps of all the major countries. When I could find the time I read voraciously although Dad sometimes criticized me for doing so much reading. By the time I was sixteen I knew the approximate population of all the cities in the world over 100,000 population as recorded in atlases and gazetteers.

In high school I joined the ROTC for three years [age 13-16] and memorized, consciously and subconsciously, all the field manuals provided plus various books in the library. I could identify every position in an infantry division at age sixteen and followed the campaigns of World War II to the point of absorbing whatever I could find on individual division histories.

I was good at math and liked the social sciences but was mediocre in the physical sciences and below average in the arts including music. My sister was always good at drawing and became a professional artist.

I was not good at mechanical things, partly, I believe, because Dad was a poor teacher. He would make me stand beside him while

MEMORIES OF ANOTHER TIME

he tinkered with the engine of his car, when he had one, or when he was soldering or mixing cement or whatever and expected me to learn from watching him. I usually couldn't see what he was doing and he never explained anything. An exception was painting and paperhanging which he explained well and which I learned thoroughly. He was proud of my work. One day we painted a new house on a blistering hot day with the sun reflecting off the wet white paint. On the way home we stopped at the tavern and Dad ordered three whiskeys and three beers and the three of us drank them. I was probably fifteen but Dad's attitude was that I had worked like a man and would be treated like one, age limits be damned.

I did well in both grade school and high school but would have done even better except for the drain of poverty and the need to work after school, particularly in the years I worked in the grocery. I was skinny, partly from natural build, but also the result of some malnutrition. I had a deep sense of shyness and suffered a magnified sense of inferiority about my physique.

When times got better I suddenly shot up in height to six foot two or three inches while, in my imagination at least, I was getting even thinner. I wrote in for the Charles Atlas course in bodybuilding for the considerable expense of perhaps thirty dollars and practiced "dynamic" tension. It helped my strength but the visible results were meager. The Atlas's ads began with "I was a 97 pound weakling". I felt I remained a 97-pound weakling.

When I finally succeeded in enlisting in the army at seventeen, I had built myself up to 120 pounds on my six foot three frame but it was war and I was accepted. The upshot was I never had a date until I was in my twenties; I was too bashful and unsure of myself.

In the three years of ROTC, I knew more than anyone else but never got higher than sergeant and squad leader. I was disappointed not to have been made a cadet officer but probably couldn't have afforded the uniform anyway. I did become a member of the City champion crack drill team that performed at some municipal events.

Of most significance for later life was the fact that the regular squad I headed in my senior year included my life-long buddy, Allen Fuehrer. He was a young man as poor as myself and one who had to endure, always with his own humor, the natural gibes induced by his name, particularly in that decade.

And so, at age sixteen, I graduated from Northeast High School in June 1942, shortly after America's entry in the Second World War. Allen and I tried to enlist that summer but we were clearly too young.

I soon got a job as a guard at the Nelson Art Gallery for $15.00 pr week and also enrolled at Kansas City night school for two college math courses. Salaries were going up due to the competition of higher paying defense jobs while labor was becoming scarce because of the military draft and war production. Dad had been working for six months or so at a steel products plant devoted to war production. He got me hired there at $45.00 per week. It was hard, physical labor but I had no problem once my hands became callused. Meanwhile, I was still going to night school and was now into my second semester of classes.

Now seventeen and eager to serve in the military my friend Allen Fuehrer had learned of a new program called the Army Specialized Training Program [ASTP] which provided for going to college for a year in the army with a perspective of an officer's commission thereafter. We enlisted on July 31,

CHAPTER 17

1933: *A* Summer's Adventure

By
Charles B. Downer

In the summer of 1933 I was eighteen and had just finished my freshman year at UCLA. During school vacation Joe Hartman and I decided to go to Smith Valley, Nevada, where Brother Robert had a haying job on a ranch. Joe and I thought that maybe we could get a job. We hitchhiked up the San Juaquin Valley to Sacramento where we grabbed a freight train going across to Reno. That being in the depth of the Depression there were lots of people traveling by freight train. The railroad police and brakemen were almost accommodating so long as you didn't give them any trouble. They understood the situation. Sometimes they would even tell you which trains were going where.

It was a little bit spooky going through the snow sheds along the mountainside up near Donner Summit and over the pass through the snow sheds. Riding on a flatcar back of the huge locomotive used on heavy grades, the thought was "This is great". Once into the snow sheds the big coal burning trains engine continued putting out this dense, black, poisonous smoke. Breathing the choking smoke made us feel ill. It was lucky the seemingly never-ending snow sheds didn't continue very much further.

When we got into Reno we found there was a narrow gauge railroad called the Virginia and Truckee running to the south. We climbed into a sheep car. It was a double decker type of cattle car with less headroom than beef cattle have. The brakeman came by and locked the door. The rolling stock was very, very old. There were brass plates on the decks of

155

the passenger cars ahead that were dated in the Civil War years. The engine had a great big, bulbous spark arrester. Our first stop was to take on a load of wood slabs to fire the engines.

We were locked in and concerned about getting out when we got to Carson City. We called the brakeman and he let us out. On foot again, we hitchhiked to Topaz Lake and then to Smith Valley. But first we took a swim in Topaz Lake, it then being mid summer.

We continued on to Smith Valley and the Fulstone home where we were greeted by Grace Fulstone, the mother of Robert's two friends, Al and Don Devoe, and her husband, "Hike" Fulstone.

Hike was a blacksmith who was as skinny as a rail and practically lived on 16 cups a day of coffee with lots of sugar. Grace had come out to Reno with her two children to get a divorce from Mr. Devoe. After the divorce she met and married Hike and settled down on his ranch. A registered nurse, she assisted Hike's sister-in-law, a MD, in her practice.

When we told her we had taken a swim in Topaz Lake on our way, she was horrified. Rabbit Fever [Tularemia] was prevalent. Rabbits would get into the lake and die. We recalled seeing lots of dead rabbits on the road and near the lake. She drew a tub of water, gave us a bar of Fels-Naptha soap and made us get in there and scrub down. Fels-Naptha was laundry soap with very high lye content. No dirt and probably no bacteria had a chance after that treatment.

Anyway, it was near the end of the haying season and there wasn't a job for us there on the ranch. We had an interesting time just horsing around.

One night Robert, Don, Joe and I walked up a road towards the home of an elderly German who lived beside a stream and made his own beer. Don knew that in the late afternoon he usually came down the road to the little, tiny town for an evening of socialization.

We hiked up to his place and took a case of his home brew out of the cold creek where he stored it. We took it out on the road where we could open a bottle by catching the cap on the barb of a barbwire fence. Half of it would squirt out the top.

We were starting to feel that beer—it was powerful stuff—when we heard some singing. It was the old fellow coming back from town.

MEMORIES OF ANOTHER TIME

He was higher than a kite. We went through the barbwire fence to hide out in the darkness until he passed by.

We were there at the Fulstone's about a week. Grace was really feeding us. Her idea of a breakfast was to spoon out heavy cream that was thicker than whipped cream onto our cereal, and follow that with bacon and eggs. Of course her figure showed that was her diet. Just the opposite of her husband!

Joe and I decided that we would go back to Chicago to the World's Fair. Robert decided that if we were going to do that he would too. His friend Don also decided to come. The four of us started out in Robert's 1926 Chrysler Imperial 80 sport roadster, which had cost him $150.00 in 1932. It was really a nice car.

We drove to Reno, leaving the car with his girlfriend at the U. of Nevada. Next, we caught the Western Pacific Railroad going north from Reno through the lumber country of Northern California. We discovered that running to catch moving freight trains and riding on the tops was often a very, very dangerous business.

We took a swim in the lake at Klamath Falls, Oregon and then rode that railroad on up to the city of Klamath Falls. Here there was a sign posted in the railroad yards saying, "Green lumber handlers wanted".

Money being scarce, our thought was that we might as well work in the lumbering industry to earn a little pay. We went up to the man behind the sign who heard our request. Sizing us up he decided that we were probably pretty green to handle green lumber and didn't have the physique for it. When we found out what green lumber handlers were supposed to handle, we thought we were pretty lucky to get off that easy. That is terribly hard, difficult and dangerous work sorting and handling the boards freshly cut from the log.

We weren't completely broke although we were close to it. Our other road companions, bums, were down and out victims of the depression. There was only one time when just for the experience of it because other bums did it I went into a bakery and asked for a loaf of bread. There was a very attractive young girl in the bakery. She looked at me nicely and without a word wrapped up a loaf of bread and handed it to me. That was the only time I bummed food.

On another occasion we were coming into a town early in the morning. We were all hungry. I stole a bottle of milk from somebody's front porch. A woman neighbor saw us do it. She screamed at us and threatened to call the cops. That was the only time we stole anything.

Continuing on up to the railroad yards east of Seattle, I had a bundle [often referred to as a bindle] with a blanket and spare clothes. The freight train had moved into a siding. Passing a big cherry orchard we went in and ate our fill of Bing cherries. All of the 'Knights' of the road on this freight train ran down to the orchard and started eating. Soon they were blue in the face.

After we had our fill of cherries the locomotive engineer blew two blasts of his horn, the highball signal they were going to leave. Some of the guys who wanted to eat more cherries simply broke off limbs and climbed back onto the freight train with them. If there had been a farmer around there I think there would have been some buckshot flying too. Then we headed on into town.

I had overdone on the cherries and got sick. I went into a drugstore and ordered a glass of citrate of magnesia. After drinking the cathartic, we took off to the dock area.

On first arriving in Seattle we were very tired and dirty. We decided we would rest in a hotel room and get cleaned up before proceeding any further. I rented a waterfront hotel room for fifty cents.

The plan was that two of us would sleep on the bed and two would sleep on the floor. When the other three guys joined me, Robert and I slept in the bed and the other two on the floor. During the night I felt bedbugs biting. I squashed them one by one and lined them up on the sheet. After quickly turning back the covers and seeing the inhabitants scurrying for cover, all four of us slept on the floor of this sailor's hotel in Seattle. The next morning I counted ten dead bedbugs in my lineup.

In the interest of finding employment we stopped by Alaska fishing fleet headquarters on Puget Sound to see if they needed any green fish handlers up in the Alaska waters. There too it seemed we were not of the physiques and types that would go well on an Alaskan fishing boat. Incidentally, we would have been out to sea so long it would have interfered with our going back to school in the fall.

We found out that the best way to ride the rails to Chicago was to get on the Chicago, St. Paul and Pacific railways, which departed the West Coast near Renton, WA. and now the home of Boeing Aircraft Co.

MEMORIES OF ANOTHER TIME

We hopped a freight train at Renton, WA. and within a very few miles this train, without giving us any warning whatsoever; ducked into a seven-mile long tunnel that ran through the heart of the mountain. Ice-cold mountain streams poured in on us from the roof of the tunnel. We were getting soaked. Also, the sparks from the rails in the jet blackness of the tunnel caused the air to be lit up like Klieg lights. Extremely brilliant. Somewhat to our surprise and much to our relief we managed to survive through to the end of the tunnel. The freight train went into a siding. Better late than never we were able to find an empty boxcar.

We proceeded on across the state of Washington in a visually soggy rain. Time went pretty slow across the plains, first to Spokane and on into northern Idaho. At a little town called St. Mary's, a division point on the railroad we were told it would be some hours before another freight continued on east.

Most of us went into this little town and into the grocery store where we bought a loaf of bread for something to eat. We went back to the railroad yards to eat this treat.

As a rule, eating was catch as catch can. If the freight went into a "hole", a siding, it would be close to a little town. We would race over to a little grocery store, usually the cracker box type, and get a loaf or so of bread, maybe a little butter to go with it and race back in time to catch the freight train before it pulled out. Sometimes to do so we had to catch the freight train on the fly. Then we would gorge ourselves on bread and butter.

Of course when we went through orchard country we lightened our diet with whatever was handy.

Personal needs were taken care of in areas where they had tall brush or at least ankle high brush. There were no facilities. When the opportunity presented itself, we bathed in rivers and rinsed out our shirts, pants and socks. Occasionally we had a nice snooze on the riverbank.

From St. Mary's there was a railroad spur into the city of Spokane. It was the middle of the night and I was spread-eagled and sound asleep on top of a tank car. I had left my bindle on a little platform on the end of the car. Joe and I were together. Robert and Don were on another car. The train was broken up and some of the cars, including the one with Robert and Don, were shunted off toward Spokane while Joe and I continued on the main line.

Someone stole my bindle with my blanket and extra clothes. After that, because of the cold, I tried to ride inside the boxcars with the door at least partially closed.

Robert and Don followed a day behind us all the way to Chicago. They were entirely without money of any kind and therefore unable to purchase any food.

When they got to Mulbridge, ND, where the railroad crossed a bridge across the Missouri River word spread throughout the train that the Catholic hospital had a soup line. We were almost destitute. The railroad was quite a ways from the town so we got in the soup line and had a couple bowls of the most delicious soup we had ever eaten. That improved our spirits quite a bit.

The train proceeded on east through ND, Minnesota and finally to La Crosse, Wisconsin. By this time we were just about down to our last cent. Unable to buy enough food to get by we went into a Greek restaurant and asked the owner if he would provide a meal in return for washing the dishes or sweeping or whatever. He did exactly that. He gave us a good meal and handed us a broom and a rag. We worked around there for a couple hours and then caught the freight down to Chicago.

As we continued eastward we let our folks know what we were doing by mailing penny post cards. We had agreed that if we got separated, we would go to the Central Post Office in Chicago and look for a postcard in general delivery. The first person to get there would find a room, come back and leave a postcard telling the others where he was.

When we got to Milwaukee I was sound asleep in the far corner of a boxcar. There were probably a dozen bums in there. On arrival the railroad policeman ordered everyone off the train. Everybody got off except me—I didn't wake up. The railroad cop, who proved to be a kindly fellow, nudged me with the toe of his boot and told me to get out. I asked him "where is everybody?" He said, "They've gone that way". I ran after them but I couldn't find them. Joe had gotten out with the others and thought I had too.

With Joe nowhere in sight, I inquired when the next train would be going to Chicago and caught it. Arriving in the railroad yards at the West End of Chicago, I was dirty from coal smoke and sleeping on boxcar floors. Walking into town I stopped at a service station with an

MEMORIES OF ANOTHER TIME

outdoor faucet and washed my face and hands as best I could. Then at the Central Post Office I left postcards saying I was there and was looking for a room. There was also a most welcome letter from Dad enclosing a few dollars.

I found a room for 75 cents a night on Calumet Ave. opposite one of the entrances to the World's Fair. I went back into town and posted some more cards giving my address. Within a day everyone else showed up. We washed our clothes and all lived in that 75-cent room while we enjoyed the World's Fair.

It was just a short walk to the Fair. If there was an admission fee it wasn't very much. I remember seeing some strange and wonderful things. I walked past a big box and could see myself walking along on closed circuit TV—something I didn't know existed.

For the next few days we really revved it up seeing the free sights at the World's Fair and swimming underneath the World's Fair in the waters of Lake Michigan.

The Underwood Typewriter Company featured the world's fastest typist demonstrating the standard No. 5 Underwood. His record speed was 128 words a minute. That was well before electric typewriters were in general use. The Fair was a real eye opener, with many scientific marvels shown years ahead of their public use. For me, that made the whole trip worthwhile.

Robert and I had a Carpenter relative who was working as a sales clerk at Marshall Field in Chicago. I went down there to see him. While there I had enough money to go into their bargain basement to buy a new pair of pants for a $1.50. I also scoured my grimy cords with a bar of Fels Naptha soap so with clean cords and with that new pair of pants I was more presentable.

By this time Joe's uncle back home had lined up a job for Joe working on a freighter sailing out of L.A. harbor. Joe bummed back west to take the job, and Don went with him as far as Reno.

Robert and I decided to visit our relatives in Iowa. We went down to the railroad yards in the south of Chicago. Once there we got into a refrigerator car and fell asleep. Two railroad policemen came along and ordered us out of the car. Just aroused from a sound sleep, we objected angrily to our sudden awakening. One of the cops said "you're talking to the wrong man this time" and hit me on the side of my head with a blackjack. The man was still there so Robert kicked him in the neck. We jumped down on the ballast and ran about a half mile down the track to lose him. We never heard anymore about the incident.

Traveling on freight trains is an extremely dangerous, grinding, thankless business, not least of all due to the "Yard Bulls". My ear was ringing.

We went first to Muscatine and visited with Uncle Will and Aunt Jane. The next morning Aunt Jane noticed there was some discharge on my pillow. She asked me about my ear and I told her what had happened. She took me to her ear, nose and throat doctor. He treated my broken eardrum and fixed me up with a little kit big enough to carry a small bottle of alcohol, a dropper and some cotton. He told me to put a drop of alcohol in the ear daily and plug the ear canal with cotton to keep it clean. Fortunately, that was the right treatment as the ear had healed by the time I got home.

Hitchhiking from Muscatine to Rock Rapids, we stopped half way at Cedar Falls to stay overnight with Aunt Alice and Uncle August. The next day they took us to the edge of town to hitch hike, let us off and before we caught a ride they came back. They gave each of us a five-dollar bill. In 1933 a five-dollar bill provided purchasing power that was like $100.00 would be today. That financed us home.

From there we hitchhiked northwestward to Rock Rapids where my mother had grown up. We stayed with Uncle Ralph and Aunt Gwen and cousins Dick and Brud in their home. It was a big house on the highest place in Rock Rapids. There was a small field in the back of the house.

Dick and Brud saddled up a horse and invited me to take a ride— my first time on a horse. I got on this animal and didn't know what to do. I wasn't holding the reins tight so the horse took off running like crazy around the field. I almost fell off and was holding on to the pommel for dear life. Luckily, the horse didn't trip so I survived that.

From Rock Rapids Robert and I continued by rail on west. We came in to Manhattan, Kansas on a passenger train riding the blinds on the forward end of the first car, just behind the locomotive. Because it was illegal to bum a ride on a passenger train, we had been reported when we were seen catching it. When we reached Manhattan a railroad policeman with a drawn pistol greeted us. He ordered us off the train.

MEMORIES OF ANOTHER TIME

Luckily for us, he was at heart a fatherly kind of guy so he walked us up the ivy-covered bank beside the tracks and sat with us until the passenger train left. He said there would be a freight train along that we could catch. We were hungry so we went into town and bought a watermelon and ate it beside the tracks while waiting for the freight train.

We were thinking that the road west from there was the Union Pacific. Without giving it a thought we climbed aboard a Union Pacific and soon found ourselves staring down the barrel of a 44. Orders were given in no uncertain terms to "Get the Hell off". So we got off and the detective kept us in view until the freight was out of sight.

We were told, "No one rides the Union Pacific freight trains." That meant we would have to go back to Rock Island. We found out the Rock Island had a line that went down through Kansas to Bellevue, Kansas. There the line went west. We went south on the Rock Island to Bellevue as figured and got off and located a freight headed for Colorado. We jumped aboard.

We were standing in the coal tender of the locomotive when I noticed the coal moving under my feet. The fireman, much to our surprise, ordered us forward into the cab, explaining that the engine used an automatic coal stoker, a large auger that drew coal from the bottom of the tender. It could draw our feet in too. It was a cool evening, in fact rather chilly. I thought that was rather nice to be invited although as it turned out, they did have an ulterior motive. They showed us where the coal "hogger" from the coal car was pushing crushed coal into the firebox. That provided the steam for the locomotive.

He told us that at times the drain moistened the coal and caused it to cake and harden. The augur wouldn't pick up the hardened chunks. Our job was to take shovels to the coal, then break it up so it would fall down into this little trough in the bottom where the augur kept moving it forward into the fire box. This work became an addition to the warmth of the firebox. We were very comfortable and enjoyed congenial company.

About a hundred miles east from Bellevue we stopped at a little town. There a very attractive young lady wearing bib overalls and straw hat came aboard. She asked if she could stay in the cab and get warm. The engineers again were very obliging and she sat there all the way to

Colorado while we kept the train going by breaking the crumbled coal down so the augur could move it into the firebox.

Once, when we were riding with some other bums in the empty ice compartment of a refrigerator car, the train stopped at a station and another bum, reeking of perfume, joined us. We asked him about the perfume. He said he had stolen it from the "two bit whore" he had just visited.

Arriving in Colorado we went on to Pueblo. There we again made a change of railroad companies. We decided to ride the Denver and Rio Grande west over the Rockies and the Continental Divide.

To do so we had to hike up to Canyon City, which is also the site of the Colorado State Prison. There we were able to catch a freight train hauling lumber up the long grades. Climbing up the grade we could have walked along side the train very easily without falling behind. Finally it topped the summit and started rolling westward. Running downhill it really picked up speed. In fact, I was a little bit worried that it might jump the rails. Fortunately, nothing like that happened.

The rest of the trip west we were getting tired and not taking time out to nap very often. By this time train travel, with its constant groaning, rattling, swaying, lack of rest and infrequent opportunities to eat was getting to be something out of a nightmare.

We crossed Colorado, Utah, the Great Salt Lake flats, and finally into Nevada and the Pequot summit. Then we began the long grade down into Wells. Here I was truly alarmed at the speed that this freight train was traveling. The cars were lurching, bumping, careening and rocking. I thought our time could have been coming during that particular stretch of the railroad.

We continued on out to Reno where Robert was due to register for the fall term at college. I was due to reenter UCLA so didn't linger long in Reno.

Don decided to come with me so we grabbed a freight train and again traveled over the Donner Pass. This time we were smart enough to ride a car at the end of the train where the smoke going through the tunnels and snow sheds wasn't quite so bad.

We changed trains in Sacramento and continued down through the San Joaquin Valley and over the Tehachapi Pass to San Bernardino. Forgetting about tunnels, Don and I were sitting on top of a boxcar about three cars in back of the engine. When the train was on a curve we could see the side of the engine. It was called a Malley, with the cab forward. The cab forward feature was especially useful going through tunnels because crewmen were ahead of the smoke.

We saw the fireman leaning out the window looking back toward us and making a rolling motion with his arms. We didn't understand the signal but we soon found out. We were entering a tunnel. Since we were way forward on the train there was no chance to run back to get away from the smoke. All we could do was lie down flat on top of the boxcar and breathe through a handkerchief. The tunnel was long and the hot smoke was very uncomfortable. That taught us a lesson. Out of the tunnel, we ran much farther back on the train.

Arriving in San Bernardino, we hitchhiked the rest of the way home to Alhambra. And so ended an extraordinary experience and a most memorable adventure.

CHAPTER 18
FAMILY, CARS AND OTHER THINGS

By
Frank S. Preston

MY FATHER, Howard Hall Preston, had left the family farm at age twenty-four to go to college and was later to earn his Ph.D. He and my mother, who had helped him, were proud of his accomplishments. From the earliest I can remember, he was addressed as Doctor or Professor.

After his college graduation in 1912, he began his teaching career at Mason City, Iowa, teaching history and coaching. He loved that life, but realized that he couldn't raise a family on what high schools then paid--and he wanted to marry his college sweetheart, Lucy Steele. He began working on his doctorate and applying for college positions. In June 1916 he and my mother were married, and though still working on his Ph.D. in economics, he was hired in 1917 to teach at the University of Texas in Austin. He had found his life career; now they could start their family.

My parents returned to Iowa for the summer, to the Steele home on the outskirts of Cedar Rapids. There Dad continued his doctoral work at the University of Iowa in Iowa City, commuting daily via the interurban streetcar.

Mother, of course, stayed at home--helping with cooking, washing, picking fruit, canning, feeding chickens and gathering eggs, and all the other summer work needed to run a farm.

167

When I was to be named, Mother's father, Franklin W. Steele, accepted having the baby named for him.

My parents had expected to settle in Austin, but that year the University of Texas was caught up in a major political upheaval. "Ma" Ferguson was elected governor, after the earlier reign of "Pa." The new governor claimed she believed in "the little Red School House," but didn't trust "those godless college professors in Austin." The University suffered major budget cutbacks and political repression.

The song "The Eyes of Texas" was written at this time and described the situation.

For the fall of 1920, my father had a chance to move up a step in collegiate rank at the growing University of Washington, so my parents moved from Oberlin to Seattle, Washington. I was only two. Mother was pregnant with Mary Belle, but I was probably not following that event.

I don't know when Dad bought a first car for our family, but it was more likely in Seattle than in Ohio.

From age two to about four I was vaguely aware of the car. On trips, Mary Belle and I usually rode alone in the back seat. Mother was in the front with Dad. He was always doing the driving. Mary Belle and I enjoyed standing up and hanging out the sides or onto the back of the front seat.

We sometimes took visitors or guests on trips around Seattle and up to about a hundred miles away. We were one of the small percentage of families with cars but I did not take this in until I was about five.

The car was a 1915 Buick of the style I associate as a touring car. It had a fold-down top and no roll up windows. I don't remember ever seeing evidence of side curtains (removable) or the top opened. When it rained, we all tried to move back away from the open sides. It had no heater and it could get cold on trips. It was a black four-door which by today's standards would be huge.

It barely fit into the length of the garage and had to be parked carefully so that Dad could have room in front to crank the car. To get into the car it was one step up to the running board and another to the door thresholds. The windshield was of two pieces and could be folded down but I don't remember this happening even once. I believe the engine was either a straight six or eight cylinders. It moved along

MEMORIES OF ANOTHER TIME

with traffic and seemed to have no trouble moving as fast as the roads would then allow.

The car wheels had yellow wooden spokes and wheels that were large by today's practices. A wheel could be unbolted from the axle after jacking up the car. The entire assembly consisted of a tire with inner tube and rim that was held on the wooden wheel with some lugs. It was also possible to remove the tire (with inner tube and rim) from the wooden wheel with the wheel remaining on the car.

What you did when you had a flat tire depended on the circumstances. If you had a usable spare, then it was fastest to remove the tire and wheel together and replace it with the spare. Then when you got back from the trip, you could either repair the tire and tube or drop it off at a service station.

If you were unlucky enough to need to repair the inner tube out on the road, it was customary to remove the tire assembly from the wheel and lay it out on the ground. Down on the ground you always got your hands grimy and your clothes muddy. It was something you dreaded doing at night or in the rain.

To get at the inner tube, the rim was made as a split ring. This had to be pried open with two tire irons (levers) to open up the split. The rim could then be slipped out from the inside flanges of the tire. After you had freed the tire from the rim, the inner tube—now flat—was pulled out from inside the tire.

You hoped you could see if a puncture had occurred, and if so, where on the tube. Fixing the inner tube was another adventure.

Normally, inner tubes were repaired with hot patches at service stations or at home. This was possible but less successful on the road. For road repairs, cold patches were usually made but these seldom worked for long and were generally replaced later when the trip was completed.

To assemble the repaired tube and tire, the process had to be reversed—only with more effort, pounding and cussing.

To repair a flat, you needed to locate the cause of the flat. This was sometimes difficult to find. At a service station, the inner tube was pumped up and immersed in a water tank to search for bubbles—something not easy to accomplish on the road. On the road you used a hand pump to pump the tube to extra large size. Sometimes you could hear the air escaping. Alternatively, you could hold the tube near your cheek and slowly turn it while trying to feel the air on your skin.

Blowouts produced large ruptures and sometimes reduced the tube to shreds. If that happened, the tube couldn't be patched and had to be replaced.

Once the size of the needed patch was determined, a piece was cut from a sandwich of gum rubber with glue on one side and waxed cloth that was pulled off like on a Band-Aid. The tube was roughed up with a scraper and the patch pressed on. This was nearly impossible to stick on in a heavy rain. This task finished, one would then have to reassemble the tire and wheel combination.

At my age I wasn't much help. I could fetch tools and had one assignment—to place the jack under the axle and remove it when the job was done. This involved some crawling and reaching and careful placement of the jack. It was always a dirty job.

Our Buick had been thoughtfully designed. It had two spare wheels on a rack at the car rear—no trunk of course. Thus, we could make a trip and if we started with two good spares, we could have two flats without a great problem. Most of the all-day trips involved up to 100 miles each way. We often seemed to have about one flat per round trip. The trip was successful unless we had more than two flats.

Roads then in the Pacific Northwest were mostly paved between main cities and in the cities. Once out of town and not on a major highway, the roads were gravel, or in farm areas, merely dirt.

I remember that out from the city we would be either in open country (farms, or fields) or in the woods. At that time, the woods came down within about ten feet or less of the road shoulders—which were often only 3 or 4 feet wide. That meant that we would then be driving down a canyon formed by tall evergreens. You could not see far into the woods and sometimes the branches nearly formed an arch over the road. At times like that, the feeling was almost church-like. We enjoyed both the open areas and the forest "primeval".

When we drove in the mountains the roads were often steep and narrow with no (or inadequate) guardrails. There often were big drop-offs on the side and sometimes the passengers would express their fear of going off into sure death. Some would ask to get out and walk, and carsickness was not unusual. Where the road was only one-lane wide

MEMORIES OF ANOTHER TIME

the going got rough. The passengers would cry out, "What if we meet another car?" Everyone had to drive slowly for this. Coming up on sharp, blind curves, the driver honked his horn to warn other possible drivers, and sometimes someone would have to walk ahead and motion if it was safe to proceed. There would be a turnout at not too frequent intervals where one or two cars could pull off the main track to let you pass. Problems big time!—if there were many cars.

One time in the mid-1920s we were following a friend's car up the Mt. Baker Highway. We were in an open area with no trees and a vast slope of rock to each side of the road. I happened to be in the second car—about 100 yards or less behind our friends. A huge boulder showed up high above us to the left, bouncing down the loose rock. It hit the shoulder on the left and rolled between the two cars missing each by about two car lengths. That boulder was at least as high as the car ahead was tall.

When we drove east in 1928 a higher percentage of the roads were paved. But the roads gave us a worse impression because they were much more crowded. It became a problem to pass a car ahead on a two-lane road. I don't remember seeing more than two lanes in the east -- except in cities.

Out west we had paved, three lane roads and rarely even a four-lane road. Along the West Coast there were motels consisting of small cabins. East of the Rockies these stopped. There we stayed with relatives or in hotels -- which were pretty seedy.

Tires were not the only problem. I remember one time we were stuck at night far out in the country. Dad fixed the carburetor with the rubber eraser cap of a pencil that mother supplied. She felt like a hero.

Starting the car was a problem every time we went out. I was gradually drawn in as a participant to help Dad. He always cranked the car because it took considerable strength. He began by engaging the crank in a hole in a slot in the drive shaft, low in the center of the exact front of the car. Then he would turn the drive shaft for a full turn. Usually, this turn was not fast enough to get the engine to start firing but did prime the cylinder with gas. He had to continue the cranking until the engine caught and began to run. The faster turning engine would then push the crank out of the engagement slot.

The engine was fairly easy to start if it was still warm. It became a difficult chore if the car had sat for a while without being used. When the weather got down near freezing, the friction increased and it became harder still to crank. To turn the crank, it was necessary to stand sort of with one foot inside the bumper and the other outside and crank from a bent over position. It was a difficult posture.

Cranking the engine was only half the battle. The engine control levers for spark and fuel had to be set right and this varied with the temperature of the engine and the air. A wire with a ring on the end ran through the radiator to the choke control at the carburetor. There was also a lever on the steering wheel that moved the same control. In order for the engine to run smoothly controls had to be changed as the car began to warm up. The levers had to be moved carefully to avoid killing the engine or letting it die.

It was all Dad could do to crank and quickly run around to reach in to change the throttle and spark advance levers on the steering wheel. These settings had to be changed as the engine warmed up. A too rapid change in the spark could cause the engine to misfire or backfire. By throwing the crank backward against the person cranking this could be a disaster. Dad knew that care was the watchword. While still on the farm he had broken his arm while working with some farm machinery.

When I was five I was put behind the steering wheel to operate the spark and throttle controls while Dad cranked. While he cranked he yelled commands at me. In doing so he impressed on me the heavy weight of my responsibility. I feared that some day, through some mistake or no fault of my own, I would be at the wheel when Dad broke another arm. Dad was not one to swear in front of his son but there were times when I was never sure if he was mad at me, or the car, or both.

If everything worked, we would make trips to visit or sightsee. I remember these with pleasure that balanced the problems we had to surmount with tires, getting started, weather and the roads.

*   *   *

Sometime around 1926, our Buick disappeared and was replaced by a 1924 Studebaker. This car was entirely different and up-to-the latest. It

MEMORIES OF ANOTHER TIME

was a four door closed sedan rated for five passengers. Its most improved feature was an electric starter! That meant no more hand cranking for Dad. It also had one flower vase attached the sidewalls of the rear seat area. It had no trunk. Overall, it was more nearly the size of today's cars. I don't remember that we had much trouble with tires.

Dad did all of the driving. Often I got to sit in the front seat while mother sat in the back seat with my two sisters.

*   *   *

In 1927 Dad accepted a complicated exchange professorship at Dartmouth College in Hanover, New Hampshire. For that school year he was to replace someone who was taking a sabbatical in Europe. In order to take the job he needed to find someone to cover his own position at the University of Washington for one year.

Arrangements were made with a professor from Michigan to come to Seattle. For this to work Dad agreed to teach his courses for the summer. Further, the Michigan family was to live in our house and have the use of our car. We were to live in their home in Ann Arbor for the summer.

When the time came, we drove to the railroad station, parked the car and gave the keys and the location of the car to the station agent. We left by train and a day or so later, the other family arrived by train, picked up our car, and drove to our house—following the map left in the car.

At Ann Arbor we lived near the campus and did not need a car. Thinking ahead to the fall and transporting his family to Hanover, Dad bought another car. By chance, it turned out to be a 1924 Studebaker! It was exactly the same as our other one except it had more flower vases. It also had a spotlight mounted to the windshield that could be turned to look for something at night.

We used the car to sightsee in Michigan. In late summer we started out for New Hampshire. Dad had a wooden box made that bolted on the driver's side running board. This box held food and other things for our trip. This was before motels in most of the country.

We drove through to Virginia and did a lot of sightseeing in the Civil War areas.

174   A STORY TO TELL

Then it was off via the two lane Boston Post Road to Hanover via a short detour to include Maine in our itinerary.

                    *   *   *

In New Hampshire the car was mostly used for short trips. When winter came, it was put up on blocks and the battery was brought into the house to keep it from freezing. While we lived in Hanover my baby sister Genevieve died at about 18 months of age. She had been born with a heart defect that would have been easily repaired in modern times. At the end of the school year Dad decided we would travel back to Seattle across the entire U. S. by car.

I don't recall just what we did with suitcases for the family, but the lunch box did very useful duty. Despite having five in the car, Dad was forever picking up hitchhikers. Somewhere out in the prairie states we saw *a* young country dressed fellow and offered him a ride. I had to move over, and ride crowded in the front seat between Dad and the stranger. From his driver's side, Dad noticed the small feet and from other signs, decided we had picked up a girl. Girl hitchhikers were very unusual and this girl was passing as a boy. She stayed with us for a couple of days before getting out in an unremembered town along the way. My parents even paid for her hotel room while she was with us.

In Sioux Falls, South Dakota we stayed with Dad's brother, our Uncle Archie. Other than staying with Uncle Archie in Sioux Falls, we usually found some kind of hotel to stay in at night.

Coming west from Sioux Falls, we got along fine until we reached Montana. There the dirt roads became "gumbo" when it got wet. After a rain the mud was sticky and slippery. Dad would drive and Mother and I walked along and pushed the gumbo out of the fenders -- using umbrellas. If we didn't push the gumbo out of the fenders, the car would finally stall.

On these occasions, where it was hilly, Mary Belle and Anne got out and walked. I know Mother and I pushed but I don't recall that the girls did. They were too small for the job.

When we would meet sheep going the opposite direction, we would stop and wait for them to pass. Sometimes the bands seemed to be about one mile in length. The band tended to cover the width of the road

MEMORIES OF ANOTHER TIME

plus about 10 feet of shoulder on each side. When we were heading the same way as the sheep, Mother and I would get out the umbrellas and walk ahead of the car and hit the closest sheep on the back, whacking them out of the way. How they would bleat and try to climb the backs of other sheep to get out of the way! I was embarrassed--but Mother was determined. It would sometimes take what seemed to be an hour to get past them.

On one especially slow day we met one band of sheep, and had to swat our way through two others going our own direction. We were racing to get ahead of the thunderstorm we could see darkening the western sky ahead, the roads were terrible, and of course, we were eventually drenched by the onslaught of rain.

Having no need for two cars, when we got to Seattle Dad sold one of the cars.

*   *   *

Dad was a very good driver, and until sometime in the first half of the 1930's Mother did not drive. Unknown to us children, Dad began to teach Mother to drive. One day Mother was backing out of the garage. She put the car in a forward gear rather than reverse. When she let out the clutch the car jumped forward and was stopped by the small curb on the concrete floor. When she hit the front wall of the garage, it was pushed about eight inches forward. Nothing was broken because the footer was not secured to the wall. The nails pulled out at each corner while the wall pivoted on the top edge. The door in that wall still worked.

Dad and I got some timbers and hammers and drove the wall back into place—none the worse. Mother was embarrassed. She didn't like to be teased by Dad or us so she told us she would never drive again.

*   *   *

Growing up on Puget Sound in Seattle, our family frequently spent vacations and outings at the beaches on that Sound and on the Pacific Ocean, as well as beside the many lakes in the area. I always enjoyed the time at the beaches and in the water. However, as natives know and visitors soon discover, the water is unusually cold. The summers are not very long, and the ocean currents flowing down from Alaska, or the snowmelt forming the lakes, make for very cold conditions. Often the water was so cold that my arm would ache if held in it for just a few minutes.

For my part I found that I could run in to the water, play vigorously, and get out but not do much swimming. As a result, I managed to learn to swim well enough to avoid drowning but remained a poor swimmer and never enjoyed diving. Dad enjoyed swimming in the Seattle area and seemed able to withstand the cold.

On one remembered occasion, neighbors invited me to go with them to swim in the Montlake canal below the University. Their dog willingly jumped off a diving platform 15 feet above the water. I only jumped feet first from the canal wall into the water about five feet below, and always dreaded doing so. The dog could swim and dive much better than I could.

At my age nine to ten, while we were at Dartmouth College, Dad took me regularly to the college pool. At thirteen, while we lived in Palo Alto and Dad was teaching at Stanford University, he took me to the Stanford pool. I greatly enjoyed those occasions with Dad. He worked on my sisters to become swimmers and perhaps divers without any success. Finally it came out that he had always wanted to be a champion diver and never had the chance. He wanted his children to fulfill his ambition.

I preferred individual sports and became adept at Ping-Pong. I took up horseshoes because we could play during lunchtime at our high school. I built a horseshoe pit on a vacant lot within our block and would go there after school to practice. In the winter this would be after sunset and near darkness. I learned to throw without seeing the stake and could tell by the sound pretty much where the shoe struck. Finally I got to the point where I got 50% of my throws around the stake. In competition I won a few horseshoe tournaments at our high school and other high schools.

During high school and college I was serious about playing tennis and skiing. I was fairly good at tennis and average at skiing

I enjoyed sports—both as participant and observer. I was about average in most things I tried.

MEMORIES OF ANOTHER TIME

While skiing on Mt. Rainier on the Fourth of July with several friends we were coming down a steep grade when the guys yelled for me to stop. They went over the edge and I was unable to stop and went over with them down a very steep patch of snow and ice. There were bare patches with exposed rock face and all rocks at the bottom. We all hit those rocks with a bang. I broke both skis off, in front and behind my boots, but fortunately was only scratched up a bit. . . . I gave up summer skiing and did only a bit of skiing at graduate school.

*   *   *

In the spring of 1936 I was still a high school student. For many years Mother had student girls living in our house. They lived like members of the family and each worked a couple of hours a day helping Mother with food preparation, ironing, dishes, cleaning and other light house-work. We three older children also had our chores to do. Mine was to wash the clothes and keep the furnace going.

The student girls shared the upstairs front bedroom on the second floor—a room that was intended as the master bedroom. Mom and Dad used the intended den on the first floor as their bedroom.

This work-study arrangement worked to everyone's advantage. It was during the Depression and the girls would not have been able to attend college without some kind of aid. The same girls generally came back yearly until they graduated. We maintained contact with them and their families after they had moved on.

Margaret Runnels, one of the student girls, was a lovely blonde with an engaging personality. She was about three years older than I was. I believe she looked on me as a younger brother. We played Ping-Pong together. She was quite good. On occasions I would help her with her work so she would have time for table tennis.

We were both sports fans; I attended many U. of W. sports activities with my Dad. Aside from an occasional talk, Margaret and I maintained our separate social lives. Her steady boy friend was a football player at Washington State College, in eastern Washington.

In our living room we had a piano and radio-record player that was universally called a "Victrola" (for RCA Victor). We used the Victrola occasionally, but a frequent activity was to sing around the piano as a

178   A STORY TO TELL

family group as Mother played. Aside from talking and reading in the living room, it was mainly used for entertaining guests. Margaret played popular songs on the piano, particularly "Stormy Weather," and got us all singing it.

In my room I had a crystal radio and later a two-tube receiver I had made. In 1932 I talked Dad into buying a large, cabinet-style radio that incidentally included a record player. After that radio was an added entertainment for the family.

I enjoyed listening to the play-by-play of sporting events—mostly football and diagramming the plays. It was the only way to follow the game when you were not in the stadium.

About 1935 or '36 the University of Washington was to play a homecoming game against Washington State—the "cow college"—at Pullman. The U. of W. was highly favored to win. Margaret's loyalty was to the U. of W. except when we were playing WSC. Her boyfriend was a first string backfield star of WSC. She arranged a visit home for Thanksgiving. While there she was also able to attend the game.

Football day, I sat by the radio and diagrammed the game. For the first half Washington was beating WSC soundly. I don't remember the second half and probably stopped diagramming and even listening.

I do remember how excited Margaret was later when she told me WSC had won and her boyfriend Chuck had scored the winning touchdown. Our team was disgraced for the season.

Some time months later in her room, I was talking to Margaret and her roommate, who were lounging on their separate beds. I was sitting in the window seat in the front bay window. It must have been time for Margaret to get ready for work or something so she got up and went into the rather small and crowded clothes closet and shut the door. There was barely room for her to move. We could hear her banging into the door. She emerged in a different dress. Trying to kid with her, I said it wasn't necessary for her to close the door of the closet. She replied, "It wouldn't bother me but your Mother would be very upset."

She then sat by me on the window seat and told me her story about the big U of W—WSC homecoming game.

She had been seated in some special seat for team guests. At half time the teams went to their locker rooms to for a brief rest while preparing for the second half. Chuck, her boyfriend, came out and asked

MEMORIES OF ANOTHER TIME

Margaret to come with him. He took her to the coach and left them. The coach told her the team was in the shower room and asked, "Would you be willing to walk into the shower room? Perhaps the shock would wake up the team." She agreed to do so. The coach had not specified how she should act, but she decided to go in NUDE. It did energize the team. And that was her story of how her boyfriend and his team pulled off the upset of the year!

Now I know how Samson got the will to pull down the Temple.

*　　　　　*　　　　　*

By 1937 I had begun to drive a little. Our 1924 car seemed out-of-date to me. I began to lobby for a new car. Dad was not much for this, but Packard came out in 1937 with a Depression response of a car called the Packard 120 (inches of wheelbase). It cost about half of what a "real" Packard would cost and was nearly competitive with Buick and Oldsmobile, etc. in price. I thought this car represented a good value.

After some months, Dad went with me to the agency and looked at and drove the car. Somewhat to my surprise, my rock solid Scotsman father bought the car in the height of the Depression.

For some time after Dad bought the Packard he hesitated to drive it. Mainly he walked to the University, but when he drove, I found out that he was parking in the student lot, not in his accustomed place. It was obvious that he didn't want his associates to know that "The Dean" had bought a new car—and an extravagant one, in his view.

*　　　　　*　　　　　*

In my younger years I had little interest in grade and high school classes I was forced to attend. As a result, and with few exceptions, I did rather poorly.

In 1936-37 I was a U of W freshman. Attending the U of W I was on my own. There I did well enough to achieve a cum laude ranking, much to Dad 's surprise. Even with that achievement I still found it somewhat difficult to be known as the son of a Dean.Engineering students were required to take two or more courses in Business and Economics. Dad was well known at the school so most of my school associates knew who my Dad was. During my growing up years we were introduced to most of the faculty and graduate students because we entertained them regularly. They knew me on a first name basis. I did not want to take a class that Dad taught. Being the son of a professor was always a pain in the butt in grade and high schools. As a result, for me there was little attraction to being called Dr. Preston.

*   *   *

The University of Washington varsity crew won the 1936 Olympics and took great pride in its nationally recognized racing crews and its coaches.

In the fall of 1936 as a freshman at the University I rowed on the 150-pound crew. Talk about tall and thin! That meant always less than 150-pounds. I was near the upper limit in size and could hold my own. My endurance and general fitness was good enough that I could jog all day up and down the hills and mountains.

We started out rowing barges and then graduated to smaller and lighter shells in at least two steps. It was hard – especially in rough waves. If you didn't keep in unison, you either hit the back of the rower ahead of you or you got your back hit – and that hurt. If you "caught a crab", the oar could lift you right out of the boat and into the water. Considering everything, it was great in good weather but not fun in the rain.

I had to walk from the upper campus down to the crew house and back every day and that took time. It also complicated scheduling.

During the summer of 1937 I worked as a day laborer in the Cascades and gained about 50 lbs. Back in school I was slotted into the JV crew but even there I was on the small side compared to some of the farm boys, etc. My size and the problem of combining crew practice with a required surveying course meant that I had to choose one. I dropped crew.

With my interest focused on engineering, I was doing well enough that I received several offers of graduate scholarships including a scholarship award from Cal Tech and the Massachusetts Institute of Technology. The latter was considered one of, if not the best, engineering school in the country. Just as importantly, it was located in Boston,

MEMORIES OF ANOTHER TIME

across the continent from Seattle. There I knew I would be on my own and no longer known as the 'son of the Dean'.

In part due to my earlier experiences, I had an aversion to getting a Doctor's degree although I ended up doing the equivalent amount of work for my Master's degree. Although it made no difference to my technical qualifications, I would have had a definite advantage with the more prestigious degree. At the time it was not important to an engineer unless I wanted to teach or work for the government. Worse, I was deficient in German for my masters and would have had to take another language for the Doctorate. And I hated languages that were of little use to me. I did write a doctorate level thesis but would have had to take at least one more year of courses as well as pass orals. Doing so seemed out of reach under the other restraints imposed on me. It was only later in my professional career that I found that some positions that I was professionally qualified for were behind an unseen but closed door that could have been opened with a Doctorate. .

CHAPTER 19
THE APPEAL OF PHYSICS

By
Henry Fairbank

I WAS BORN in Lewistown, Montana, which is right in the center of the state. I lived in Hobson, which is 25 miles away by a dirt road. Hobson had a population of about 250 people.

Dad started out as a salesman for the Washington-Crosby Milling Co. in Minneapolis. In 1917 the U.S. was preparing to join with the WW I allied forces in Europe. Wheat flour was a really booming business. Desiring to be an independent businessman, Dad was encouraged to start a flourmill in Hobson, Montana. There, with the help of investors, he started a mill called Hobson Flour.

Married and with two children, Dad was not drafted for service in the war. He built a house in Hobson in anticipation of bringing mother and the two children, Sister Elizabeth and Brother Bill. The house was ready to move into when it caught fire and burned to the ground. Hobson had no real fire department. So he rebuilt the house.

My mother's father, the son of a minister couple, was vice president of a railroad in the mid-west. He was successful. Mother, the middle of three daughters, came from a business family. She grew up in Minneapolis where the family ran a retail store.

As a result of her mother's father going to Colorado during the gold rush and successfully founding a couple of mining companies there, her mother's family became comfortably well off. They bought a home in Minneapolis and traveled in comfortable societies. She went to Wells

College in upper New York near Syracuse. Dad met her when he had come at Christmas time with a friend to her home.

When mother joined Dad in Montana she had no experience in small town life. She had to learn to do her own cooking. She canned everything out of the garden that we needed for the winter. Starting with me, three of the children were born in Montana. As the mill did OK we had a sort of Nanny, a maiden lady, who helped raise the kids. Mother did a lot of the work herself. Father was gone a lot of the time because although president of the milling company, he was also the sales force.

I was born two days before the end of WW I on Nov 9th 1918, about a year after the family first moved to Hobson. The day I was born was a false Armistice. The papers were full of the news that the Armistice had been signed but it hadn't been. My birth was registered with the Bureau of Records in Montana on a form filled out by mother. She spelled my name Farrbank. The birth certificate came back with an S on it. That caused me a little trouble later on to get that fixed.

Hobson, originally populated by homesteaders, was the center of a wheat and sheep growing area, many of the original homesteaders were still there. Their children were essentially running the place at that time.

We were very good friends of a wheat farmer who lived near by. They had five children and we ended up having five children. Every Sunday after church we would go out to their place and have a wonderful chicken dinner with home made ice cream. The ice cream was made from their own cream separated by their separator from the milk from their own cows.

One of the joys was to go swimming in an irrigation ditch. Sometimes we would get to go up in the barn and play in the hay, jump around and have a great time. Eventually we got old enough to try to fish in the largest stream there. It was about three feet across. We had a wonderful time growing up there. We had a very enjoyable childhood.

Bill and I had a great time collecting gopher tails for which we could get a penny a piece. We trapped them with the old-fashioned spring trap. It was kind of a brutal thing. Weasel tails were ten cents. We never found any weasels. We would come back with our pockets full of gopher tails much to my mother's delight.

MEMORIES OF ANOTHER TIME

We went to a small four-room school that serviced eight grades and seemed huge. There was a little hill that in the wintertime we used to slide down on our Flexible Flyers all the way to the railroad tracks.

Things went along pretty well. In 1927 my father bought the flour-mill, with help from borrowed money that was available in Lewistown. It was very successful in 1928. We moved to Lewistown and then the Depression hit. Hobson Flour and Milling Co. was devoid of any business and had to default loans and went bankrupt.

Dad had a good friend from Amherst College who was general agent for National Life Insurance in Seattle. He moved to Seattle and got a job selling insurance. Dad was a very loyal alumnus of Amherst College as were my forebears. Grandfather and great grandfather also went to Amherst. We kids had become very loyal Amherst people who knew all the songs and everything like that.

When father went to Seattle seeking work, mother was left with all the children. Suddenly she had to become responsible for doing everything for herself. She worked very hard and was a tremendous supporter for her children and the family. She had an absolutely marvelous sense of humor.

I was ten when we moved to Lewistown. Our economic situation had changed from good to bad.

We stayed another year in Lewistown so my older sister could finish highschool. When we finally followed my father to Seattle we moved in with Francis Foster Powell, a very good friend of my father. The seven of us moved in with the five of them in their home in Laurelhurst.

We lived with them for our first summer after moving to Seattle. By that time Dad had lived with them for a year.

Now that I was twelve I was given lots of opportunity to make my own way. I had paper routes; it was one of these throwaway papers. I got a great deal of fun out of it.

It was a marvelous summer there. At the end of the summer Francis Powell's bank went bankrupt. As a result he was out of a job and had to give up the house.

We found a house nearby at the low end of Laurelhurst, which my father bought for $4,200. My grandmother, who lived in Minneapolis, was kinda funding us during that period. We were not dirt poor but we were scrounging pretty much. Dad was selling insurance but that wasn't a very high priority for anybody at that time. He worked very hard. He was a very bright, very hardworking, very nice man who, over time, became very well known and prominent in Seattle. Eventually he made a reasonable success in the insurance business before he retired.

After his bank went bust, Francis Powell moved down next door to us. His son Addie was my best friend. When his father died suddenly that left his mother to support the family. She was a very active woman, became a public servant and served as Seattle City councilman. She was just a marvelous lady. The only real advice I ever had about the things every boy should know came from her. She didn't tell me much but she was just a great person. We were fortunate to have such nice friends all our life. For the most part though, my best friends have always been my own family members. This has been a tremendous blessing.

My father and my mother were arch Republicans. They thought Franklin Roosevelt was a bad man with divorces in his family. Basically they weren't sympathetic to the New Deal. Dad was an ardent supporter of Alf Landon and while I was still at Whitman, Wendell Wilkie. I began to be converted over to the democratic view when I went away from home.

As my father struggled to keep food on the table, mother was the efficient and caring source of strength to all of us. Dad was out almost every evening.

Advanced education was something we took for granted; we never considered anything else. It was something we knew we were going to do. Mother had a Masters degree from Wells College. Both parents read a lot. When we were young they read to us. We played all kinds of games as family activities.

Our life was partly centered in a small Methodist church. Later on we were Presbyterian. Eventually we ended up where my fore-bearers were as Congregationalists. Dad was a superintendent of Sunday school. Sunday night after supper we would have a family songfest. I enjoy singing and have sung in church choirs all my life. We learned almost all the church hymns sitting around singing in the evening in my own home.

My whole childhood was very much family centered. While we fought like most normal kids do we stopped short of killing each other.

MEMORIES OF ANOTHER TIME

Bill and I fought but he was bigger and older. Even so it was pretty even going. We slept in a double bed so we fought over the blankets. Saturday morning we had to make the beds. It would take us all day. In the meantime we would play some baseball, play dice, and learn how to juggle.

Mother had such a marvelous sense of humor. For example when Bill and Jane married mother dutifully packed their bags and sewed up the pajama legs with rice in them. They got up to the Olympic peninsula being careful not to let anyone know they were newly married and low and behold, rice spilled all over the place. Jane spent the night picking up the rice. Or so we were told.

I was in the Boy Scouts and had lots of good experiences there. One summer when I was 12 we went to Camp Parsons. A highlight was the seven-mile hike up the mountain. Our sleeping bags were a bunch of army blankets pinned together with safety pins. We learned all kinds of good songs that delight 12 and 13 year olds. It was a wonderful experience.

At home we played lots of games. We played charades where we acted out various things. My parents had a Ma Jong set and we played cards a lot. Card playing was a sin to the Methodists.

When I lived in Laurelhurst as a teenager we went out regularly to play in the streets. Kick the can was a favorite game. That was a kind of hide and seek thing. Then of course on Halloween we did a variety of bad things. Most of it was not really destructive. We would throw the master switches on the porches of people's houses to leave them in the dark. One time some of our engineer friends found a master switch that put most of Laurelhurst in the dark. Sometimes there were roadblocks put in front of the bus.

Things were such that all of us had to work. Bill and I were essentially self-supporting from the age of twelve on. I had 12 lawn jobs during the summer, for which I got about twenty-five cents per lawn. They got their money's worth. I delivered the Seattle P.I. every morning. I sold everything under the sun.

One summer I started out selling Saturday Evening Posts on a crew. The crew leader took a group of five or six boys in his car to outlying districts in Seattle. As a result, we got to know Seattle very well. I enjoyed that; it was a great experience. We went to all these outlying districts, north, south, east, west. We even went up to Skykomish. We went door to door down the streets selling the Post for five cents. For doing this we were paid fifteen cents an hour. We worked about an eight-hour day. If we had a real good day we would sell as many as four or five Posts. Not everybody did that well. I learned a little bit about economics because the Curtis publishing Co. was trying to fulfill advertising contracts and they had to legitimately sell the magazines. This was what they were doing to do it.

In the middle of the summer the NRA [National Recovery Act] was formed by the Roosevelt administration. It had a minimum wage provision of thirty-two and one half cents an hour in it. When that became effective our wages went up to that amount. We were paid up for the rest of the week and then we were fired. Our magazine selling had been a loss leader kind of selling.

I took up the piano, didn't get too far, and then broke the neck of the violin! We couldn't afford to get it fixed so I just had to quit and go out and play football and other things in the streets. There were some accusations regarding my accident with the violin!

I was very interested in sports. I was never big enough or good enough to do anything until I became a junior in high school. Then I started to grow a little bit. I was good at track and field.

I did collect stamps. We had a lot of stamps because my fore bearers? grew up in India. There were volumes of stamps that various family members collected but that didn't last.

The only jobs available were in selling. I got a job selling house numbers. I only sold two house numbers. I sold one to my parents, one to my parent's friends and I essentially had to buy one as a demonstrator.

For a couple years I had a great deal of success selling real silk hosiery. By seven o'clock in the morning a bunch of highschool boys, I think, went down to Second Avenue to a second floor loft where Real Silk Hosiery was located. We had a pep meeting put on by the Assistant Manager in which he went over various things with us and took our orders. The culmination was for the general manager to come in and announce leaders of the day. He sent us on our way charging out the door. Part of this was a religious revival kind of thing. We sang songs that I know to this day. Then we got on the streetcar and went back to our assigned territory in Seattle.

MEMORIES OF ANOTHER TIME

I actually won an all paid trip back to the mills in Indianapolis as the leading new recruit in the western region. The reason I won it was because my father, a very supportive person, gave me lots of help. When he saw I had a chance he told all his friends and relatives they probably wanted some socks. There were a lot of orders that came in with some assistance from family.

Dad used to travel a lot when he had the milling company so he arranged for the train tickets for the trip to Indianapolis. When I got on the train I found I had a berth. I was very well aware of the economics of the situation. I found out from the conductor how much it was costing me to sleep in a berth. It was costing me a week's wages, a lot of money to sleep one night. I thought that was a pretty poor deal. I got the ticket changed to a coach and got a refund on the Pullman.

With that money I went back to Washington DC and to New York, a wonderful experience. To me, Washington DC was the most wonderful place I had ever seen. There, I virtually fell in love with beautiful cousin of mine. She was of my age but eventually I realized it was a hopeless situation.

With all that selling experience I learned something else. There were a lot of things I didn't want to do the rest of my life. When I got into physics later, I thought, "Gee, this is a real racket".

Our family was very close. We did a lot of things together. We enjoyed each other. I was shocked a few years ago to learn that my sisters thought the two boys in the family were especially privileged. That our parents gave them all kinds of special considerations. I never perceived anything of that when I was growing up.

I was ready to go to college and had accepted a scholarship for two hundred dollars at Whitman. The rest of my expenses were essentially taken care of by working although I did have to borrow from the Hickman fund in Seattle.

Bill, who was two years older than me, had come to Whitman one year earlier. He had taken an extra year to get money to go to college.

My sister Elizabeth had come over three years earlier. She got some help from our grandmother. Women weren't nearly as privileged as men in those days as far as work was concerned. She was a great role model for all of us because she loved Whitman. All of her stories of her Tri Delts made me a thoroughgoing Tri Delt by the time I went to

College. I was also a converted TKE because my brother had pledged Teke despite the fact our father was an ardent Beta.

I have two younger sisters, Ruth and Janet. Later both came to Whitman and both married spouses from Whitman.

I came and lived in third floor Lyman House with other people who were on scholarship. It was a very privileged thing. Bob Hosakawa was in my class. I mention Bob because after the war started in 1942 he was sent to a Japanese relocation camp in Idaho.

I fell in love with Whitman. It was a wonderful place. I had no idea what I wanted to major in. I had Paul Jackson in English. That was a wonderful experience. I took a French course that was difficult. I was never any good in languages. The main language that was helpful for me was the Latin I took in highschool. It was very helpful in many ways. Later on when I did a lot of traveling I dearly would have liked to have known French better.

In highschool track I ran the quarter mile and the half-mile. At Whitman I immediately turned out for track. It was a great experience. I really enjoyed that.

I played intramural football and was pretty good at it. I had a certain amount of speed relative to my fellow amateurs but I was near sighted. I couldn't see anything so if I went out for a pass I had a hard time being sure which was our man. We made up our plays in the huddle. Bill and I both played regular eleven man tackle football using discarded uniforms from the school team. The game was changed to six-man football when it was discovered they didn't have enough uniforms.

In six-man football everybody is a star. Everybody is eligible for the ball. For me as a track person it was perfect because speed is an advantage. We weren't very good at tackling and blocking. It was sorta touch football that sometimes ended up with a tackle.

Academically, I came to Whitman College not knowing what I was going to major in. I enjoyed everything I was doing. My brother had a good friend who became an optometrist. Bill and I thought that was a good field. We liked economics but didn't do much with it.

In my sophomore year Carol Zimmerman and wife came to Whitman. He was a very bright 26-year-old who had gotten a master's degree from Duke University but had not gotten his Ph.D. yet. He had been teaching at George Washington University where the stars at that time were two refugees from Europe, George Keller and George Gamoff.

Within weeks of coming to Whitman he had people deciding they wanted to be physics majors. I had him for a course and he opened my eyes to how exciting physics could be. This was a time when the electron was being discovered. The positron was discovered not too long ago. The accelerators were beginning to be built so there was an excitement about the field with all kinds of mysteries that needed to be solved. Zimmerman expressed that excitement to all of us in a very real way.

Bill and Jane Davenport, his girlfriend, were chemistry majors. Caught up in the Zimmerman enthusiasm, they changed from chemistry to physics majors. That added an extra year of schooling for them. In the 4 years Zimmerman was at Whitman I think there were twenty students who went on to graduate school in physics.

I majored in physics. Both Bill and I were lab assistants. We might have even been paid a little bit for it, which was very necessary. Bill and friend Art Nelson lived in the house of Zimmerman because they couldn't afford anything otherwise. They did some nominal jobs like mowing the lawn.

In my senior year I decided to go on to graduate school. Zimmie as we called him, wrote letters and recommended several places to apply. I got offers at all the places I applied to including Yale. I went there as a teaching assistant. Yale was a great place. I had an incoming class of five people.

I quickly learned there were a lot of smart people in the world who knew a lot more about a lot of things than I ever did. My background in mathematics was quite limited. I had to take some extra course work there. The confidence gained at Whitman allowed me to succeed.

My own children were frustrated in that regard but my grandchildren came along. My granddaughter was stroke of the Brown crew for four years. She majored in neuro-science and has now almost finished medical school but athletics were a tremendous thing for her.

Sister's Elizabeth, Ruth and Janet all graduated from Whitman College. It was a time of life when girls got degrees but they didn't go on to careers. It was the expectation that wives would become mothers and homemakers.

Janet married Reg Thompson who was a local Walla Walla product. He was a star athlete as a baseball player.

Ruth married fellow Teke Bob Roberts. Bob Roberts was a star basket-ball player. His mother and father were highly motivated people for educa-tion. He was an avid reader. He read prodigiously but as far as Whitman was concerned, he really majored in my sister. When it came time for an exam he opened the book to see what was there and did better than satis-factory work. He frustrated some of his friends because he made it seem it wasn't necessary to study hard. Bob was so able and a very fine historian as was his two twin younger brothers. David and Clayton. Both had doctorates and both became history professors in nineteenth history America history.

When he got to his senior year he looked around and wondered what he was going to do next. He recognized his friend Ruth wasn't interested in being a basketball coach's wife and decided he ought to prepare himself for something more serious. He started studying for his comprehensive senior exams and did very well.

When he graduated he went immediately into the Navy. When he came back from the service in 1945 he was admitted to the University of Chicago.

Eventually he went on to become a history professor and head of the Social Sciences in San Bernardino State College. He was picked as one of three people to plan the new college of San Bernardino State. They spent a year or more deciding on curriculum, what participation in athletics, and so forth. It turned out to be quite a successful venture and has now turned out to be a large place.

Although careers didn't appear to be an option for the female gradu-ates of Whitman, in later years my sister Elizabeth had a career in writ-ing and sister Ruth worked to help support the family working in a de-partment store in San Bernardino. Sister Janet became Administrative Assistant to the Superintendent of Schools in her district.

There is no question in my mind these girls could have had distin-guished academic careers in anything they wanted to. Or careers in other professions.

My wife, who was a wonderful mother, had her hands full with three children. When they finally graduated and left home she followed a music career and became minister of music at her church and did a wonderful job.

My three children, two girls and a boy, are all career people. Their husbands have their separate careers.

CHAPTER 20
SUMMER ADVENTURES IN IOWA

By
Frank Steele Preston

LET ME tell you a little bit about working in Iowa in 1939. We hadn't come out of the Depression yet. I had worked the summer of 1937 in a construction camp in Washington as a laborer. Jobs were hard to get. In 1938 I couldn't find anything to do so I went to summer school at the University of Washington.

In 1939 I was looking around when Uncle Otis contacted me and asked if I would like to come to Iowa and do some electrical wiring. I had done a few things that he knew about and I agreed to come. Uncle Otis had hired an electrical contractor to wire up his two farms, one in Tipton and one in Keota.

He had bought these farms in the depths of the Depression. He had saved a lot of money so he was able to buy half-million dollar farms for under one hundred thousand dollars. He wanted to build up the farms and wasn't interested in making money off them. He had tenant farmers on these farms who were raising cattle or growing alfalfa or various things that would improve the productivity of the soil. They got the money from selling the pigs or the cows. Uncle Otis was not trying to turn a profit. He thought if he built them up that he would have something. Otis was not a farmer but he knew farming.

The electrical contractor Uncle Otis had picked to wire these farms hired me. The REA (Rural Electrification Authority) was building power lines that went along the farm roads.

The farmers thought the electricity was going to change their crops — oh, they didn't want the change. Most of them didn't want their houses wired either. But the REA was going to get the wire in there and it was up to the individual farms to do the wiring. They were wiring the farm areas whether the farmer wanted them there or not. It was going to be a year or more before the roads in front of Otis' farms were actually electrified.

Otis wanted to be ready so I was doing the rough in wiring of the houses and a little on the barns. The electrical contractor was going to come in, finish up, and put in the fixtures when the power was finally available. I got zero supervision from the contractor. I guess he had enough confidence that he could repair anything I did that he didn't like. I suppose he knew I knew the code and had some experience. Also, he knew he could fix up any problem I got into.

I got zero instructions from Otis as to what he wanted, other than doing what the farm wife or farmer wanted. I would ask them what they wanted. I was used to the houses in the city where we had a few outlets in each room. They were used to visiting a farm friend of theirs who had electricity who had a light on the porch and one in each room with pull chains and similar simple wiring. I knew that wasn't enough. I kept asking them what they wanted and I would embellish it.

The farmer wanted two things: lights in the barn and the motor for the pump instead of the windmill. He didn't care whether the house was wired or not. After twisting his arm he said it would be nice to plug in the radio. The farmer's wife wanted a place where she could plug in an iron. She didn't want anything else but lights and an iron!

This was an old house and not very well constructed – plaster walls and not much, if any, insulation. I had to work from a dug cellar and an unfinished, small attic. I had to snake the wires into this existing house. This house was built before they used the box frame construction. You couldn't figure where the studs were. Vertical walls went from the basement to the attic in one piece. There was no easy way to get to places.

Uncle Otis had hired three or four other people. Two young men were called fencers and tilers. They put fences around the fields and dug ditches and put in drain tiles in the valleys. One of the men was a carpenter of sorts and had the necessary tools. If I needed a floorboard taken up, he could cut the tongue and groove boards and lift it out while

MEMORIES OF ANOTHER TIME

I put the wiring in, then he put it back down. I didn't have to do a lot of the construction work. None of them would get near the wiring.

The toughest work of all was working in the attic. When it was 90° outside it was unbearable in the attic. It was easily 140° to 150° up in there. Nobody had been in there since the house was built 60 years or so before. It was not really dusty, but it was covered with fine black grime – a very, very fine powder. You would get it on yours hands and you could hardly wash it off. It got in your clothes and was incredibly difficult to get out.

Of course there was no power so I had to work with a gasoline lantern. To do the wiring, I was sitting bent over working in up to 150° heat and being bathed in the heat from the gas lamp. I sweated like you can't believe. The sweat would run down over my eyes and be dripping off my nose so bad I couldn't even see. It was miserable work.

To compound my problems, the code required that you solder all joints. So I had a gasoline-heated blowtorch with a soldering iron putting out more heat. I'd be trying to solder with the water rolling off my hands on to the soldering iron and making steam. I was bathed in the steam. I wore glasses and I couldn't see because of the steam on my glasses. If I wiped my face it was black with the grime.

At that time the code required that you tape the solder joints with rubber to keep the water out of the joint. The rubber would deteriorate and crack so you had to put friction tape on the outside of the rubber tape to protect the rubber from the air (ozone). Friction and rubber tape doesn't stick when wet. The water pouring down my fingers and getting the friction tape wet meant I had one horrible time. The junction boxes were small. You had to be very careful you didn't make a big fat glob of tape so that you couldn't get all the joints in the box. It had to be carefully done. I had a miserable time.

My clothes just got black. By the end of the week I could take off the pants and stand them up from the sweat and the grime that had solidified in the pants. My Grandmother had volunteered to wash my work clothes. She had two washing machines that Otis had bought her, so I thought that would work out. On the Fourth of July holiday weekend, I saw her washing my dirty pants with a scrub-board out on the back lawn. I asked why she didn't use one of the washing machines. She replied that you could get clothes cleaner by hand. She said she used the machine with the wringer (not the one with the spin dry) because her hands were getting weak. (She was 76 at the time.)

The farm lady raised chickens and sold the eggs to get house money. By the way, I milked cows for my board and room at this farmhouse. I would get up at four in the morning and milk cows for a while, and then I would go do my wiring. The day would proceed like that. She would feed us around noon. Then we all took about a half-hour to relax because it was pretty tiring work.

When Otis bought the farm it was overrun with mice and rats. The mice were the most troublesome. When I had the ditch dug for the pig feeding floor there would be two or three mice down in that hole in the morning that had just fell in there in the night. The farmer would get cats from the Humane Society in town — two or three at a time. If you wonder why he needed so many, they were eating so many mice the cats were dying after four or five weeks. He needed to keep replacing them. He had about thirty or forty cats at a time. They lived in the barn. At milking time we would place a garbage can lid upside down and fill it with milk. About thirty cats would try to get in to this milk. That was about the only time you saw them in any quantity. They were kinda secretive, running through the barn. I was able to catch them one at a time. There were clippers the farmer had for clipping horses hair. I learned that after lunch I could place the cat lying upside down on my lap and clip their hair. The cats would struggle and fight it until I began working with the hair and then lie quietly. I started with the tail and would cut all the fur off the tail except a little tuft at the end of the tail. Then I cut all the fur off the body except for a little piece around their feet and left a shaggy front so they looked like lions —- little tiny lions. They were neat looking cats. Each day I would catch one and cut all the hair off. They were happy. They were running around the farm, all these little lions. Again, neighbors would come just to see these cats. That was the way I spent my half-hour at lunch.

This farmer's wife was raising chickens. I had read enough about chickens to know there was a pecking order but I didn't really know very much about a pecking order. I got the biggest rooster, an all-white one with a nice tail and with all the trimmings roosters have. I took him down to the fifty gallon drum and dipped him in tail first so the entire tail was red —- nothing else. Here I had this beautiful white rooster with

MEMORIES OF ANOTHER TIME

a nice red tail. Of course, all the red trimmings on a rooster are part of his sex appeal to the hens. So he had either more or less of it, I wasn't sure which it was.

I let him out into the chicken yard with all the other chickens. He looked like a regular chicken except the tail no longer stood up but stuck straight out in the back. He was a streamlined chicken. He had no appeal to the other male chickens. They didn't like that at all. They started chasing him. They never really chased him fast enough to catch him; they just kept him moving. One would chase him five minutes or so and stop; then another rooster would chase him. At the end of the day that poor rooster was dead. They had just run him ragged. I felt terrible about that. I compensated the woman for the loss of her rooster.

Fourth of July came and we had fireworks. When it got dark we had Roman candles and that sort of fireworks. I saved enough firecrackers that the chickens could also celebrate the Fourth of July. I lit some firecrackers and threw them into the chicken house. I knew it wasn't going to hurt the chickens. There was a big explosion and all the chickens fell off their roosts. It was pitch black dark in there. The hens couldn't see to fly up in the dark. They would fly up and knock others down. All night long hens would try to climb up to the roost in the dark; fly up, hit another on the roost and down they would come. They made noise all night long. I was entranced with that. That was great sport.

The farmer had been raising Guinea hens. Those are the most miserable things to have on a farm. They make enough noise that the neighbors living a mile away don't like Guinea hens. They won't roost in a hen house –- they roost in trees. They were roosting in the fruit trees across the road on the farm.

I went around to the trees to help the Guinea hens celebrate the Fourth of July. There was a big bang and they kept falling out of the trees like ripe apples. They too made noise all night –- that was great. They wouldn't lay for a time after that so for several days we had no hen's eggs and no Guinea eggs. So I compensated the lady for Guinea eggs, too. That's the way the summer went. It was pretty good stuff. By the way, I'm sad to admit I was 21, and somehow my normally good adult behavior slipped a little.

I would spend five or six days at the farm, then come back to Cedar Rapids which was 30 to 40 miles away for Saturday or Sunday or both.

Otis had recently completed his house — built in the old fashioned way. He wanted several things done electrically. By the way, I did it free. I know that is what Otis expected and I was happy to do it. It wasn't part of my week's work. It was something I did because I enjoyed it and he expected it. If I had given him a bill, he would have paid me, I'm sure.

Anyhow, he wanted a light on the porch in the back. They had enclosed the porch for a breakfast and sitting area. When built, this porch had a light on it so the former porch light was now inside. He wanted a light out by the porch entrance steps and he wanted a light on the corner of the windmill (which they retained when the house was built) so it would light the way coming from the car into the house. Then he wanted a couple other things in the basement wired.

The electrical contractor had told him it was impossible to do what he wanted. I think that perhaps it was impossible to do it the way Otis wanted it because I don't think Otis wanted anybody tearing up his house. What Otis wanted was a switch at the kitchen door to turn on the light on the windmill and another for the light over the steps. The kitchen door was hung from a solid brick wall about twelve inches thick. It sat on the basement concrete wall also about twelve inches thick.

There was no way you could get into that wall from below or above or anywhere else. I was stewing around about this. Ray heard me talking to Emily. He said, "You cut two holes in the wall at the top and bottom and I'll drill a hole between the two." I thought that was a fair deal.

I could have put two switches in a small single gang box but I decided I wanted a double gang box so I would have room to work in this terrible location. I cut the two holes about 4" square and about 5" deep. I cut them with a cold chisel, just breaking the bricks. I had two holes about 50 inches apart, one in the kitchen and one in the wall below the floor I went about my work doing all the rest of the wiring Otis wanted.

Ray went to his shop. He was down there the better part of two days. Then he came back up and started work drilling the hole. He didn't want or need any help; he did the hole drilling. He just wanted to know from me on how big a hole and where should it go.

He had made what was essentially a tiny drill press that would hold a drill. It had a pulley around the drill holder. He could put the press inside the hole and turn something to move the drill up. I don't remember exactly the details. It would feed the drill up so he could drill an inch or so. Then he inserted a threaded piece on to the drill end and do another inch or so. He had all these little pieces and a carbide drill.

He drilled a hole maybe 3/4" in diameter. That was big enough for me to run all the wires in. I didn't need any conduit or anything. He used an electric drill on the outside with a belt and pulley arrangement to this thing inside and it all worked fine.

The fact he could drill it at all didn't surprise me. What surprised me is that he could drill it straight enough so that he would hit the hole above and not come out in the front or miss it to the back or to either side. He came pretty close to where he wanted it.

I put the metal boxes in the wall and we plastered it up and covered it with a switch plate. They were pleased as punch they could light the light out by the driveway and the light at the steps. From a workmanship standpoint, we didn't have to do any painting or any patching of the plaster in the kitchen. I thought that was a remarkable piece of craftsmanship. Ray built this special drill and drilled a blind hole.

There are all kinds of electrical drills available that you could drill in a small space and by bending the drill, if you were very careful, you could probably stay within the wall. But you can't go very far.

If you had asked an electrician to do that he would chop the brick all the way to make a groove. Then he would put in the wires and plaster it solid. That's the way they do the houses in Mexico; they put them up with concrete and then they go in and chop grooves for the wire. Otis didn't want me to chop into his wall!

Another thing Ray did that was kind of interesting. It showed considerable ingenuity. It was kind of typical of Ray that his ideas were not marketable. When they built that house, the carpenters fitted everything perfectly. In the winter all the doors would stick.

Ray went in and carefully planed down the doors so they no longer stuck. You have got to give them three coats of paint on the edges that had been cut. Ray did that and a year later; they stuck again. He did it a second time with considerable reluctance. He decided that was the last time he was going to do that.

He went to his shop and made some hinges. They were conventional looking hinges but they did what European hinges do that are made for cabinets. You could adjust them in or out, up or down, both ways. He made these hinges but they were not adjustable like the European ones.

He had taken the hinge pin out and made it eccentric so you could turn them. The screws that held the hinges against the door and jam fit into bored holes and through washers that were eccentric. He could place the hinge position where he wanted it and then place the washer where it was needed. The screw would go in the wood and retain the position.

He made all these special hinges, for many of the doors in the house. They were made starting from regular brass hinges. Nobody was going to buy those hinges because they were too expensive. There must have been eight extra parts, at least, for every hinge. Of course, with mass production the machining wouldn't add too much. But with all the extra parts, the first carpenter who tried it would say, "I'm not going to waste my time with this".

When I got ready to leave Iowa, I planned spending the rest of the summer traveling to go see both the New York and San Francisco World's Fairs. When I left, I went to Iowa City to catch the train and that day happened to be my birthday.

I was born in Iowa City, moved away when I was 6 weeks old and this was sort of the first time I was back in Iowa City other than to drive through it going someplace. So I left Iowa City July 30th, 1939 on my 21st birthday, which I thought was kind of remarkable.

CHAPTER 22
PREPARING FOR WAR

By
Robert H. Wells

I HADN'T CONSIDERED the possibility of college until one day early in June that summer of 1939. On that day a young man named Pat Kilby stopped by our home, introduced himself and told me he had seen me run the hurdles at the District track meet. As a recent graduate of Whitman College in Walla Walla, a place I had never heard of, he felt the Track coach at Whitman would be interested in talking to me. I pointed out there was no way that I could afford to go to College but of course, would be happy to talk to the coach. A day for a visit was agreed on. In selling the idea of college to me, Pat tried to encourage me by talking about scholarship and work opportunities. I didn't see my grades as being of scholarship caliber but agreed I was certainly willing to work.

On the day Bill Martin, the coach of the Whitman College track team came to town to meet me I had been working for the city, washing down the paved main street with a fire hose. This was normally a two-man job. It required dragging the hose to a fire main and hooking up the hose. Then with the water at full force I needed to drag the hose down the street while washing all debris into the gutters. I ended up washing the accumulated material to the end of the block. Our city maintenance man, after observing I could handle the job by myself, went off to other chores.

After finishing the street cleaning, I went home for lunch, still stripped to the waist. I arrived there in time to greet the coach. After

201

demonstrating a few stretching exercises for him he apparently decided I looked like a hurdler. He also expressed some interest in my football and basketball playing experience but indicated his primary interest was in athletes for the track team he coached. After checking out my high school grades, he asked if I would like to attend Whitman. I really hadn't expected an offer, in fact, had given no thought to going to College, rather, had expected to join the Civilian Conservation Corps, about the only paying job I knew of after summer haying. However, following a discussion of my financial situation, basically an estimate of what I could hope to earn during the summer, he promised me help with the tuition and enough work to pay all my expenses.

Mother was thrilled with the thought of my going to college, something we had not considered almost until that moment. She encouraged me to accept what sounded like a wonderful offer. Practically speaking, this offer was in effect an offer for full time employment. Without question, it did seem a better job opportunity than the CCC's.

Work seemed more plentiful that summer of 1939, whether because I was now a seventeen-year-old adult or as a result of recovery from the depression, or a combination of both, I'm not sure, but I had a fairly busy summer. Summer jobs began with the two-week National Guard camp held near Seaside, Oregon shortly after school was out. At one dollar a day that meant my summer earnings would be off to a good start.

Older fellows in the unit had talked of camp as an exciting opportunity for new adventure. After getting into our uniforms, we were driven to La Grande. There we boarded a train that was to take us to an area near the town of Seaside, Oregon where there was a large, permanent National Guard camp.

Many of our group had been to the camp before but for me, everything was new and different. We were assigned to a large WW I tent mounted on a wood frame with a wooden floor. Immediately we arrived, we were given canvas cots wrapped in a bundle and handed a mattress ticking, a pillow and two blankets. Our first act was to assemble the cot and fill the mattress ticking with straw. Not so bad, our Boy Scout beds on the ground had been much worse.

After getting set up in our tent space, we had a few minutes to explore the area before our first meal in the mess hall, an unusual expe-

MEMORIES OF ANOTHER TIME

rience for me, as I had never eaten cafeteria style before. Immediately after breakfast the next morning came my introduction to the true meaning of military service. Our entire group was put to work policing [a truly military term] the campgrounds for cigarette butts. At the time it was an activity for which I saw little military relevance, especially as I didn't smoke.

Living together with a large group of mostly strangers seemed just a little on the threatening side. Friends were from the hometown so we tended to stick together. As part of our clothing issue we were all given a broad brimmed felt hat known as a "Campaign" hat, another leftover from WW I. On my first day in camp my Campaign hat disappeared sometime while we were seated in the mess hall during our mid day meal. At first, I couldn't believe I could have been so careless as to lose it. It was even harder to believe that someone might have stolen it. In so far as I knew people just didn't steal. Back in Company quarters, I reported the loss immediately. The shocking word was I would have to pay for it. As the pay for the two-week encampment of one dollar per day wouldn't have paid for the hat, a compromise was reached and I was given another hat and a punishment detail for my carelessness. Later it was suggested that the hat was probably stolen, as they were popular civilian items.

The big event of the entire two-week exercise was an overnight bivouac out on the beach. Summer time on an Oregon beach can be and usually is quite cool. We appreciated the fact we were wearing a woolen uniform and at night, even the wool uniform wasn't enough to keep out the chill. Not that we initially had time to get cold. Somehow, I found myself part of a two-man team whose job was to tow our communications cart through the sand dunes. That cart held all the reels of wiring for the field telephone lines. The only relief from the heavy weight came as the wire was strung out between command posts, actually foxholes dug in the sand dunes.

Maurice Hand, the opposite side tackle from our football team was my teammate in towing that cart. How we got so lucky I don't know although I suspect it was because we were the biggest of the new recruits. By the time we had towed that heavy cart through those sand dunes for much of the night, we were exhausted. Our lieutenant had designed the cart and our demonstration of its use earned him a commendation. For the two of us it earned unwanted blisters and a lasting sense of the adventure of it all.

On our way home from the encampment, we stopped in the big city of Portland where I saw my first stage variety show followed by a movie. Walking around the look alike streets of Portland I was afraid I would be lost, not knowing anything about the use of street signs. Staying together as a group of uniformed "Guardsmen", we tried to handle our ill ease with a certain amount of bravado.

My longest job that summer was with a farmer who offered me a haying job and then kept me on as he started cutting grain. During the time I worked with the threshing crew, I left home about 4:30 AM to walk the three miles out to the farm, getting there at six, in time to harness my team and have breakfast. The work demanded both stamina and strength, the days were long and we continued until dark or first dew, which ever was sooner. The only rest was on the drive to and from the thresher and during the noon mealtime.

Shortly before leaving for college, I got a job chopping wood for a neighbor. One of my more serious accidents with an ax occurred as result of my failure to stop and stack the cut pieces. As I was swinging away, gripping the ax handle at the midpoint, the end of the handle caught on a chunk of wood and deflected the ax head into the thumb of my left hand holding the wood chunk I was splitting. The blade glanced off the bone of the thumb, leaving a large V shaped cut about an inch in length.

With blood flowing in great gushing quantities, I walked home for bandaging and care. Mother took a careful look and determined that the wound was beyond her first aid skills. She sent me on to the Doctor. Before going, she wrapped the hand in a cloth to control the flow of blood. If that sounds casual, it really wasn't. We didn't have a telephone or car and there were no telephones in the neighborhood so the quickest way to receive help was to go to the Doctor.

Doctor Gilmore was a general practitioner who made his basic living as much by barter and exchange of services as by cash payment for services rendered. He undoubtedly depended for some part of his income from a small farm he owned a couple miles out of town.

He had received his formal education at the University of Nebraska and once told me that as a student playing football, the practice had

MEMORIES OF ANOTHER TIME   205

been to jump on exposed limbs in a pileup, hoping to break the exposed arm or otherwise incapacitate the opponent. When the U of Nebraska came to the Rose Bowl in the 1940's, the townspeople took up a collection to send him to the game as a gesture to demonstrate their gratitude for his many years of largely unpaid service.

As a Doctor he attended all births and delivered with the help of a mid-wife / practical nurse. Known to everyone as "Old Doc", he had been responsible for delivering a large portion of the people of the town, including twin brothers Dean and Gene, Wayland and Marydith, so we grew with a feeling of loyalty toward him.

Fortunately, old Doc was in his office. Without many questions, he unwrapped the hand and after a quick examination, reached for a bottle of Iodine and a cotton swab. He dipped the swab in the Iodine and with his other hand, grabbed my arm and laid the wound open. Then, with the Iodine-saturated swab, he ran it over the length of the open wound. Even now I can feel the sting of the Iodine as it covered the open wound and as it turned out, effectively killed the saturated flesh.

Having disinfected the wound, he got out his needle and surgical thread and sewed the flesh back in place with three stitches. He suggested it might hurt a little when he sewed the wound but the fact is the only memory of hurting I have is of the Iodine as it seared the flesh.

The wound itself healed in time, leaving a V shaped patch of white, dead flesh that didn't develop a blood supply and appearance of health for more than ten years. I massaged the area several times a day for all those years.

Leaving his office, I went back to finish the wood splitting job; after all 25 cents an hour, in a day when ten cents an hour was the usual wage for common labor, was not to be lost due to a minor injury. However, before I started splitting again, the large stack of split wood was carefully stacked.

*   *   *

In April of 1941, Hitler sent his armies into Belgium, Holland and northern France. With the "Blitzkrieg" threatening all of Europe, the impregnable French Maginot line was bypassed and the French troops scattered. Britain was forced to evacuate her troops at Dunkirk. Under the force of out of control events, the United States itself began to sense a threat to its peace and security.

One would think that events that were soon to prove to be of such a world shaking nature would have the general population reacting with a high degree of excitement, concern and possibly anxiety. Not true. For the student population, as best I remember, there was no discernible ripple of interest or concern. For my part, I had only the vaguest awareness of world events, events that for the most part left me totally unconcerned. From my point of view, and I suspect for most Americans, the war in Europe was just a sideshow that had nothing to do with Fortress America.

*   *   *

Meanwhile, the Whitman College was host to a government sponsored and funded Civilian Pilot Training program, a program that had also been offered the previous summer for those volunteers who had completed their sophomore year of college. This was a program I now know was designed to develop a cadre of trained flyers in anticipation of our country's entry into WW II. At the time though, military service or even American involvement in the European war was still far from my mind. Caught up in the glamour and excitement of flying, I was eager to learn to fly. I applied for the program as soon as I was eligible that spring.

While taking a thorough preflight physical the examining physician wanted to disqualify me because of the eleven-inch differential between my waist size of thirty-one inches and my chest size of forty-two inches on a 180-pound frame. It didn't make sense to me but I asked him to measure again. On the second try I was able to push out my waist to a thirty-three inch measurement and while that hadn't really changed anything, he reluctantly passed me. After all, it seemed rather obvious I was as healthy a physical specimen as he was apt to see. Oddly, I had no trouble with the eye examination. Not that I expected trouble as I considered my vision to be exceptional. The eye chart was a cinch. Depth perception was tested manually by pulling strings to align two objects about ten feet away. A more thorough eye examination would have discovered what later kept me from flying in the military. There,

MEMORIES OF ANOTHER TIME

my eyes tested 20-15; I had some astigmatism, was thought to have poor depth perception and as a result was never allowed to fly.

Flight instruction began almost immediately following the end of the school semester. Already working full time at the cannery I discovered I needed to get up at four AM, ride my bicycle out to the airport and begin my flying lessons at five AM. Sleepily riding my bicycle into the early dawn was a struggle but the exercise served to get me awake. By the time I arrived I was alert and ready to fly. Fortunately, I have always been a morning person.

On first arriving at the Airport my first act was to check out my parachute in hopes I could be in the plane and in the air by five AM.

The first eight hours of flight time were with the instructor. I soloed after eight hours and from then on was given instructions on the maneuvers to practice with the instructor coming along only to demonstrate and check on my progress.

The airplanes were Piper Cubs, single winged and powered by a forty-five horsepower engine. In many ways they were like a large, powered kite but with an enclosed cabin and two tandem seats, the student sitting forward. Dual controls enabled the instructor to take over in an emergency. Most emergencies occurred when the frightened or panicked student froze to the "stick". Looking back, I have to think the Instructor had to be out of his mind to go up all day in such a rickety craft, especially with people who had never flown and weren't all that adept.

If all went well with the flying, I was back on the ground by six and went directly to work from the Airport, stopping for breakfast on the way. More often I was delayed and reported to work without breakfast. As work breaks were unheard of, that led to a long morning until the noontime meal break.

As we approached our forty hours of flight time, we had to complete a cross-country flight to test out the navigation skills learned during those sleepy classroom hours. The course we were to fly was Walla Walla to Pendleton, Oregon, Pendleton to Pasco, Washington and return to Walla Walla. It was unbelievable to me that the country and its landmarks could look so different from the air. Flying to Pendleton wasn't difficult as there was only one road there from Walla Walla and I could guide on it. Finding Pasco was another matter. After sighting the Columbia River, it was no problem to follow it up stream.

Unfortunately, Pasco was fogged in so after locating Wallula, I turned back heading for Walla Walla. Apropos, I might note we not only had no radio; airport traffic was light enough that we could expect to fly in and land with no notice and no permission.

The last leg of the flight was the return to home base. I took a compass heading for Walla Walla and judged by the Columbia River that I was headed in the right direction. I'm never terribly confident about directions but felt that it would be impossible to miss a major town like Walla Walla. As the minutes went by and I couldn't find a familiar landmark in all those rolling hills, my assurance began to diminish until I was feeling something akin to panic.

I knew I could land in most of the wheat fields I was flying over because we had practiced emergency landings until we were coming in with wheat on the wheels and even on the wing tips. However, the embarrassment of being lost and not qualifying for my license was too much to face. Fortunately, before panic had taken hold I saw a town, in the wrong direction from where I was flying, but I flew over to get my bearings and found myself heading for the Walla Walla airport. Glory be and thanks to the luck of fools, which I have been pleased to accept on more than one occasion, I was returned safely and passed my last flight test.

My cannery job was in the warehouse. I started by hand trucking cases of cans just out of the cooker into the warehouse where the cases were to be stacked. I quickly became adept trucking the cans, as handling the hand truck required simple skills of balance and timing.

The heat in the warehouse was difficult for many to cope with. When outside temperatures were 95 to 105 degrees, the heated cans tended to increase the inside temperature by twenty degrees. On many an occasion I tracked coworkers by the trail of sweat dripping from their pants.

Thirteen hour days, seven days a week in weather usually in the nineties and much hotter in the warehouse, required a great deal of stamina and persistence in work that was repetitive and physically demanding. I enjoyed the challenge and the newfound riches and to this day look back on it as a very satisfying work experience.

When it came time to enroll for the fall semester, the foreman asked me if I would stay on. By this time we only worked six ten-hour days

MEMORIES OF ANOTHER TIME

for twenty-seven dollars a week. I had cleared my previous years tuition debt but didn't have much saved yet and thought I needed money for the coming term. As girlfriend MaryBelle had graduated the spring semester before and I was getting out of debt and looking to put a little money aside, I was easily persuaded. I continued with the job until laid off in mid December.

CHAPTER 23
SHIPBUILDING IN WW I & WW II

By
Frederick G. Greaves

SETTLED NOW in Seattle, I progressed in my work to the point I was feeling financially secure. In June 1916 my Milwaukee sweetheart, "Tillie" came out. We were married in that rental house I was sharing with my mother and my three half brothers. Three weeks later mother married John Bayne. They took two of the boys with them to live at Cedar Falls. Arthur stayed with us.

In 1916 WW I was raging in Europe. It appeared imminent that the United States would enter it, so I enlisted in the Navy as a Reservist. Owing to the work I had been doing and my education, I was rated a Warrant Machinist. A year later when we entered the war I tried to get into active service, but because by then I was quite experienced in certain phases of Navy shipbuilding, the Navy insisted that I stay on my job, as we were building Navy ships.

In a few more months it was found that transports and freighters were needed much more than combat vessels, because at that time England had the largest Navy in the world. Our shipyard was almost in the heart of Seattle's waterfront. Already the demand for docks was beginning to be felt, and there was no room to expand the plant. The Todd Dry Dock Company of New York had bought out Seattle Construction & Dry Dock Company, which had bought the plant from Moran Brothers in about 1912. Moran, with the aid of the people of

Seattle, had obtained a contract from the Navy to build the battleship Nebraska. Some of the cleanup work for that job was still being done when I arrived in Seattle, so Todd moved the new construction work to a new yard in Tacoma, on Commencement Bay.

I was not anxious to go to Tacoma, and was offered a job at the Standifer Shipyard in Vancouver, WA. This was only a few months before the war ended. We moved to Vancouver, and were there when the war ended on November 11, 1918. Soon after my old boss at Todd's asked me to come back and settle in with them in Tacoma. We moved to Tacoma in late 1919. Todd's had a big contract to build three Scout cruisers: The Omaha, Milwaukee and Cincinnati. I was made chief draftsman in the machinery division. We stayed in Tacoma until the contracts ran out, about five years later.

Perhaps the most significant happening of this time was the birth of our only child, Fred Greaves Junior, born January 30, 1923.

By 1925-1926 shipbuilding had dropped down to almost nothing. Disarmament had been agreed to by the big three, United States, England and France, so no Navy ship contracts were available. We built one or two private ships, but by early 1926 there was no work in sight. At this point I decided I had better try some other line of work if we wanted to stay in the Pacific Northwest.

After considerable endeavor, I took charge of the Seattle office of the Harnischfeger Corporation as a machinery salesman-engineer. This job lasted about six months

The Electric Steel Foundry in Portland needed a sales engineer to open an office in Seattle. After several weeks in Portland being indoctrinated, I worked for ESCO for five years.

In 1929 business was beginning to show signs of being grossly inflated. With the fall of the stock market, everybody became scared. It seemed that people throughout the world began to hoard their savings and stopped buying anything but absolute necessities. Many banks with limited assets closed their doors. Thousands of businesses failed, and hundreds of thousands of employees were thrown out of work.

There was much suffering, as many people had no savings to fall back on. My father-in-law was retired and living on his savings. He and his wife had worked hard all their lives, and had just enough saved to live decently. For a while in 1930 he could not draw any money from

MEMORIES OF ANOTHER TIME

his savings accounts. He died in 1933 and we all knew the Depression had hastened his death, since he lost considerable in the banks.

In 1930 I was persuaded to leave ESCO and join the Lake Co. on a commission basis selling feeding concentrates to the feed and flourmills in Washington State. I soon found the company had grossly overstated the possibilities but now that I had some experience they wanted me to take over their Portland office.

The bottom fell out of the market on most commodities in late 1930. The Lake Company had material enroute, including about 350 tons of meat scraps from Australia, which we had purchased at $60.00 a ton. I had sold 150 tons in the Portland district, but before it arrived the price had dropped to about $30.00. Most dealers refused to take delivery unless we lowered the price so we had to swallow our losses. We struggled along for another year, hoping to recuperate, but conditions were against us and Lake finally quit. Since I had been working on a commission basis we had been using up our savings to a large extent.

While still living in Seattle I had invested in a business making fishing tackle, in partnership with Donis Bardon. He had some ideas that looked good in new designs of spoons for both commercial and sports fishing. My role was to provide engineering and shop experience.

He seemed to have reached a point where he could use my services if I gave part-time to the shop and part-time to selling, especially if I brought some other lines. So we returned to Seattle after a year and one half in Portland and moved back into our house, which we had kept rented.

Business did not go much better for the Bardon-Greaves Company and the winter of 1931 was particularly bad financially. Since business was so bad I found it necessary to take some small engineering jobs, primarily drafting, in order to earn a little money for food, as our savings were then gone. Not only had we used up our savings, but also I had borrowed quite heavily from friends and had let our mortgage payments lapse. We were about $12,000 in debt.

With business practically non-existent we decided to liquidate the Bardon-Greaves Company.

I arranged to work for W. C. Nickum, the outstanding naval architect in the area. I had met him when he came to Seattle to do naval architecture for the Todd Company. Nickum's work was also intermittent. He needed someone to do his machinery layouts, and he graciously allowed me to set up the Fred G. Greaves Company in his office, sharing his phone. His two sons were working for their Dad.

Nickum had been unable to keep a steady crew, because jobs designing new ships were mighty scarce. However, there were some short jobs making plans of alternations and improvements, etc. One day in confidence W. C. said to me, "Fred, I don't know what I am going to do. I have used up my resources. If I don't get a job within the next thirty days I'm going to have to let my sons go." Fortunately, he got a new small boat to design before the month was out.

During the winter I got an engineering and drafting job making all the equipment in the coalmines for Northwestern Improvement Company, a division of Northern Pacific Railroad. For several weeks I went to the mines at Roslyn, WA, then did the balance of the work at home.

The next year business began to improve a little, and I was able to get a few machinery orders for the Fred G. Greaves Company. Moreover, in view of my contacts with the feed and flourmill trade, and through studying the needs of smaller mills, which were popping up in many of the small towns in the Pacific Northwest, I went about obtaining more lines that would go together for that trade.

Starting a small business is no joke when you have no money. Wife Tillie did the books for the Company. This was in addition to doing all the housework and even included making underwear for our son and me. He was going on ten years of age and helped out by carrying papers and selling the Saturday Evening Post and the Ladies Home Journal.

By about 1935 I had built up the Fred G. Greaves Company to the point that it was all my wife and I could do to keep up with the paper work, especially since I was on the road most of the time. I usually traveled after working hours in order to be in the next town early the next morning. I was covering practically the entire Pacific Northwest, including British Columbia, Alberta and Western Montana.

On Labor Day 1939 Tillie and I had gone to Vancouver Island, partly on business and partly for pleasure. While we were driving around Victoria we heard on the car radio that Hitler had invaded Poland. I said to Tillie, "This is bad. I'm afraid it won't be long before we are involved in a worldwide war." I am not proud that I saw it coming.

MEMORIES OF ANOTHER TIME

Todd had reopened the shipyard in Tacoma in 1939 to build small airplane carriers and freighters. As they had to use steel, I naturally kept in close touch with them. In 1940 the Navy asked Todd if they could establish a yard in Seattle for the special purpose of building destroyers, which were badly needed. In the latter part of 1940 the President of Todd asked me if I would consider getting together an engineering department for the new yard and serve as its Chief Engineer.

At first I was inclined to turn down the offer. After thinking it over, I realized that if we went into the war the Navy would very likely ask me to go to some distant place. On that basis I felt it was highly advisable to work things out so I could accept Todd's offer. By so doing I would be able to stay in the Seattle area where I could keep the Fred G. Greaves Company afloat.

Fortunately, I was able to obtain the services of a man who had some machinery experience but was not likely to be called into the service. He worked out so well I later made him a partner.

As a result, in November 1940, I was able to take the position of Chief Engineer with the Seattle-Tacoma Shipbuilding Company. At this point we had a contract for ten destroyers of the Navy's 453 class. Later we received a contract for fifteen of the 445 class and a little later six more 445's. Still later we had a contract for fifteen of the 692 class, and finally three "AD" submarine tenders. The latter were finished in 1946 and 1947, at which time we also built the "Chinook" for the Puget Sound Navigation Company.

At the beginning of 1947 it was clearly evident that my work at the yard was coming to an end. I felt my best interests lay with the company I had founded.

Fred Junior came home from the war in 1946 and returned to his studies at the University of Washington. About a year later he came to work for me. Sufficient to say he gradually came to be my right hand man. The business continued to go along fairly well, giving both of us and two or three others a fair living.

INDEX OF CONTRIBUTORS

Introduction, Disease and Family Survival, Growing up Poor, & Preparing for War by Robert H. Wells, b October 10, 1921, excerpted from autobiography titled Country Roots, published March 2001.

Relief Check Kept Our Family Going by Harold E. "Sam" Haight born 1 December 1923. Stories excerpted by Robert H. Wells from "Canadian-Americans at Home and Abroad" unpublished manuscript 1999.

A Will to Live by Cornelius John Van Beekum born August 1926, as told to Robert H. Wells.

War comes to Seattle by MaryBelle Preston Wells born 4 October 1920. unpublished manuscript.

Westward Migration by Alexander J. Sharp, born 17 May, 1921, excerpted from "Memories of Some Forty Niner's" edited and published by Robert H. Wells, May 1994.

My Father Worked: by Theodore George Lumpkin, born 30 December 1919, as told to Robert H. Wells and excerpted from "Memories of Some Forty Niner's published 1994.

The Appeal of Physics: by Henry Fairbank born 6 November 1918 as told to Robert H. Wells June 2001-June 2003.

Malnutrition and Other Things by Robert Martens born 24 November 1925, excerpted from unpublished manuscript.

A Summer's Adventure by Charles Benson Downer, born 9 November 1914, excerpted from "Autobiography of Charles B. Downer, Colonel, United States Air Force, Retired" as told to Robert H. Wells

Family, Cars and other Things as told to Robert H Wells, memoirs by Frank Steele Preston, born 30 July 1918-died 31 March 2004

Growing up in the Early Twentieth Century & Ship building in WW I & WW II by Frederick George Greaves unpublished manuscript.

Making a Life without a Father by Ernest Giffen published May & Oct 1994 in Memories of Some Forty Niner's by Robert H Wells

Growing up in Early Los Angeles by Norton Sanders published May & Oct 1994 in Memories of Some Forty Niner's by Robert H Wells

An Alaskan Adventure by Howard Rustad as told to Robert H Wells

A Coal Miner's Daughter by Hazel Schmeil unpublished manuscript.

A Rural Upbringing by Harriet Wilkerson as told to Robert H Wells

A Will to Live by Cornelius John Van Beekum born August 1926, as told to Robert H. Wells

A Child's Memories of the 1920's by MaryBelle Preston Wells unpublished manuscript.

Reaching for a College Education by Patricia Murphy Burns as told to Robert H Wells.

Printed in the United States
63298LVS00003B/268-270